"And what can we tell from the fortune-teller's hands, Miranda?"

Lucas rubbed his thumbs lightly over her warm skin, thrilling when he felt the pulse in her wrist accelerate wildly. She bit her lip nervously and tried to tug her hands from his grasp.

"Miranda's lonely," he said with quiet certainty, tightening his grip. "And Miranda doesn't like being alone."

She started to say something, but he spoke again before she had a chance. "And Miranda's passionate, too."

Cupping her fingers gently in his, he lifted her trembling hand to his lips and kissed it softly, watching her face as she closed her eyes and unconsciously wet her lips. "Perhaps we'd be a good match after all," he murmured.

She shook her head mutely and tried once more to pull her hands free. His grip remained firm.

"I want to know more," he whispered provocatively. "Tell me more, Miranda. Tell me what's in the cards."

Dear Reader,

Welcome to Silhouette **Special Edition** . . . welcome to romance. Each month Silhouette **Special Edition** publishes six novels with you in mind—stories of love and life, tales that you can identify with . . . as well as dream about.

This month has some wonderful stories for you— after all, March comes in like a lion and goes out like a lamb! And in Lisa Jackson's new series, MAVERICKS, we meet three men who just won't be tamed! This month, don't miss *He's Just a Cowboy* by Lisa Jackson.

THAT SPECIAL WOMAN!, Silhouette **Special Edition**'s new series that salutes women, has a wonderful book this month from Patricia Coughlin. *The Awakening* is the tender story of Sara Marie McAllister—and her awakening to love when she meets bounty hunter John Flynn. It takes a very special man to win That Special Woman! And handsome Flynn is up for the challenge!

Rounding out this month are books from other favorite writers: Elizabeth Bevarly, Susan Mallery, Trisha Alexander and Carole Halston!

I hope that you enjoy this book, and all the stories to come! Have a wonderful March!

Sincerely,

Tara Gavin
Senior Editor
Silhouette Books

ELIZABETH BEVARLY

HIRED HAND

Silhouette®

SPECIAL ▼ EDITION®

Published by Silhouette Books New York

America's Publisher of Contemporary Romance

For Valerie Kane, my very first writing buddy

SILHOUETTE BOOKS
300 East 42nd St., New York, N.Y. 10017

HIRED HAND

ISBN: 0-373-09803-0

First Silhouette Books printing March 1993

All the characters in this book have no existence outside the imagination of the author and have no relation whatsoever to anyone bearing the same name or names. They are not even distantly inspired by any individual known or unknown to the author, and all incidents are pure invention.

Printed in the U.S.A.

ELIZABETH BEVARLY

is an honors graduate of the University of Louisville and achieved her dream of writing full-time before she even turned thirty! At heart, she is also an avid voyager who once helped navigate a friend's thirty-five-foot sailboat across the Bermuda Triangle. "I really love to travel," says this self-avowed beach bum. "To me, it's the best education a person can give herself." Her dream is to one day have her own sailboat, a beautifully renovated older model forty-two-footer, and to enjoy the freedom and tranquillity seafaring can bring. Elizabeth likes to think she has a lot in common with the characters she creates, people who know that love and life go hand in hand.

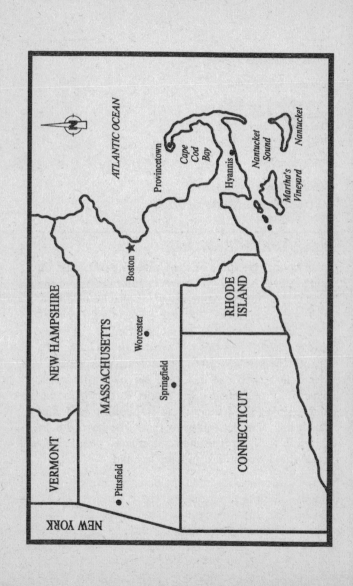

Chapter One

He was a Martian, no question about it. As Miranda True watched the big broad-shouldered, dark-haired man cross the room with easy, confident strides, she could guess without even seeing the telltale marks on his hands that he was in fact a Martian in every sense of the word. His bare chest would be magnificent freed of the expensive charcoal suit that lovingly hugged his body now, she thought. His back would be spectacular. Martians always had wonderful physiques.

His mere presence at the party tonight had cost her a great deal of her concentration, and as a result she hadn't been able to perform nearly as well as she usually did at these functions. However, she must be doing something right, she thought, because everyone in the room who had approached her this evening now gazed at her with reverence at best and suspicion at worst. Miranda sighed. Would there ever be a time in her life when she might attend a party like this as a guest instead of an employee, as an interest instead of an attraction?

Of course she had only herself to blame. Herself and her assistant, who had talked her into beginning this "gig" in the first place.

"This is fantastic!" Miranda could still hear the enthusiastic voice of the recently graduated Marcy Dolan two years ago. Awed by the accuracy of the palm reading Miranda had given her to pass some time one day, Marcy had remarked that Miranda could make loads of money with her interest in chiromancy, renting herself out to be the entertainment at social gatherings. "My mom threw a party once and rented a tarot reader for the entertainment. People went nuts. These upper-crusty Bostonians may act the proper overstuffed Victorians at those parties, but deep down, they're as fascinated by the unknown as four-year-old children. Trust me, Miranda, you'd be great at it."

And so had begun Miranda's moonlighting profession. At first the income had been sporadic, an occasional party or fund-raiser here and there, nothing to write home about. But as she'd gained some word-of-mouth publicity, a number of bookings had followed, and she'd earned more regular money. It had all seemed like a good idea for supplementing her income two years ago, when Miranda was just starting to get her shop off the ground, but she was gradually growing weary of the oddity people associated with her skill. And nowadays, she didn't really need the extra money her moonlighting as a palmist generated.

Because nowadays her storefront shop, One To Grow On, was considered one of Boston's most innovative retail establishments, offering an eclectic array of organically grown goods from gourmet foods to herbal remedies to potpourri to cleaning alternatives. If it grew out of the earth, Miranda could and would find some use for it, and then she would sell it in her shop for a reasonable sum.

She had finally arrived, she told herself. And she resolutely decided then that tonight would be the last of the moonlighting parties. Maybe now that she was a member of Boston's business community, the next time Miranda attended one of these gatherings of businessmen and women, it would be because of her professional acumen and her venture's success. No one would look at her as if she were only there because she was hired to be there, and no one would talk to her as if she didn't belong. She was a long way from the tiny community of Saint Denis, Massachusetts, now. A long, long way. No one in Boston would ever accuse her of invading circles she had no business being a part of.

And no one could tell her she didn't belong.

Almost involuntarily, Miranda began to search the crowd again for the big dark-haired man who was in attendance tonight, spotting him immediately. And maybe someday, she fantasized further, she would attract the eye of a man like him. Handsome, confident, successful, assured. A man who would love her to distraction and keep her close forever. A man who would cherish her because she was important to him, and who would never, ever lie to her.

Almost as if he could hear her thinking about him, the man turned to look directly at her, and Miranda caught her breath at the shivers of heat his gaze sent spiraling through her body. He was a man with a presence, a man who was without question in complete control of his destiny. Definitely a Martian. She was certain somehow that he owned whatever he was in the business of doing, and was immensely, enormously successful. For a moment their eyes met and held, then he smiled at her—a smile she was sure he saved for every single woman he met. Just when he seemed to be on the verge of approaching her, someone else claimed his attention and he looked away, and Miranda's heartbeat slowly, gradually, returned to normal.

Wow, she thought, suddenly feeling the need for a little break. Turning quickly, she hurried out of the cavernous white, ultramodern living room of the Devon home, down the hall to the kitchen. For some reason Miranda always retreated to the kitchens of the expensive homes where she was working when she wanted to escape for a while. No, not for *some* reason, she realized. For a specific reason. It felt normal, reassuring even, to be a part of the hustle and bustle of the big kitchens, felt almost like going home. Even if her memories of employment with the Lyndons of Saint Denis weren't necessarily happy all the time, at least they were familiar.

Miranda poured herself a glass of ice water and took a seat in the corner of the room where she could remain unobserved. Yes, tonight would be the last of these parties, she decided. She would never submit to—or even experience—the need to hide out in a kitchen again. Those days were well over. Instead she thought about a dark-haired, beautifully built man, and wondered what his name was.

Lucas Strathmoor was as edgy as a cat in a barn fire and for the life of him couldn't identify why. It wasn't just because of his preoccupation with the palmist Grace Devon had hired for the evening's entertainment—although certainly, beautiful blond-haired women always caused him some uneasy preoccupation. No, tonight his feelings of anxiety went deeper—straight to the bone. For some reason he turned to search for the palmist again, but she had vanished. Ignoring his disappointment, he reflected once again that she didn't look at all like what he would have expected of a palm reader.

She seemed awfully young. And instead of being swathed in big baggy clothes reminiscent of gypsies and hippies, she wore a simple long-sleeved cocktail dress of sapphire blue. Her hair was unbound, falling in straight shimmery lengths of pale gold to rest between her shoulder blades. The moment Lucas had seen her, all he'd wanted to do was grab a fistful of that pale gold and lift it to his lips. He shuddered involuntarily at the memory, unaccustomed to experiencing such an immediate response to a woman. Nor had he ever felt one so intense. Whatever else the woman might be, she was certainly sexy as hell.

"Lucas!"

Upon hearing the voice of his hostess greeting him from behind, Lucas turned to smile warmly at Grace Devon. In many ways, she had been his mentor, and he wouldn't be the monster success he was today without the support and guidance she had tirelessly offered him for the past twenty years.

"Great party, Grace," he said as he swept her forward into a warm hug. "As usual. Where's Peter?"

Grace waved her hand airily to the other side of the room where her husband appeared to be cutting the real estate deal of a lifetime. "Talking to some new kid in town about investing in this mega-mall scheme he has."

The "kid" in question looked to be older than Lucas's thirty-eight years, but he supposed to Grace everyone under the age of fifty was slated to be dismissed as extremely young.

"I'm sorry I haven't been able to talk to you sooner," she said now, curling her fingers through the crook in Lucas's arm, encouraging him to follow her to the buffet. "But April is the end of the fiscal year for Devon Enterprises, and I've been cornered by nearly every member of the board tonight. Frankly I'm hoping you'll ward off the rest of them for a while by pretending you have all kinds of important business to discuss with me."

"Sorry, Grace, but what I'm working on now is very hush-hush," Lucas told her quietly. "Despite the fact that you're quite possibly the only person in the world besides my father that I trust implicitly, at this point I can't even discuss the new deal with you.''

"It's Panwide Textiles, isn't it?" Grace asked bluntly.

Lucas wasn't surprised by the accuracy of her suggestion, particularly since nearly everyone in the nation's business-and-financial communities knew about his bid on the company—and about Panwide's successful efforts to stall his takeover thus far. But he had plans for Panwide that even Grace didn't know about, hidden agendas that he was just now putting into place and had yet to make public. The company that was giving him so much trouble would be his. It was only a matter of time.

"Let's talk about something else, Grace."

She offered him a knowing smile and paused by the buffet. After selecting a crab puff and asking for a glass of wine, Grace turned to Lucas and inquired, "Have you consulted my palmist yet? She might be able to offer you some guidance."

"No, Grace, I haven't," Lucas replied mildly. "Nor do I intend to."

"Oh, you really should—she's wonderful. She even named correctly the month and year of Peter, Jr's, birth, and listed quite completely my businesses successes over the years."

"Did it ever occur to you that those things are available for public examination?" Lucas asked, not bothering to hide his disbelief in such psychic mumbo jumbo. "All she had to do was go to the public library and hall of records."

"Oh, Lucas," Grace muttered. "You're no fun at all. Everyone here tonight thinks Miranda's got remarkable gifts. She's told everyone something phenomenal. You should find out what she has to say about you."

"She'll tell me what she's told everyone present tonight. That I'll meet the mate of my dreams and be very successful. I'll die a happy, satisfied man."

"Oh, she's much more specific than that."

"So she's done her homework."

"Lucas, you're such a skeptic."

"I'm a realist," he muttered resolutely.

"Same thing," Grace concluded with a haughty sniff.

Lucas shook his head hopelessly but couldn't help smiling. Except for his father, Grace Devon was the only person alive who would speak to him with such familiarity, and such fondness. Of course, she was the only other person alive who had the right. If it hadn't been for her, Lucas would have flunked miserably out of college and wound up right back under the upraised cars in Nate's Garage, fixing fuel lines and patching radiators. The tiny industrial community of Easton, New Jersey, was way behind him now. He had become a hell of a lot more than a mechanic's son. Thanks to Grace, he'd made the old man proud.

Now his father lived in one of the finest houses on New Jersey's coast, where the air was clean and the sky was blue, and buses didn't wheeze past his front door day and night. It was the least Lucas could do. Aside from Grace, Nate Strathmoor had been the only person who supported his dreams and bent over backward to help Lucas turn fantasy into reality. Grace and Nate were quite possibly the only two people he loved.

"I see one of your board members approaching, Grace," Lucas said now, smiling mischievously when she recognized his intention to abandon her. "He looks like he wants to discuss something very important. I'll leave you to him."

"Lucas . . ."

"Say good-night, Gracie."

Grace sighed in resignation. "Go have your palm read. Maybe Miranda will tell you that Panwide Textiles is a done deal." She gritted her teeth at him affectionately. "Or maybe she'll just reaffirm how infuriating you are."

Lucas smiled and slipped away, setting his empty glass on the table as he did so. Grace's parties were always very nice, and he usually enjoyed himself immensely whenever he came to one. But tonight he simply couldn't relax, couldn't shake the feeling that something big was coming. He felt anxious and uneasy, as if everyone in the room knew what he had in store for Panwide, even though he'd told absolutely no one about his plan. Everything was going along exactly as it was supposed to, Lucas assured himself. So why was he so overcome by this feeling of foreboding? And why the strong sensation that someone was watching him?

Spinning quickly around, his eyes fixed on those of Grace's palmist who was standing on the other side of the room again, and he realized that someone was indeed watching him. Her expression reflected panic when she saw that she'd been caught studying him, but she didn't look away.

Lucas was intrigued.

So what was the big deal with having his palm read? he asked himself. There was no harm in it, was there? He'd listen politely while she told him all the vague, optimistic things she thought he wanted to hear, never believing a word she said, and then maybe the two of them could go have a drink somewhere. It would top the evening off nicely. And if he could get her to come home with him—or better yet, finagle an invitation back to her place so he could leave when he wanted to—all the better, right?

As he took a deep breath and began to close the distance that separated him from the palmist, it occurred to Lucas suddenly and with uncharacteristic whimsy that he might just be approaching his destiny. Destiny, hell, he thought further. What he was approaching was simply what might amount to a very enjoyable evening.

* * *

Miranda felt an inexplicable sense of danger wash over her as she watched the man who had claimed her attention all evening stride toward her. Somehow she knew intuitively that she was in for a rough time with him. It was almost as if some sudden, invisible energy passed between them, as if they were two halves of one whole being drawn together by some force outside their knowledge.

Just calm down, Miranda commanded herself. He's a man, only a man. Albeit a thoroughly unsettling one.

Without speaking, he stopped before her and extended his left hand, palm up, for her inspection. Instead of taking it immediately as she had for the others present that evening, Miranda paused a moment to study his face, trying to gauge precisely what kind of personality he possessed before reaffirming her suspicions by surveying the lines on his hands.

A Martian, she thought again. And very, very handsome. His near-black, expertly cut short hair was kissed by more than a few threads of silver amid the chestnut highlights, a perfect complement to his rusty-gray hazel eyes. Slashes of high cheekbones hinted at nobility, a full lower lip suggested sensuality. But of course, that was the case with all Martians. The man smiled at Miranda then, a smile that exuded raw masculinity and supreme self-confidence. His voice will be deep, rich and melodious when he speaks, she thought, his laughter reminiscent of a rugged, wind-swept canyon.

Yes, he was a Martian through and through.

Gingerly, cautiously, she clasped in her own the hand he still offered, picking up his right hand with her other as she did so. Her eyes never leaving his, Miranda gently massaged his fingers and thumbs, her own fingertips skimming nimbly over the rough flesh stretched across the backs of his hands, rubbing his knotted knuckles, circling his strong wrists. Finally she turned his palms back upward and let her gaze rove quickly and deftly over the array of lines criss-crossing the broad surface.

"I knew it," she said on a quiet sigh. "You're a Martian."

The man gazed at her mildly, seemingly unfazed by her comment. But Miranda saw the flicker in his eyes that other people would probably miss and realized that the man was thinking he had just allowed himself to be cornered by a stark raving lunatic.

With a mischievous smile, she continued, "I'm a Venusian myself. We wouldn't be a good match, you and I. You'd run roughshod over me, I'm afraid."

A long moment passed in which the man continued to stare at her in silence, until Miranda decided she had teased him enough and sought to clarify her assertions.

"See?" she began, indicating a small rise on the man's palm, midway between his wrist and little finger. "You have an exaggerated mount of Mars. It's more prominently pronounced than any of your other mounts." Turning her own palm up for his inspection, she guided his thumb to a point midway between her own thumb and wrist and added, "My most prominent mount is here. On my mount of Venus. That makes me a Venusian."

The man stroked his thumb softly over the warm flesh upon which she had placed it, and Miranda sucked in her breath at the sudden rush of heat that shot from her fingertips to her chest to huddle around her heart.

"If you ask me," he said in a voice even deeper and richer, even more melodious than she had anticipated, "you feel pretty soft."

"Yes, well," she whispered a little breathlessly, "that kind of goes along with the territory. Venusians are entirely too vulnerable for their own good."

"I see."

Lucas eyed the woman before him, skeptical and bemused, wondering how he'd let himself get talked into this one. He had to admit that as far as party entertainment went, Grace had outdone herself this time with her palm reader. Still, he hadn't intended to become one of the victims. Not until nearly everyone present had told him how amazingly accurate the palmist had been in assessing their pasts, and how optimistic she'd been in foreseeing their futures. Not until he had decided he had no other choice but to surrender to the constant tug of desire he'd felt running between the two of them all night.

Of course it was all ridiculous, Lucas thought now, as he peered into the clear blue eyes of the young woman before him. Yet as she continued to stroke his hands and gently bend his fingers, he felt himself relaxing for what seemed like the first time in months, and decided there was really no harm in allowing a beautiful blonde at least fifteen years his junior to hold his hand. Wasn't that the fantasy of every man his age? he thought. Or at least the beginning part of that fantasy?

When he looked at the young woman again, he was startled by the expression in her eyes, one of complete familiarity. For a moment it seemed as if she were staring right into his soul and could detect every flaw and perfection in his psyche, indeed every trait in his character.

"What's your name?" he asked impulsively, hoping to throw her off balance enough to rid her of that arresting, disturbing expression. God, her eyes were blue.

"Miranda," she replied immediately. "Miranda True."

No doubt a professional name, Lucas guessed. "And you're going to read my palm, Miranda True. Is that about the gist of it?"

She smiled at him, a smile that indicated she fully recognized and dismissed his skepticism. "If you want me to. I won't tell you anything you don't already know. If you have

questions, I'll do my best to answer them. But if you'd
rather not..."

Lucas chuckled indulgently. "Do your worst," he muttered with a carefree shake of his head. "Tell me the usual
rot about how happy and successful, how rich and famous
I'll be. Tell me what you've told everyone else this evening."

Miranda bowed her head to look once again at his palms,
and only then was Lucas spared the intense blue scrutiny
that spoke of more experience than anyone her age should
claim. As he studied the crown of her head, he noticed a
number of silvery strands mingled with the pale gold hair
that fell past her shoulders, and was surprised. Perhaps she
wasn't as young as he'd thought.

"You're already very successful and rich, and you're famous in your own way," Miranda told him in response to his
earlier statement. "However, you're not entirely happy."

Lucas bristled at her suggestion that he wasn't completely fulfilled, choosing to ignore that such a suggestion
was correct. "Well, Ms. True," he retorted, "considering
the fact that you're working a cocktail party in one of Boston's finest homes and were hired by Grace Devon, one of
the city's most prominent businesswomen, I guess it's a
pretty safe bet that everyone present tonight is successful,
rich and somewhat famous. And who among us is ever entirely happy, hmm?"

Instead of buckling under his oppressive CEO voice that
normally sent underlings scattering in fright, Miranda simply smiled even more serenely. "I suppose almost none of
us ever is," she agreed. "But your unhappiness comes as a
surprise to you, doesn't it? You've always thought by the
time you were thirty-eight, you'd have attained everything
you wanted, didn't you?"

Lucas was frankly startled by her statement. Certainly he
made no secret of his age, but he knew to a casual observer

he looked several years younger than he was. And anyway, lots of people set goals they didn't see realized, he thought. That didn't mean there was anything supernatural about Miranda's evaluation. "You're a perceptive judge of people, Ms. True," he finally stated carelessly. "Not to mention quite a good guesser of ages."

Miranda continued to smile in that maddeningly peaceful way and dropped her gaze to his hands again.

"You have very interesting hands. They're very large," she pointed out unnecessarily. "That indicates analytical talents. They're also thick, and hard, suggesting a primitive, rather rough nature." Miranda's expression was speculative, almost curious, when she met his eyes again. "But you harbor an inherent honesty. You haven't always been a businessman, have you?" she went on quickly, seeming as surprised by the question as he was. "You started off performing common labor with your hands, didn't you?"

Lucas nodded silently, helplessly, feeling a gaping pit open up in his stomach. Crazily he glanced down at his fingers to see if maybe they still carried traces of grease and oil after nearly twenty years away from his father's garage. But no such telltale signs were in evidence. She really was thorough, he thought. She really *had* done her homework.

"The dark hair on the backs of all of your fingers suggests you're ardent," Miranda continued, "with a disposition toward being easily aroused."

Again that strangely ponderous look in her eyes caught Lucas somewhere in his midsection.

"Square-tipped fingers, though," she qualified in a nononsense, oddly efficient tone of voice. "That's common among successful businessmen—shows you're professional in your endeavors. Your knuckles also tell me you're an excellent financier." After a moment's pause and further inspection of his hands, she added, "You're not easily deceived and you work very hard, perhaps too hard. Your index finger leans toward your thumbs. That suggests a desire for independence. The pink, mottled color of your palms indicates an optimistic nature and general good health."

Miranda's smile became mischievous again as she flattened his hand to inspect it for a moment longer. "No health problems aside from a little nearsightedness," she added. "No suicidal tendencies."

Lucas felt his spine stiffening with every personal observation she made—every one of them disturbingly correct—repeating over and over to himself that it was all very general stuff that she could say about anyone. Except for the nearsightedness. And he hadn't told anyone about that.

"Oh! Oh, this is wonderful!" Miranda said suddenly, enthusiastically. "A cross *and* a star on your mount of Jupiter. True love *and* genuine success of the highest caliber."

"Success and love," Lucas corrected her mildly, indicating that one carried more importance to him than the other.

But Miranda ignored the distinction. "Few people ever find even one of these in life. You're a very lucky man to ultimately be endowed with both." With another glimpse at his palm, she added, "And in the near future, too."

"Yeah, yeah," he muttered, uncomfortable with her prediction. "What about my financial future?"

He could tell Miranda was disappointed that he held so little faith in her assurances, but she lowered her eyes again and replied with a slight shrug, "It's excellent. You're already a very rich man—monetarily speaking, anyway—and your wealth will multiply in the future."

That's more like it, Lucas thought. She was beginning to talk like a hired entertainer again. He should probably leave now on that optimistically vague note.

"This is interesting, though," Miranda went on before he could snatch his hand away. "Your mount of Mercury is very close to your upper mount of Mars. That's something normally seen in people who make a trade of fighting—soldiers, mercenaries . . . in olden times, pirates.''

Pirates? Lucas repeated to himself, mystified. *Pirates?*

"But," Miranda continued, "your mount of the Sun lies very near your heart line. That shows you have the gift of mercy, the capacity to be compassionate."

But Lucas heard little past the word *pirate*. How could she know unless . . .

Unless she reads the business section of the newspaper, you dolt, Lucas chastised himself. Quit losing yourself in the long shafts of pale gold hair and the delft-blue eyes. Quit falling under the lull of her quiet, sensuous voice. Quit thinking about how good it feels to find your hands captured in the warmth of Miranda True's.

"Your mount of Venus is also exaggerated. That indicates that you're . . . uh . . . rather . . . um . . .''

Her sudden hesitancy intrigued Lucas. He had to duck his head to catch a glimpse of her face, because she had let her own head drop until he couldn't see her expression. He was surprised to find that Miranda was blushing furiously, and noticed then that her hands no longer gripped his quite so confidently.

"I'm what?'' he prodded.

"You . . . uh . . . you have a . . . a . . . a very passionate disposition," she mumbled quietly.

"Really?'' Lucas was delighted. "What else?''

"You . . . um . . .'' Miranda sighed heavily and tried to look him in the eye, failed miserably and let her gaze drop again. "I mean, I've seen this before in a number of hands, but yours is so . . . so . . .''

"So . . .''

"So amazingly well developed," she finally concluded, blushing even more.

Lucas felt inexplicably pleased, although he had no idea what a well-developed mount of Venus might provide for him. "Thank you," he mumbled curiously.

Miranda tried one more time. "Simply put...you're a very amorous man, very physical in your...romantic pursuits. And see all these lines crisscrossing the mount?"

"Yes."

"That really affirms your...your..."

"My very romantic disposition?"

Miranda swallowed with some difficulty before meeting his gaze again. "Uh-huh," she whispered.

Suddenly Lucas forgot that he considered this entire experience a ridiculous bit of parlor-room voodoo. Suddenly he only knew he was standing at the edge of a crowded room near a secluded alcove, with a beautiful woman who had the gentlest, most soothing hands he'd ever felt. And suddenly *he* wanted to be the one who made suggestions.

He flattened his palms against Miranda's before sliding his hands slowly forward to circle her wrists with the thumb and middle finger of each of his hands. Then he tugged gently but insistently until she was following his progress toward the alcove hidden behind one of Grace's many potted plants. When they were safely obscured from prying eyes, Lucas turned her palms upward, and pretended to study the numerous lines that zigged and zagged across the surface.

"And what can we determine from Miranda True's hands?" he murmured quietly, rubbing his thumbs lightly over her warm skin, thrilling when he felt the pulse in her wrist accelerate wildly. He noted she wore rings on nearly every finger except the one that would have stood for something. "She's single," he said softly, strangely glad to realize it.

When Miranda's eyes met his, they reflected a quality Lucas recognized all too well, because he'd witnessed it in his own mirror reflection lately. "And she's become aware recently that her life has gone way too far without her ever having planned any of it."

Miranda bit her lip nervously, and Lucas knew he'd struck a discordant note precisely. And when she gingerly tried to tug her hands from his grasp, ducking her head once more to hide the melancholy he'd seen in her eyes before she'd had a chance to hide it, he knew he had her pegged exactly.

"Miranda's lonely," he said with quiet certainty, tightening his grip somewhat to prevent her from freeing her hands. "And Miranda doesn't like being alone."

She started to say something, but Lucas turned his attention back to her hands and began to speak again before she had a chance. "She's . . . Venusian?" he asked, glancing up only long enough to see her nod her head slowly. "Venus," he repeated. "That's the . . . the *mount,* is it?"

Again she nodded.

"That's the mount that indicates one's very passionate disposition, is it not?"

Miranda only gazed at him silently when he looked up this time.

"So Miranda's passionate, too."

Lucas rubbed his thumb over the pad of her palm directly below her own thumb and felt her tremble. Cupping her fingers gently in his, he lifted her hand to his lips and pressed a soft kiss over the area he had just caressed, watching her face as she closed her eyes and unconsciously wet her lips.

"And Miranda is easily aroused, too," he murmured against her warm skin. "Perhaps we'd be a very good match after all."

Miranda drew in her breath sharply, then let it out again on a soft, ragged sigh. But she opened her eyes and fixed her gaze on his as she replied levelly, "That's another thing about Martians. They tend not to notice other people's feelings. It's not that they don't care, mind you. It's just that they don't always...notice.''

Two bright flames flickered to life at the center of her pupils when he replied in a quiet voice, ''I notice more than you think, Miranda.''

She shook her head mutely and tried once more to pull her hands free. Lucas's grasp remained firm.

''I want to know more, Miranda True,'' he coaxed quietly. ''I want...'' He paused for a moment, feeling as if everything were going too fast, as if he had completely lost control of the situation and now things were being orchestrated by another hand. ''Tell me more, Miranda,'' he whispered provocatively, trying to slow things down a bit and regain some semblance of command. ''Tell me...tell me what's in the cards.''

Chapter Two

Miranda ceased her struggles and stared at the man who'd been making her heart skip and dance and thump erratically ever since she'd first laid eyes on him. His hands had told her quite a lot, and there were a number of things about his character she could have voiced but had chosen not to— things that she wasn't sure she wanted to explore further herself.

Miranda knew most people considered palmistry to be no more than silly, affected mysticism and popular hocus- pocus, but she felt otherwise. To her, hands were reflective of life experience in the same way faces were. Just as lines grew more pronounced around lips and eyes and across the forehead as one aged and lived, so did they develop on the surface of one's hands. And in just the same way that doc- tors detected physical maladies elsewhere in the body by checking eyes, ears, nose and throat, so did indications of illness and good health appear in the features of the hand.

The more Miranda had studied chiromancy, the more she had discovered it went much deeper than silly hocus-pocus.

"Come on, Miranda," the man was urging her again. "They told me you read cards as well. What say we give that a look?"

Yes, to Miranda, the hands were definite windows into the soul. Tarot cards, however... tarot was something Marcy had convinced her to include in her "act," but Miranda had never quite mastered them. They were too inconsistent, too iffy. Hands were hands from one minute to the next. But cards came up different every time.

"Gee, I don't know," she stalled. "It's getting awfully late. Mrs. Devon only hired me to be here until ten and it's already—"

"Not even nine-thirty," the man informed her.

Terrific, Miranda thought, with an impatient sigh. But she knew it was senseless to argue with a Martian—they never backed down. Oh, well. She'd been faking it with the cards since arriving and no one had seemed to notice or care. Maybe she could bluff her way through one more hand.

"All right," she conceded, then indicated the nearby window seat where she had pretended to read cards all evening. When they were seated, each facing the other, she reached for the worn deck of oversize, brightly illustrated cards. "But just a small spread. I'm not getting into a major category spread like some people have asked for this evening."

"What's that?"

"Dozens of cards," Miranda told him. "It can take hours."

"What other... spreads, did you call them?"

Miranda nodded.

"What other spreads are there?"

She placed the deck of cards in front of the man who had become entirely too inquisitive to suit her mood. "Shuffle," she instructed before explaining. "There are several versions of the Celtic cross. Then there's the zodiac spread, the calendar spread, the three-card spread..." She sighed in exasperation because she couldn't remember any more, although she knew there were as many different spreads as there were interpreters of tarot cards. "Look, we'll do one I developed called the pyramid spread, okay?"

"Can I stop shuffling now?" the man asked, clearly impatient to get on with it.

"Not until you think about a question you want answered."

"Question? What kind of question?"

"Any question," Miranda told him with a shrug. "Whatever might be concerning you, anything you have reservations about, something with which you've been very preoccupied lately."

Panwide Textiles, Incorporated, Lucas thought immediately. That damned company had kept him in knots for months now. Every time he thought he had them in his possession, those slippery little bastards in their legal department found something to keep him from seizing control.

Miranda True hadn't been off the mark at all when she'd compared his hands to those of a pirate. He'd been called a pirate and worse in nearly every boardroom in the country, but never without grudging respect. Lucas Strathmoor was what people in the business community politely referred to as a corporate raider—and more accurately as a shark. He preyed on companies that were gasping and floundering in the sea of big business, consuming them first with seemingly ineffective nibbles and then with great gaping bites, until finally swallowing whole what feeble, trembling part was left. Then he turned them around and sold them to someone else for an enormous profit.

But Panwide Textiles had proved to be stronger than the usual target. They'd fought off every maneuver Lucas had attempted, both subtle and overt. However, he had one plan left, one final option he had described to no one for fear that there might be a possible leak emerging in his band of privateers. It was a plan that would work beautifully as long as he claimed the element of surprise. Soon enough Panwide Textiles would be his.

"I have a question," Lucas finally answered resolutely.

"Okay, don't ask it out loud, but stop shuffling the cards whenever you're comfortable."

Lucas stopped at once and replaced the cards on the window seat between them.

Miranda retrieved the cards, handling the deck gingerly, reluctantly, turning the first card faceup into a position by itself. Beneath it she turned up two more, and beneath those three more, and beneath those four more, until she had an irregularly placed pyramid. She studied the cards for a long time, remembering the significance of some of the illustrations, but totally oblivious to what the others stood for. Why had she ever agreed to try tarot? she asked herself miserably. Cards were simply too inconsistent. There were a million things they could mean. With a resigned flick of her thumb along the remainder of the deck, she set it aside and began to interpret the spread before her as best she could.

"This card," she began, pointing to the one that stood alone above the others, "represents you in the scheme of things. How you see yourself and how others see you." Normally those would be represented by two separate cards, Miranda knew, but having assessed the character of this man earlier from his palm, she also knew those were one and the same in his case.

"The king of wands," she continued. Well, this one she remembered well, and she marveled at its appropriateness now. "You're ambitious, headstrong, confident and capable, but are also inclined to be short-tempered, self-centered and impatient. Your career probably revolves around construction or development of some kind. Certainly you spend a lot of time planning things.''

Lucas shifted a little uncomfortably in his chair.

Miranda turned her attention to the next row, moving left to right, relieved to see another card she recognized. ''This card represents your personal wealth. The high priestess. You've been waiting impatiently for something that will expand your finances to a large degree.''

Lucas shifted again.

''This card represents pleasure—where you find it, how you pursue it. The justice card. You like buying things and, once again, planning and productivity bring you enjoyment.''

Again, Lucas squirmed uneasily, involuntarily edging away from the offending cards. His gaze began to wander erratically, trying to find something to focus on that would provide him with a more settling diversion. Almost immediately his eyes fell on the length of shapely leg encased in sheer, smoky silk that extended from beneath the hem of Miranda's blue dress. He let his gaze wander up to the perfectly rounded hip and the dip of slender waistline, up to the generous swell of her breasts.

Yes, this was just what he needed, Lucas thought. Forget Miranda's lucky guesses with the cards and focus instead on how you might go about getting lucky with her.

''This card,'' she continued, feeling restless and edgy as she became all too aware of the frank, appreciative inspection of her feminine charms, ''is representative of your working conditions and your relationship to other employees.'' The two of cups, she thought dismally. What on earth did that mean? Because she had absolutely no idea, Miranda went back to the original card she'd upturned, thinking that if he was a man of the traits she had listed, she could pretty well figure this one out on her own.

"You're the boss," she began cautiously, detecting only a glimmer of confirmation in his pale gray eyes, marveling at the way the brown flecks made the irises seem deeper somehow. "You...uh...you worked your way up from meager beginnings to become a huge success." After all, he'd already affirmed that he used to do manual labor, hadn't he? "Your colleagues and employees offer you grudging respect, although they sometimes...they sometimes think you go too far in your pursuits."

There, that was suitably vague, wasn't it? Miranda thought. And perfectly reasonable to assume, after the way he had gone too far in kissing her hand earlier. When she saw the man's left eyebrow arch in just the slightest fashion, she knew she'd been right on target. This bluffing business wasn't going to be so difficult after all.

"This next card, the fifth one, refers to partnerships and mergers."

Without saying any more, Miranda saw the man growing visibly uncomfortable. That was odd. Recent divorce? she wondered, having already noted the absence of a wedding ring on his left ring finger. No, he clearly had no taste for romance and therefore had probably never married. He was first and foremost a businessman, so... *Mergers.* That was the word he had responded to. He must be getting ready to take part in a merger. Glancing down at the card to find it was the five of pentacles—another she didn't recognize— Miranda was more than relieved by the escape he'd offered her without realizing it.

"You're getting ready to take part in a merger." She voiced her suspicion out loud and nearly chuckled in delight that she had obviously been so accurate in her guess. He flinched as if she had slapped him. "And it isn't going as well as you'd hoped it would," she added for flavor when she saw that his reaction wasn't a favorable one. She suddenly felt buoyant and confident, as if she suddenly claimed some sixth sense about this man's life-style. When she saw that he was seated with a stiff spine and an even stiffer expression, she knew she had hit a nerve. So she jumped on it with both feet.

For the remainder of the reading, she used every bit of body language he offered her to describe his character and "predict" his future. Over and over again Miranda could tell she was hitting unseen targets exactly, and by the time she reached the tenth card, she knew she could do no wrong. The man was as clear and transparent as a summer sky.

Without realizing what he was doing, he helped her to relate accounts of vague childhood experiences, and unknowingly made her aware that he had experienced some difficulty in college but had been aided by the guidance of another person. He reaffirmed her suspicion that he had never married and suffered workaholic tendencies. And in a silent parlay that bordered on brilliant, Miranda had led him to reveal that he was working on a very important project. All the while, she did whatever necessary to make it seem as if *she* were the one who had uncovered these facts, in no way indicating she had received any help from his own reactions.

"This last card represents the one obstacle you'll need to overcome in order to see your project through," she told him nearly a half hour after they had begun. Once again she was relieved to see a card she remembered, and once again she was startled by how appropriate it was in this situation. "The chariot," she said simply.

"And just what the hell does that mean?"

Boy, was he angry, Miranda thought. He'd been prickly almost since she turned over the first card. Okay, so his hadn't been the best reading in the world. So it had been filled with less than positive omens and portents of bad luck.

She hadn't actually told him he was going to fail, had she? She hadn't said anything negative that couldn't be overcome by his own perseverance. And besides, these were *cards,* for goodness sake. He couldn't *possibly* put any credence in them, could he?

"It means you're in for a confrontation. Maybe a conversation with another person is going to cause you trouble, and you're not going to have someone there to comfort you when you most need it."

"And just what the hell does *that* mean?" he repeated.

Frankly, Miranda wasn't sure, so she searched for a suggestion that might sound plausible, pretending to scrutinize the card while she thought of something to say. "Someone...someone you thought you could count on will be...will let you down." There, that sounded reasonable, didn't it? People were always being let down by others they thought they could count on. It happened every day.

Lucas glared at her for a long time in silence, repeating to himself over and over again that this entire experience was grounded in malarkey. "You realize of course that you're full of it," he finally snapped impatiently.

He'd had enough of this ridiculous exercise. Gorgeous, leggy blonde or not, Miranda True was annoying as hell. Never mind that she'd been gut-wrenchingly correct in just about everything she'd described. She'd also been vague enough for him to reassure himself that it was all lucky guessing. And that's all it was, he asserted to himself again. Lucky. Guessing. No one could tell what he'd been through or what he had planned by staring down at brightly colored bits of paper. And no one knew what was in store for Panwide except him, right? Right?

A cold, dark feeling slowly seeped into Lucas's midsection as he studied Miranda. Unless... Could it be that she... Was it possible that... For a moment, it took every ounce of willpower Lucas claimed for him to contain his growing rage. No, it couldn't be, he tried to tell himself. It was too crazy to even consider. She couldn't work for Panwide. That was too farfetched an idea even for that company. Miranda True couldn't possibly be a plant, a corporate spy sent to the party this evening in some weird, last-ditch effort to catch him off guard and make him spill his guts about his intentions.

Or could she?

"Excuse me," Lucas said suddenly, standing abruptly to make a fast, awkward departure.

Miranda watched the man as he made his way across the room again, thinking that despite the strange encounter she'd just had with him, he did indeed have a marvelous back. That spectacular Martian physique.

It was just too bad she was a Venusian.

After one final glance at the cards, Miranda collected them and went to find Grace Devon. She had enjoyed herself this evening despite the strange interlude with the dark-haired man. Or perhaps that interlude was precisely what led to her enjoyment. She wasn't sure. Whatever the reason for her oddly cheerful disposition at the moment, Miranda knew it was pointless to even dream. He wasn't a man for her. Besides, she didn't even know his name.

She located Mrs. Devon with little difficulty, because the other woman completely dominated a room with her stately silver-haired presence.

"It's after ten, Mrs. Devon," Miranda told her employer. "I'll be leaving now if there's nothing else."

"Oh, do call me Grace," the other woman instructed. "And don't go, Miranda. You're much too much fun to have around."

"You only paid me until ten."

"I'm not asking you to stay as my entertainment. I want you to stay as my guest. Everyone adores you, and you've completely rattled Lucas to the point where he had to call it a night early.''

"Lucas? Which one was he?"

Grace bit her lip playfully, and Miranda could tell she was doing her best to hold back peals of laughter. "Oh, my dear, you're an absolute wonder. Every woman here tonight would gladly surrender her pension plan for one wild week-end with him, yet you didn't even bother to get his name."

Suddenly Miranda knew exactly who Grace was refer-ring to. "Oh, you mean the last gentleman I gave a reading to."

"Yes, that's the one. Although I don't think anyone much refers to Lucas as a 'gentleman' anymore."

"He was very polite," Miranda defended him.

"Oh, I'm sure he was," Grace said with a knowing smile. "He probably never let on that he was mentally undressing you and making plans for the ruination of your reputa-tion."

"Actually he wasn't quite able to disguise that," Mir-anda confessed with a small laugh. However, for some strange reason, his unquestionably lustful intentions hadn't bothered her, though she was normally put off by men who were so forward and obvious. From this man, Lucas, though, it had been rather...exciting.

"At any rate," Grace went on, "he left with his feathers all ruffled, something I haven't seen happen to him in a very long time. We all want you to stay and tell us how you did it."

Miranda smiled but shook her head. "Thank you, but I really should be getting home. The shop is closed tomor-row, but I have some paperwork and yard work that I need to see to before Monday, so I have to get up early anyway."

"Well, maybe next time, then."

"Thank you," Miranda replied, delighted that a pillar of Boston's business community would invite her to be included in her next social gathering. "I'd like that very much."

"Be careful going home, dear."

Miranda lifted a hand in farewell, retrieved her purse and black cape from the cabinet where she'd stowed them in the kitchen and went out to her car. With a steady growl, the engine rumbled to life, and then she was easing down the long, cobblestone driveway and onto the street below. As she wound her way through town to the other side, she hummed along with a song on the radio, a throaty Carmen MacRae tune from the fifties that Miranda had always loved. But her mind didn't dwell on the lyrics this time. At the moment, all she could think about was a pair of steely eyes that were filled with an unknown fire, and a pair of hands that had wreaked havoc upon her very soul.

In a sleek, black coupe following six car lengths behind, Lucas Strathmoor turned down his radio to quiet the strains of an old standard lifting from his speakers, and wondered exactly what kind of game Miranda was playing. He picked up the phone nestled beside his seat and punched a series of familiar numbers.

"Lawler," he stated with feigned casualness when someone answered at the other end of the line. "I need your help. I want you to check someone out for me. A woman by the name of Miranda True, although I doubt very seriously that's her real name. Rents herself out as a palmist for parties—worked Grace Devon's tonight. I want to know everything you can tell me about her, and I want to know by tomorrow morning. Thanks."

Without awaiting a reply, Lucas settled the receiver back in its cradle, fully confident that the information he'd requested would be in his hands by the time he was enjoying his Sunday morning coffee and reading about the upcoming Sox season. It didn't prevent him from wanting to follow Miranda, however, to discover her home base. Just in case she was as slippery as everyone else Panwide seemed to hire. One never could tell about corporate spies, he thought. So often, they took the most unlikely form.

"Come on, you guys, grow. You're about to make history."

Miranda stood with her hands settled impatiently on her hips in the greenhouse cornered in her tiny backyard, staring dismally at the minuscule seedlings barely poking their green shoots up through the black soil. She was experimenting with hybrids of certain herbs, something she attempted every year, but was meeting with as little success as usual so far. For some reason she couldn't begin to understand, the plants never made it beyond the seedling stage. They simply refused to grow.

"I understand your reluctance," she said sympathetically to the numerous rows of tiny terra-cotta pots she used for phase two. "Really, I do. This isn't the best world to be growing up in. But I promise I'll take good care of you. I promise you won't go hungry or be out of work or get hurt by someone who doesn't truly love you. You'll like life. Honest. It's not so bad once you get used to the rules."

The seedlings quivered in the early-morning April breeze that crept in through the open door, but offered no other response. Miranda sighed and tugged on the hem of her red hooded sweatshirt, leaving a black streak of potting soil behind. Picking up a hand spade, she offered the seedlings one last longing look and left the greenhouse, closing the door very quietly behind her as one might do a nursery door on a sleeping baby.

It was a glorious morning, cool and crisp and clean in preparation for the appearance of the sun, which had yet to rise fully above the earth. Miranda loved her Sundays. It was the only day when the shop was closed, and she could completely devote herself to the land. Both her front and back yards, though very small, were essentially no more than gardens, consisting of a series of plots devoted to specific flowers, vegetables or herbs. The effect on the whole was beautiful, beginning in late spring when everything began to burst open in splashes of pink, purple and yellow, and lasting well into the fall when her asters and chrysanthemums, her pumpkins and squashes, all ripened into the colors of fire and sunset.

And the smells, she marveled, inhaling as deeply as she could to enjoy the rich, loamy aroma of soil and moss. Even this early in the growing season, when things were only beginning to stir below the earth's surface and peek through the dirt, Miranda loved to simply sit outside, watching and waiting, listening and smelling. The subtle changes that occurred in her yard over a period of weeks and months were amazing. Sometimes things came up so quickly, it was almost as if she could watch the flowers open. And after the blossoms arrived, then came even more life—bees and ladybugs, hummingbirds and snails. It was a little ecosystem all her own that Miranda sustained through care, attention and love.

A little plot of land and someone to love, that's all she'd ever really wanted in life. Something and someone to call her own, something and someone she would be responsible for, something and someone to be hers to take care of. For a while, back in Saint Denis, she thought she'd found exactly that. Mr. and Mrs. Lyndon had been nice enough to allow her use of a little section of their huge backyard to grow things, mostly vegetables and herbs and spices that eventually wound up on the Lyndon dinner table. But Miranda had always taken some home to fix for her mother, too, in spite of the fact that her mother seldom ever noticed.

If only things had been different back in Saint Denis, she thought now. It was a question she used to ask herself every day, but one that only cropped up occasionally after the passage of nearly twelve years. And if only Patrick Lyndon had been a different kind of person.

But things hadn't been different, she reminded herself, and Patrick had turned out to be a complete stranger in the end. And even if Miranda hadn't found true love, at least she'd gotten her little plot of land. Now she never let a day go by when she didn't sit on her back porch to enjoy it. Today was a very beautiful day. And after thirty-two years of what seemed like continuous struggle, hers was finally a very good life.

For hours Miranda worked outside, preparing the earth for the plantings that were to come, tending to the seed-lings already secured in the ground who were brave enough to fight their way through the soil while there was still a chance of frost. Her hair, so neatly braided when she'd stepped from the bathroom at six-thirty that morning, gradually fell apart into a series of petulant strands of gold. And by the time the sun hung fully overhead at its apex in the sky, Miranda was happily stained with remnants of the earth—her face smudged and streaked with dirt and perspiration, the knees of her jeans and elbows of her sweatshirt black, her short fingernails caked with soil. Scooping her bangs back from her eyes, she knew she had left another dark stain amid the ones already present on her forehead, and smiled. She liked the idea of becoming one with the earth, but sometimes she overdid it a little.

Lunchtime, she decided at noon, pushing herself away from a freshly tilled plot of soil she would use for annuals this year. When she turned to head back toward her house, she stopped dead in her tracks, staring at the man who sat on her back porch, feeling her stomach drop to her toes even as her heart leaped into her throat. It was the man she had met last night at Grace Devon's party—the man the other woman had called Lucas.

He sat with his feet planted firmly on the bottom step, his elbows rested on his knees, his hands forming loose fists over his mouth. Despite the fact that it was Sunday, and he in no way seemed the churchgoing type, he wore a dark suit and charcoal-gray overcoat. He appeared very comfortable, though, as if he'd been watching her for a long time. Several moments passed, but he said nothing, simply returned her gaze levelly, as if he had every right to be there. As if she should have been expecting him all along, Miranda thought strangely.

"Lucas," she said softly, involuntarily voicing the name that had rattled around in her head all night.

"So you do know my name," he replied evenly, that dark rich voice reminding Miranda of the wrist-deep soil in which she'd spent her morning.

"Mrs. Devon . . . Grace . . . told me last night after you'd left."

"Uh-huh. I bet she did."

He seemed angry about something again, and Miranda thought that odd, considering the fact that *he* was the one who was trespassing.

"This is private property," she told him, aware that her reminder would probably be falling on deaf ears. "What are you doing here?"

"I followed you home last night," he replied bluntly.

For the first time since meeting him, Miranda felt a thrill of fear edge down her spine. Not because she was afraid of what he might do at any moment, but because of what he seemed capable of doing in the long run.

"Why?" she asked softly, hoping none of her apprehension was evident in her voice.

"Because I don't think you're who you say you are."

"Who do you think I am?"

Lucas took his time in replying to her question, and Miranda decided it was because he wanted to put her on edge.

She also decided his effort worked extremely well. With every second that passed, she grew more and more uncomfortable.

"At first," he began slowly, stretching his long legs out before him onto the sidewalk, leaning back on his elbows with a casualness Miranda was sure he didn't feel, "I just thought you were some cheap bit of psychic hoodoo turning a fast buck at the expense of other people's gullibility."

Miranda felt her face flame in anger and embarrassment. She was only too sensitive to such reactions from other people—the assumption that she presented herself to be something other than what she was. The entire population of Saint Denis—all nine hundred and seventeen of them— had ultimately thought of her as nothing but a cheap, immoral little gold digger, something she most certainly had never been. Even Patrick Lyndon had come to feel that way, she had discovered too late. But to hear a man like Lucas— whoever or whatever he was—charge such a thing without even trying to disguise the contempt in his voice, opened up old wounds and hurts that Miranda had thought were finally impervious to pain.

"After seeing you in action, though," he continued, again in that maddeningly careless tone of voice, "I realized you honestly believe in this ridiculous stuff, and all I could do then was shake my head in wonder."

"You still haven't answered my question," Miranda said hoarsely, feeling angrier and more defensive now than she could recall being since leaving Saint Denis. Who did this man think he was, barging in on her life this way, trespassing on her property, only to make her feel as if *she* were the one who should be making explanations? "Just who do you think I am? Tell me that, mister, then I have a few more questions I'd like answered."

That seemed to hit a sore spot with him. Lucas shot up from the stairs and took several measured strides in her direction, pausing only inches before her. Miranda had to lean her head back to meet his gaze, because he towered a good eight inches over her. His eyes were as flinty as a stormy sky, his lips pressed thinly in exasperation.

"You've got one hell of a nerve demanding anything from me," he told her.

Miranda squared her shoulders and tried to make herself as tall as possible without actually standing on tiptoe. No one had the right to try to make her feel small. Not anymore. "I repeat," she stated firmly, "*you* are trespassing. Now get off my property before I call the police."

Lucas emitted a single humorless chuckle. "Answer my questions, or your property will dry up into dust. I'll see to it that you spend so much time in jail, the planet will be a toxic wasteland by the time you get out."

Miranda's anger was overcome by her confusion then, and she felt the fight go out of her. She backed down somewhat as she asked, "What on earth are you talking about?"

"Tell me true, Miranda," Lucas demanded with a menacing grin. "How long have you been working for the Lyndons, and just what the hell is your position in Panwide Textiles after all these years, anyway?"

Chapter Three

Lucas hadn't wanted to have his suspicions and fears about Miranda confirmed. His disappointment upon coming down to breakfast that morning to find his assistant, Simon Lawler, seated at one end of the table in the massive dining room, had been surprisingly acute. And when Simon had handed him a harmless-looking manila folder, Lucas had tried to convince himself that he was prepared for the worst. Yet he hadn't been ready for the gut-burning reaction he experienced when the worst was what he discovered. Over his usual morning repast of coffee, and bacon and eggs prepared by his housekeeper, he had tried to remain nonchalant as he read hungrily every scrap of information Simon had gathered on Miranda True. And there had been a wealth of it.

First he had perused the usual stuff, noting that none of it was particularly remarkable except for the fact that she was thirty-two years of age—quite a bit older than he would have guessed. She had never married, claimed no children, was a high school graduate, had taken some night classes in business at Boston University over the past four years and was currently finishing up the semester enrolled in Marketing 201. He just skimmed briefly over some of the more intimate details of her character, wanting instead to get to her work history. She owned a shop downtown, he learned, one in a row of other trendy boutiques, and she was prospering nicely after two years in operation. Before that, she had worked for nearly ten years as a domestic in the kitchen of a wealthy Boston family, and before that . . .

Before that she had lived in Saint Denis, Massachusetts. It was then that Lucas had sat up in his chair and pushed his plate away, only to immerse himself in learning everything he possibly could about Miranda True.

He was surprised upon realizing that True was indeed her last name—and silently amused by its appropriateness. What he tried to assure himself was *not* surprising was the fact that for over four years her name had appeared on the payroll of a family known as Lyndon—and that it was the same Lyndon family who also owned Panwide Textiles in Saint Denis, Massachusetts. Miranda had been hired at sixteen to work for them as a domestic, a cook's assistant. Twelve years ago, however, her name had disappeared from the roster, and Lucas wanted to know why.

The following page of the report furnished him with an answer, describing in detail a two-year dalliance between Miranda and the eldest Lyndon son, Patrick, four years her senior. Apparently the two of them had gotten involved shortly after Miranda turned eighteen, and had kept their relationship secret from everyone in town. When the liaison was finally discovered, Patrick severed his ties to the kitchen help, and the family sent her packing. It sounded like the oldest story in the world as far as Lucas was con-

cerned. But there was still something about it that had
bothered him.

Now as he stared into the seemingly guileless eyes of
Miranda True, it bothered him even more. If she'd loved a
Lyndon once, she might love him still. And if she loved him
still, she would probably do anything for him, right? Including breaking the law. Including spying on the competition.

"You've been spying on me," Lucas accused her evenly,
his voice belying none of the turmoil tearing him up inside.
She looked so innocent, so incapable of the charge he was
levying against her. With her face free of cosmetics, and
black smudges of soil decorating her cheek and forehead,
she looked almost like a child who'd been playing in a dirt
pile all morning. How could someone so beautiful be guilty
of deception? Crazily Lucas realized he suddenly wasn't
certain whether he was angrier at the fact that she might be
spying on him, or the fact that she might still be carrying a
torch for some jerk who'd treated her so shabbily twelve
years ago.

Miranda's expression went from confused to completely
dumbfounded. "What?" she asked, her posture telling Lucas she was less assured than she was letting on.

"You work for Panwide Textiles, don't you?"

Boy, there was a name she hadn't heard for a long time,
Miranda thought, as her confusion compounded. How on
earth was Patrick's family's business even remotely related
to what was going on here now? "I...I'm sorry," she
stammered. "But I really don't have any idea what you're
talking about."

"You work for Panwide," Lucas repeated, turning the
question into a statement.

Miranda shook her head. "No, I don't. I own a shop
downtown called One To Grow On. I never worked for
Panwide."

"Your name appeared on the Lyndon payroll for four years," he reminded her.

Miranda took a deep breath before replying, trying not to betray any of the apprehension swirling around her midsection. The knowledge that a virtual stranger had easily managed to pry into her background was startling, to say the least. When she spoke again, it was slowly and evenly, as if she were weighing the consequence of every word before she uttered it. "Not that it's any of your business, but I worked for the Lyndons in their home, not their mill. Just what are you driving at? I don't like to play games, Mr. . . . ."

"Strathmoor," he obliged, his expression just short of a sneer. "Lucas Strathmoor. As if you didn't already know."

"No, I didn't know. Now cut to the chase, Mr. Strathmoor. If there's a question about me you want answered, ask it. But don't pull this suave, corporate-exec routine with me. I'm not impressed."

Lucas inhaled deeply before finally conceding. "All right. I want to know about your relationship with the Lyndons and Panwide Textiles."

Miranda studied him for a moment, then replied simply, "No."

"Excuse me?" he muttered, raising his eyebrows in unmistakable surprise. Apparently her reply was the last thing he expected to hear. Lucas Strathmoor was clearly a man accustomed to getting exactly what he asked for, exactly when he asked for it.

"I said no," Miranda repeated blandly. "It's none of your business." Wiping her hands on the front of her sweatshirt in what she hoped he would interpret as a symbolic gesture, she pushed past him with a quietly uttered, "Now get out of my yard before I call the cops."

She leaped over the two steps leading up to her porch and grasped the knob of her back door feverishly. Propelling herself forward with a savage lurch, she pushed the heavy

door and herself into her kitchen in an effort to escape the
very disturbing Mr. Strathmoor. But her action was in vain.
Obviously he was indeed a man who expected to be obeyed,
because instead of being put off by Miranda's dismissal, he
followed her up the stairs and into her house. If was then
that Miranda began to panic.

"I repeat, Mr. Strathmoor, you are not welcome here.
And I won't hesitate to call the police."

"I only want to talk to you, Miranda," he assured her in
a voice that was anything but assuring. As if to illustrate his
intent that he meant her no harm, however, he came no
farther into the room, instead leaning casually against the
doorjamb with his hands in his trouser pockets and one foot
crossed over the other.

Miranda placed herself on the other side of the kitchen
table, near a butcher block that housed an assortment of
very sharp knives. It was a position Lucas duly noted.

"So talk," she instructed. "But make it fast."

"If you'll tell me the truth, I promise I won't take any
action that might land you in trouble with the law. All I
want to know is what I'm up against, where the Lyndons are
concerned. All I want to know is what they have up their
sleeves."

"I'm truly sorry, Mr. Strathmoor, but I can't help you."

"Why not?"

Miranda glared at him furiously. "Because I still don't
know what you're talking about."

Silence hung over the room for several moments, until
Lucas finally relented. "Okay, fine," he said. "Let's pretend for a moment that you really don't know what I'm
talking about. I'll just give you a quick rundown, shall I?"

"Please do."

Miranda tried to slow her accelerated heartbeat and
breathe evenly. But the longer she stared at Lucas, the more
erratic her pulse became. No one had ever put her on edge

the way this man did. However, she realized to her chagrin, the uneasiness she was experiencing had little to do with the fact that a strange man had just entered her house uninvited, and quite a lot to do with the fact that she wasn't honestly certain she wanted him to leave. Despite the antagonism that hung thick in the air between them, there was something about Lucas Strathmoor that intrigued Miranda. The realization was crazy, she knew, but she couldn't shake the feeling that there was more to their odd relationship than either of them realized.

Lucas continued to lean lazily in the doorway as he explained the situation, but withdrew a hand from his pocket to trace a crack in the paint as he spoke. "Miranda, I'm in the business of...acquiring things. Businesses. Most recently I set my sights on Panwide Textiles in Saint Denis. They resisted my efforts to buy them outright, so I started buying them up piece by piece. When they caught on to what I was doing, they began trying harder to keep me out. So I had to resort to maneuvers that were a little...underhanded. But perfectly legal," he added quickly, turning his attention from the crack in the paint to meet Miranda's gaze levelly. "Yet every time I'm ready to finally close the deal, they shut me out somehow."

"I'm not surprised," Miranda said softly. "That company has been the lifeblood of the Lyndons for more than a hundred and fifty years. It would kill them to lose it."

Her comment must have rankled him. As if he couldn't stand being still any longer, Lucas pushed himself away from the door and began to make a slow circuit around the table toward Miranda. For every step he took in her direction, she took a step backward, until they had completely traded places and she stood near the back door, ready to bolt at any moment.

"Then they should have taken better care of it," Lucas muttered through gritted teeth. "The business has been declining for nearly a decade. They can't hang on to it much longer without pumping more money into it than they have. Now, may I continue?''

Miranda nodded slowly but remained silent.

"Thank you. Last night I went to a party and met a woman who seemed to know an awful lot about what I was doing and what I had planned. I later discovered that this woman is, coincidentally, from Saint Denis herself, and also, coincidentally, worked for the very people I'm trying to oust from power."

Although Lucas slowly began his progress around the table once again, Miranda remained where she was standing, reasoning that she was better off near an exit than near weapons, because surely this man could overpower her with little difficulty. She didn't dwell on the realization that he could no doubt outrun her as well, and instead stood staring helplessly as he drew nearer and nearer with every step. All she could think about was that she now understood how a partridge must feel when cornered by a snarling wolf.

"Some coincidence, don't you think, Miranda?" Lucas murmured when he stood only inches away from her.

Miranda nodded silently again at his roughly uttered question, and Lucas smiled grimly at the recognition that he had succeeded in putting her so clearly off her guard. Maybe now she'd live up to her name and answer his questions honestly. "You would have done anything for Patrick Lyndon back then, wouldn't you?" he pressed further. "You'd do anything for him now. You're still in love with him, aren't you?"

The fact that Lucas Strathmoor had so thoroughly checked up on her infuriated Miranda to the point where she could feel nothing but anger. What she had experienced with Patrick was intensely private and very much a part of her past. This man had no right to uncover things that she wanted to keep personal. And there was no telling what else he thought he knew about her.

"You've got some nerve," Miranda bit out crossly, her anger putting her quickly on the offensive. "Just who do you think you are?"

"A businessman," Lucas replied immediately. "A businessman who wants a particular business and knows how to go about acquiring it."

"Acquiring it?" Miranda repeated doubtfully, forgetting now the precariousness of their positions. "*Acquiring* it? Sounds to me like you stop just short of stealing it."

"I do not steal—"

"Sneaky, underhanded tricks, no matter how perfectly legal, amount to nothing more than theft in my book. If people don't want you to have their businesses, then you have no right taking them."

"I have every right—"

"Don't you ever wonder what happens to the people you oust from power, Mr. Strathmoor? What does happen to them, huh?"

"Oh, don't lose any sleep over it, Miranda, they all do just fine—"

"They don't have what once belonged to them," she reminded him, trying to hold back tears that seemed to come from nowhere. "No one ever does *fine* after something like that."

Lucas gazed down at Miranda, stunned by the vehemence of their verbal exchange. Where had all this anger come from? he wondered. They were both shaking from their barely restrained fury, their voices rough and ragged from their efforts to keep from screaming at each other. Suddenly it dawned on Lucas why Miranda had defended the Lyndons so quickly and passionately.

"You do still love him, don't you?"

Miranda was slowly trying to calm herself down and didn't understand the implication of Lucas's assertion. "Who?"

"Patrick Lyndon. That's why you launched into me like that. You're still loyal to the Lyndons. You still love Patrick. That's why you're spying on me for them."

Miranda closed her eyes in a silent bid for patience when she realized that Lucas Strathmoor still thought she was guilty of corporate espionage. If the situation wasn't so utterly bizarre, she might double up with laughter right now. Miranda True, corporate saboteur. Really, it was simply too, too funny.

"Mr. Strathmoor," she began a little breathlessly, still trying to regulate her respiration. "I can see how a man who does what you do for a living might experience some obsessively paranoid behavior, but I assure you, I am not spying on you for the Lyndons. And although I find your checking up on me reprehensible, I'll comment on what you've uncovered nonetheless, if for no other reason than to remove you from my life once and for all.

"It's true that I grew up in Saint Denis, and I did go to work for the Lyndons when I was sixteen. But I worked at their home, in the kitchen. I never worked for Panwide, and wouldn't be able to tell you the first thing about company affairs. It's also true that Patrick and I were...romantically involved . . . but that was a youthful indiscretion that ended twelve years ago. Shortly after that, I left Saint Denis, and have been back only once, six years ago, to attend my mother's funeral. I saw none of the Lyndons then, nor have I spoken to any of them since I left.

"I'm sorry if you suffered a sleepless night because of this weird coincidence, but I assure you that's all it is . . . a very weird coincidence."

Miranda waited patiently for Lucas's reaction, hoping he would accept her explanation at face value and refrain from probing further. Mostly she hoped he wouldn't press the issue of what she had termed her "youthful indiscretion" with Patrick. To say she had been "romantically involved" with him was a gross understatement. She had fallen for Patrick Lyndon with all her heart and soul the moment she'd laid eyes on him when she was sixteen. And when he'd returned from college two years later and began to take an interest in her, Miranda's infatuation had become full-blown love. Patrick had been her first lover. And her only love.

But he had also been the oldest son of Saint Denis's most prominent family, and she had been the illegitimate daughter of a waitress who lived on the wrong side of the tracks. Up until the time that her relationship with Patrick was discovered, the Lyndons had treated Miranda as politely as they did everyone who worked in their household. But she had never quite been able to escape the stigma that went along with being poor and insignificant. Patrick's honest affection for her back then had made her begin to hope that perhaps her time for happiness had finally come.

However, Patrick had been as much a victim of social stigma as she. Miranda never doubted that he had cared for her on some level, but he felt the constraints of society, too, and thought it would be impossible for him to spend his life with someone like Miranda when he was the kind of man he was. And when word of their relationship got out, the citizens of Saint Denis had drawn their own conclusions. Miranda True was a fortune hunter of questionable virtue, an immoral little money grubber who was no better than her sleazy mother. Ultimately even Patrick had bought into the allegations, and she'd known then there was no hope for a future with him. He'd broken off their relationship, telling Miranda she would never belong in his world. After that, Miranda had wondered if she would ever "belong" anywhere again.

These days, she knew that she did. With the success of her shop, she'd managed to carve a niche for herself in Boston, a good distance away from the rolling green hills of Saint Denis, and far from the people who had so thoroughly misjudged her. And that little niche didn't include corporate espionage in any way, shape or form. With any luck at all, Lucas Strathmoor would realize that and never bother her again. She pushed away the odd pain that twisted through her at the thought of never seeing him again.

He still looked thoughtful when he said, "If that's the truth, then how did you know so much about me last night? Try as you might, you'll never make me believe that you learned of my intentions by staring at a deck of cards and the lines of my hands."

Boy, she'd really rattled him with that reading, Miranda thought. Shrugging nervously, she told him honestly, "I was guessing."

"You were guessing," he repeated, clearly unconvinced.

Miranda nodded and sighed deeply, realizing that the least she could do was explain truthfully about the previous evening. "I'm not much of a tarot reader," she confessed. "In fact, most of what I told you was purely fictitious."

"No, it wasn't," he countered. "It was right on target, every last word."

She paused for a moment before revealing, "Then I'm a lot better at reading body language than I thought."

Lucas gazed at her blandly for a moment before requesting, "You want to clarify that for me?"

Miranda's shoulders dropped in defeat. "No, not particularly."

When he continued to gaze at her in silence, his expression unwavering, Miranda sighed again. "Okay, okay. I guess the least I can do is own up to my fraudulent behavior last night."

Lucas sucked in a quick breath of air before stating softly, dangerously, "So you admit that you've been misrepresenting yourself."

Miranda nodded. "Yes. But not in the way you think. I've been passing myself off as a tarot reader, when the fact of the matter is that I don't hold any more belief in the prophetic qualities of tarot cards than you do. What I told you last night during your reading—anything I might have described accurately—was purely a result of how *you* responded physically to my suggestions."

Now Lucas was the one to be confused. "Come again?"

"Mr. Strathmoor, you may not realize it, but you're an open book where facial expressions are concerned."

Lucas took a proprietary step forward, causing Miranda to take a defensive step back. Her action landed her flat against the wall, and Lucas took advantage of her position by planting his hand and upper arm firmly against the doorjamb between Miranda's face and her only means of escape. The action also served to bring his body closer to hers, something he suspected they both found rather disconcerting.

"That's funny, Miranda," he murmured softly. "Because I've always prided myself on maintaining an excellent poker face. A good deal of my success has resulted from the fact that very few people, if any, ever really know what I'm thinking."

"It's your eyes," Miranda said quietly, unable to tear her gaze away from his. "They're..." Her voice trailed off when she realized she was about to say "beautiful." Instead she took a deep breath, met his steely gray gaze levelly and told him, "They're...very expressive."

Miranda was helpless to say more, because about that time Lucas Strathmoor's eyes began to change. The stain of brown surrounding his pupils became darker, making his eyes seem larger, deeper somehow, and the pale gray irises turned stormy. Suddenly her kitchen seemed to fade away to nothingness, and Miranda felt as if she and Lucas were the only things living and breathing in the universe. For a moment, Miranda thought she heard thunder outside, then realized it was only the pounding of her heart. Lucas was standing so close to her. Close enough that she could smell the spicy man scent of him and feel the warmth of his body. Close enough that she could just tilt her head back and kiss him, if that was what she had a mind to do.

"If what you say is true, Miranda, then what are my eyes telling you right now?"

Slowly, as if giving her the opportunity to stop him if she wanted, Lucas flattened his other palm against the wall on the other side of her head, pulling his body as close to hers as he could without touching her when he did so. Miranda felt herself growing warmer, felt parts of her body that had lain dormant for years stirring to life with a burst of fire. Her pulse ran more rapidly as she answered his question, replying bluntly, "You're . . . you're aroused."

At her utterly frank statement, Lucas's eyes grew even darker, even more intense. For long moments he returned her gaze, then slowly he began to smile, a seductive, dangerous smile that was full of intimate promise. "So are you, Miranda," he said softly, his voice full of wonder at his realization that he could recognize her thoughts as easily as she could his. He lifted his hand from the wall to brush the backs of his bent fingers over her heated, flushed cheek. Then his voice dropped in volume and tone as he repeated, "So are you."

Miranda couldn't deny his assertion, as much as she wished she could, but she said nothing that would give her emotions away. Instead she ducked deftly under Lucas's other arm and headed out the back door into her yard. Fresh air, that's what she needed, she decided. *Cold* fresh air. Lots and lots of fresh . . . cold . . . air.

As she gulped in as much as her lungs would hold, Miranda heard the sound of her screen door creaking open behind her and knew that Lucas had followed her out into the yard. Turning to meet his gaze, she realized he was still more than a little angry, and still more than a little suspicious. If she was ever going to get rid of him, she had to convince him once and for all that she did not work for the Lyndons or Panwide.

"Mr. Strathmoor, I'll try one more time to explain, then I want you to leave my house, and leave me alone." She straightened herself to her full height, commanding her voice to be supremely matter-of-fact as she concluded their conversation. "Last night, I was able to appear to tell you things about yourself, because every time I made some vague suggestion, you either verified or denied it without saying a word. I wasn't reading your cards last night, I was reading your reactions to guesses and suppositions I voiced. Your reactions to my suggestions told me everything I needed to know. It was easy to put together the pieces of the puzzle you offered me. As I said earlier, you're an open book."

Lucas listened intently as Miranda spoke, realizing that there was some degree of sense in what she said. However, he also knew that he was better than most people at hiding what he felt. If she *was* able to pick up on his thoughts by interpreting his body language, then she was a lot more perceptive than the average person.

"And the palmistry part, was that all conjecture, too?" he asked.

"No, that part wasn't," she replied honestly. "I know most people think chiromancy is a lot of hooey, but to me it makes a lot of sense. Still, even if I'd never seen your palm, I could have told you everything I did because you're such a perfect example of the kind of man you are."

"And what kind of man is that?"

"A Martian," Miranda told him simply, the ghost of a smile playing about her lips. "Aggressive, self-confident, domineering, charming, ruthless, passionate, handsome..." Her voice trailed off when she realized that what she was saying would reveal how completely preoccupied she'd become by thoughts of him. He would think she was utterly enthralled by him if she wasn't more careful, she told herself. And of course, such a suggestion was ridiculous.

"How can one man be all those things?"

Miranda shrugged. "Not many men are. You're an exceptionally well-developed Martian."

"Why should I believe what you've told me?" he asked aloud, though he wasn't sure whether he was posing the question to Miranda or to himself.

As Miranda watched him watching her, the cool breeze kicked up again and nudged a stray piece of gold hair across her eyes. She lifted her hand to brush it away, but Lucas beat her to it, threading his own fingers through the soft strands of blond to tuck them back behind her ear. Before he drew his hand away, he traced the line of her jaw with his thumb, then raked his fingers softly over her lower lip. Miranda's skin came alive everywhere he touched her, and involuntarily she parted her lips as if expecting him to kiss her.

"Why should I believe you, Miranda?" he asked her again.

When she answered him, her voice was filled with a quiet conviction that dared him to dispute her. "Because I'm telling you the truth, that's why."

Lucas wasn't sure whether he believed her or not, but he wasn't quite as certain of her duplicity now as he had been that morning. It wasn't so much what Miranda had said to explain and excuse herself from his accusation, but more the way she had behaved since he'd confronted her. She wasn't the only one who was good at interpreting body language—Lucas also prided himself in being able to read people and their reactions. It had contributed largely to his success in business. And Miranda True simply didn't *seem* like a liar and a thief and a spy.

Lucas said nothing that would either confirm or deny his belief in her assurance. Instead he only gazed at Miranda a moment longer before turning on his heel to leave. He didn't look back, didn't offer her a farewell, just continued walking until he reached his car. Once inside, he immediately gunned the engine to life and sped away from Miranda's house, his thoughts a jumble over what had transpired between them.

There was no reason for him to believe she was anything other than what she claimed and appeared to be—a woman who was quite adept at studying people, at seeing subtle nuances and interpreting facial expressions that other people, himself included, would overlook. Lucas had to admit that she did seem to claim an earthy, amazingly perceptive sense of what was what.

But there was still a good chance that she was just an exquisite actress, adept at disguising the fact that she was also an exceptionally good spy, working for the Lyndons to help ward off his advances. In either case, he would be wise to keep an eye on Miranda True. And for more than just the obvious reasons, Lucas thought further. The way he saw it, there were two possibilities he had to consider.

If Miranda *was* still working for the Lyndons, then it was absolutely imperative that he know what she was up to every minute of the day in case she had uncovered some weakness in his maneuvering that she could report to her employers. However, if she *didn't* claim ties to the Lyndons anymore, and had been able to tell what he was thinking by the way he reacted to her statements, then she *must* be damned good at reading people—a good deal better than he was at it himself.

It was with that realization that Lucas began to form an even better plan than the one he'd been entertaining previously to gain control of Panwide. Miranda would be a gift from the gods to someone like him. She could guess accurately what his adversaries and targets were thinking or planning, based on how they reacted to certain questions or suggestions. And whereas Lucas's corporate targets were always on guard around him, Miranda's guileless eyes and bewitching charm put others at ease immediately. Simply put, people would trust her. They would feel comfortable around her, even open up to her. For a man whose livelihood depended on guessing and predicting what other people were going to do, Miranda True could make things a hell of a lot easier.

Unfortunately this second version of Miranda also came across as a very ethical, virtuous, gentle woman who would be hesitant about even squashing a mosquito. There was little chance she would ever go along with any venture Lucas might plan along those lines, even if he offered to pay her extravagantly for her talents.

He grimaced at the harsh squealing of his tires as he took a turn too quickly. Therefore, he thought, it would probably be better if she never figured out what was going on.

He could do it, Lucas thought. It would be so perfect, so completely fitting. He would just use Miranda's talents this once, he promised himself, to get Panwide Textiles, because they'd been so difficult. It was perfectly acceptable as far as he was concerned. The Lyndons deserved it after the crummy way they'd treated Miranda all those years ago. Despite the fact that she seemed in no way the avenging type, Lucas thought it was possible that she wouldn't mind being instrumental in the downfall of the mighty Lyndon family.

Besides, he reminded himself, there was still a chance that Miranda *was* involved in some kind of shady corporate espionage, no matter how effective she'd been in shaking his earlier conviction. She and the Lyndon kid had been lovers, after all. It would be a good idea to keep close tabs on her until this deal went through. And anyway, he concluded selfishly, he could pull this off without her ever knowing what hit her.

As Lucas steered his car to a halt in the street directly in front of his Cambridge town house, he made his decision. He would use Miranda True and her perceptive qualities to his own advantage. And seeing as how the two of them had reacted so... favorably to each other on two occasions already, what better way to hook her than by pretending to have a romantic interest in her? If he was lucky—and he usually was—things would indeed get very romantic between them. And if he did this thing up right... Lucas smiled wickedly.

If he did this thing up right, he wouldn't have to pretend at all.

Chapter Four

Three days later found Miranda working late. Her shop closed at six, but it wasn't unusual for her to stay until eight or later taking care of paperwork—orders for merchandise from her suppliers, scheduling, payroll or any number of other things that might arise. Tonight was just such a night. In her tiny office, surrounded by soft strains of Mozart emerging from a radio on the filing cabinet, Miranda steadied on her nose the glasses she wore for close-up work as she added a column of numbers that refused to total the same thing twice. Glancing at the clock that was nearly obscured by a mountain of paper at the edge of her desk, she decided to call it quits. She hadn't eaten for nearly seven hours, and her stomach was loudly insisting she fill it.

Miranda decided to forgo organizing what little she could of the mess on her desk, and instead removed her glasses and tucked them into the top drawer. Tossing her cape on over her seawater-green suit and retrieving her purse from the filing cabinet, she then switched off the lights, turned on the alarm and locked up the shop behind her. Before she had taken two steps toward the bus stop, however, she heard a familiar male voice call out her first name, turning the simple, three-syllable word into a sensually murmured promise that felt like the soft caress of comforting fingers upon her restless soul.

When she pivoted toward the direction from which it had come, Miranda found herself staring at Lucas Strathmoor, who was bathed in the yellow glow of a street lamp, leaning against his car as if he had all the time in the world. Which of course wasn't true at all, she realized further, because he was illegally parked in a loading zone in front of the shop. Still, he looked marvelous in his expensive suit, with the wind ruffling his dark, russet-stained hair.

Miranda had to remind herself sharply that she wasn't on the best of terms with the man, then wondered helplessly why she even bothered. Regardless of how much she tried to bear in mind that they were barely one step away from being adversaries in some undeclared war, she nonetheless found Lucas Strathmoor to be an extremely compelling specimen.

"Mr. Strathmoor," she greeted him coolly. "What brings you out into the night air?"

He pushed himself away from his car and strode confidently toward her with his hands tucked casually in his pockets. Miranda suspected he was nowhere near as harmless as the gesture made him seem.

When he stood directly in front of her, he gazed down into her eyes levelly and declared simply, "You."

His frankness shouldn't have surprised her after the bluntness he'd shown only a few days before, but it succeeded in putting Miranda on her guard. The last time he was this frank, she reminded herself, he accused her of spying on him.

"Why?" she asked warily.

"I think we need to talk."

"Oh, I think we did plenty of talking on Sunday," Miranda told him mildly. "You said more than enough." And then you turned and left without even saying goodbye, she added to herself, hating the fact that his abrupt departure had actually hurt her feelings.

"And that's exactly what I want to talk to you about now."

Miranda reached into her purse for her gloves, not because her hands were particularly cold, but because she suddenly felt the need to keep them occupied. "I don't know what you mean," she said as she struggled to tug one on.

Lucas watched her actions with much interest, and Miranda felt her skin heat up at the way he was looking at her. It was how he had looked at her before, when he'd had her cornered in her kitchen—aroused. How could he possibly find something erotic in the act of putting on gloves?

Ever since he had taken Miranda's hands in his at Grace's party, Lucas had been fascinated by how soft and delicate they were. More than once over the past few days, he had found himself wondering what it would feel like to have her hands splayed across his naked chest or tangled in his hair. It was a curiosity he hoped to have assuaged in the near future. But for now he knew he would have to remain patient. Miranda True was a wary woman—wary of him, and for very good reason, he knew. Yet he couldn't quite keep his thoughts from skirting around sexual images. The woman brought out the beast in him.

"I owe you an apology," he said. "And I'd like to buy you dinner to make up for my behavior on Sunday."

Miranda gazed at him for a long time as if trying to decide whether or not his invitation was earnestly offered. When she apparently came to the conclusion that it was, she went back to donning her gloves and shook her head.

"No, thank you," she told him simply, certain it was the right decision, even if it felt like the wrong one.

Lucas wasn't used to hearing the word "no" from people, especially with such quick conviction. Miranda's resolute declining of his offer, not to mention the dismissal he detected in her voice, put Lucas's back up in a big way. Suddenly, convincing her to say yes became the ultimate challenge.

"Why not?" he demanded as he took another step toward her that left little room for argument.

Miranda's eyes met his in the dusky light of the street lamp, and Lucas could have sworn he saw a flicker of something combative ignite in their blue depths.

"Because I'm not hungry, that's why," she replied.

As if to betray her, Miranda's stomach chose that moment to growl ferociously, and Lucas smiled triumphantly.

"Sounds to me like you're hungry."

Miranda's expression was deadpan. "It's indigestion."

No doubt brought on by his appearance, Lucas thought mildly. "Come on, Miranda," he cajoled. "Let me make amends for being so erroneous and obnoxious Sunday. I really am sorry I overreacted the way I did. I just jumped to conclusions, that's all. You have to understand that I was only trying to protect my interests."

"Oh, I don't doubt that for a moment," she told him with a mirthless chuckle. "Nor do I doubt that *your* interests far outweigh any responsibility you might feel toward other human beings."

"That's not true, and you know it. You're deliberately misunderstanding me and misinterpreting what I say." Lucas tilted his head toward the sign over Miranda's store. "You'd do whatever was necessary and within your power to make sure your business flourished, to be certain no one undermined you, wouldn't you?"

"I wouldn't accuse someone of spying on me."

"You would if you honestly believed that they were."

Miranda placed her fists firmly on her hips, tilted her head back to glare at him and countered, "Maybe. But I'd thoroughly research my suspicions before I started pointing a finger. You, on the other hand, came barging right into my life—invading my home, for goodness' sake—not asking me about your suspicions, but telling me outright what a criminal I was. You didn't even take a breath long enough to let me explain until I out and out demanded an opportunity."

Lucas returned her fiery gaze with one of his own, but his words were quietly uttered and full of regret when he spoke again. "You're right. I did. And I'm sorry."

Miranda wasn't sure what made her soften toward him when she did. Maybe it was because of what seemed to be an honestly solicitous apology for his behavior. Or maybe it was because of the look of complete, unmistakable worry in his eyes. She only knew that suddenly she was finding it very difficult to remain angry with Lucas Strathmoor, and she felt the fight go out of her.

"All right," she murmured wearily. "I accept your apology. It isn't necessary to buy me dinner to make amends."

For a moment he said nothing, only gazed at her as if she were something worth gazing at. Finally he continued, "Then let me buy you dinner because I'd like to get to know you better."

His quietly uttered declaration couldn't have surprised Miranda more. She took two involuntary steps backward, which he followed with three deliberate steps forward, and found herself backed against a wall with Lucas Strathmoor towering over her—again. It was becoming an all-too-familiar position, one she was shocked to realize she was beginning to find somewhat . . . intriguing.

"I don't think so," she declined softly, halfheartedly.

"Why not?" he asked again, his insistence punctuating the question.

"Because..." Her voice trailed off as she tried to think of a good reason.

"You've accepted my apology," Lucas pointed out.

"Yes..."

"So that means you've forgiven me?"

Miranda nodded slowly, only a little uncertain. "Yes..."

"You're...hungry," he added for flavor.

"Yes..." She tried to ignore the shudder of heat that shook her body at the emphasis he put on the word "hungry."

"And you'd like to get to know me better, too," Lucas went on.

Miranda wanted to assert that, no, that wasn't the case at all, that finally he had stumbled onto what was precisely the reason it would be pointless for them to have dinner together. Unfortunately she wasn't sure *that* was the case at all. Despite their rocky beginning, there was something, some unidentifiable attraction, burning up the air between them. It would be foolish for her to deny that.

However, he really wasn't the kind of man with whom she'd normally associate. He was a Martian, after all, she reminded herself, and most Martians ate Venusians for breakfast. Still, there had been successful unions between the two groups—like every rule, this one had exceptions. Miranda chose not to dwell on the funny rhythm her heart kicked up at the notion of what a union with Lucas Strathmoor might involve. The memory of his mount of Venus still burned brightly in her mind, and she knew without doubt he wouldn't be a man who took lovemaking lightly. Not the physical part of it, anyway.

Assuring herself she would be better off declining him once and for all, Miranda was surprised to hear herself say, "All right. Dinner sounds good."

The smile he offered her in response could have meant anything, she decided. Suddenly Miranda got an inexplicable hunch that dinner tonight would involve a lot more than food. And, judging by the expression on Lucas's face just then, she also suddenly felt as if he might just have the intention of making her the main course.

However, as they sat opposite each other in the elegant dining room overlooking the Public Gardens at Aujourd'hui a half hour later, Lucas ordered a steak for his dinner—very rare. His choice only made Miranda view him that much more as a predator, and she chose for herself a main-course salad, something she deemed quite suitable for small, seemingly defenseless prey like herself. She saw Lucas smile as she ordered and realized that his thoughts were probably running along the same line as her own.

"Rabbit food, Miranda?" he asked her after their server left to retrieve the bottle of wine he had ordered.

Miranda nodded, trying to exude a confidence she didn't feel. "I'm a vegetarian."

Why am I not surprised? Lucas thought. "Is that a result of health concerns or a personal moral issue?"

She shrugged carelessly. "A little of both, I guess."

Lucas certainly found no fault with the fact that she was a vegetarian, and clearly she wasn't so overzealous about it that she criticized his order of beef. However, the knowledge of this new aspect of her character simply reaffirmed his suspicion that she was perhaps too gentle and caring for her own good.

A small twinge of guilt shimmied up his spine to lodge firmly in his brain, but Lucas shoved it aside. He had no reason to feel guilty, he told himself. He was doing nothing wrong. Who was going to be hurt by this charade he was playing with Miranda? Panwide would be his in the long run no matter what, so the consequence of his plan had no bearing on that outcome. He himself would wind up with the company he'd been after for months. And as for Miranda...

Well, Miranda would find herself wined and dined and attending some very nice parties as a result of Lucas's attentions, something he was sure would please any woman. After he got what he wanted from her, the two of them could part ways with neither feeling cheated in the bargain. There was no reason for him to feel as if she were going to suffer. Where was the harm in promoting this little game? he asked himself again. As he realized how desperately he was trying to justify his deed, Lucas cursed himself sharply. Dammit, he was doing nothing wrong.

However, such assurances did little to make him feel better. There was still an annoying little part of him that mocked his dishonesty and underhandedness, an irritating little part that told him he should be ashamed of himself for using Miranda the way he intended to do. He tried to remind himself that deception went along with the job, and that as long as he remained within the confines of federal and state laws, his actions were perfectly acceptable and not at all uncommon. But for some reason, such reminders were in no way as effective as they used to be. Lucas still felt like a creep.

Their server returned then to open their wine, so Lucas decided to put his internal monologue on hold for the time being. He and Miranda sat in silence until their server departed once again, then Lucas lifted the bottle of cabernet from the table and added another inch of wine to Miranda's only half-full glass.

"Are you trying to get me drunk, Mr. Strathmoor?" she asked lightly.

Lucas shook his head and smiled broadly, and Miranda nearly caught her breath at the way his face changed when he did so. Suddenly the stern, thoughtful moodiness vanished, replaced by what appeared to be an honest enjoyment of his surroundings. He was so handsome, she thought fondly, and he had a wonderful smile. It was a shame he didn't use it more often.

"Not on this stuff," he assured her. "It's to be savored. If I wanted to get you drunk, I would have ordered the Château Night Train, vintage last week."

Miranda couldn't help but smile back at him. "I don't recall seeing that on the wine list."

"You have to ask the wine captain for it specifically," he told her in a knowledgeable voice. "One of those well-kept secrets only we connoisseurs know about, you see."

Miranda nodded, suitably impressed. "I see."

"And please, Miranda, call me Lucas," he added negligently as he replaced the bottle on the table. "Even my secretary doesn't call me Mr. Strathmoor."

No, she probably calls you Darling, Miranda thought before she could stop herself, wondering where such an uncharacteristic and jealous supposition came from. She scarcely knew this man and certainly had no claim to his affections. Nor did she even *want* a claim to his affections, she insisted. The two of them were simply going to have dinner together, after all, nothing more than that. Before the evening was out, Lucas would no doubt do or say something to which Miranda would take exception—as he had a habit of doing—and she'd find herself with every reason never to see him again. Then she would go back to living her life quietly, peacefully and uneventfully. Which was precisely how she liked it, right? Right.

"Why did you really ask me to dinner tonight?" she heard herself ask, as surprised by the question as Lucas seemed to be. She wasn't sure why she'd asked it, she realized strangely, but something in his posture, in his expression, suddenly made Miranda feel as if there were an underlying reason for his invitation that she didn't fully understand.

"What do you mean?" he asked, and if she hadn't known better, she would have thought he sounded almost... cautious.

She shook her head carelessly. "Just that a mere three days ago, we were standing toe-to-toe in my backyard, each of us about to lunge for the other's jugular. You were calling me a liar and a spy, and I was accusing you of being totally amoral and dangerously money-hungry. Now we're sitting here over wine and candlelight just as civil as two human beings can be, and I'm not sure what happened to put us here, or when it occurred."

Lucas took a thoughtful sip of his wine and said, "Three days ago we didn't understand each other."

Miranda studied him curiously. "Today we still don't understand each other."

"I disagree."

"Why?"

Lucas shrugged, then lifted his glass to his lips once again. Miranda marveled at the way his broad, blunt fingers wrapped gently around the fragile crystal stem of his glass, and she wondered what those fingers would feel like raking softly over her bare skin. A shudder shook her entire body as the harmlessly curious thought exploded into sexually graphic imagery, but he didn't seem to notice her startled reaction.

"Three days ago, Miranda, I didn't realize what a fascinating woman you are."

When his eyes met hers again, they were lighted with a strange fire, and Miranda felt her pulse quicken. What was it about this man that sent her sailing so thoroughly into a tailspin? Certainly he was about as handsome as they came, and carried himself with aplomb, but there was something else, something more. Thousands of men in Boston were good-looking and self-assured, but they didn't make Miranda's blood run wild, didn't send her sexual awareness into a frenzy. Why did Lucas Strathmoor—a man she should find thoroughly unattractive because of his obvious preoccupation with obtaining wealth and power—instead make her want to lose herself in making love with him?

What was really crazy was that, though she had had a couple of brief relationships in the past twelve years, she hadn't experienced such intense fascination with any man since leaving Saint Denis and Patrick Lyndon behind. Yet here was a man she had known for less than a hundred hours, and he was causing her to have thoughts more characteristic of a hormonally inspired teenage girl. It made no sense.

"And that's changed in such a short time?" she asked in response to his carelessly uttered statement. "I find that hard to believe."

"You find it hard to believe a man could find you fascinating?"

"A man like you, yes." She met his gaze levelly, honestly.

Lucas inhaled deeply before speaking again. "That's the second time you've called me 'a man like me.' What exactly am I supposed to make of that? That you think I'm a jerk? Or that you're impressed?"

"I don't think you're a jerk," she replied immediately.

"So you're impressed?"

That was the understatement of the year, Miranda thought. Aloud, she responded, "I think . . . I think you're . . ."

"I'm what?" he urged her in a quiet, anxious voice.

Now she'd done it, Miranda thought. She could produce a list of adjectives a mile long that would describe him, and every single one of them would incriminate her, would make her sound as if she were panting at his heels for a scrap of attention. "You're a very interesting man," she finally concluded, knowing it was a lame response even as she uttered it.

Lucas seemed to consider her statement, then smiled derisively. "Isn't that what people say about members of the opposite sex they find unattractive?"

"Oh, I don't find you at all unattrac—" Miranda made a valiant effort to halt the objection before she uttered it, then felt herself color at her quick, frank and all-too-revealing admission.

Lucas only smiled and said quietly, "I see."

The remainder of their dinner was spent in somewhat stilted, at times awkward, conversation. Theirs was an odd situation, Miranda thought, because it was almost as if they were reluctant to get to know each other. Although it was obvious that there was a certain significant attraction between them, there was also the presence of enormous philosophical differences they couldn't deny or ignore. How could that be? she wondered. How could she find a man so fascinating when she didn't approve of what he did for a living? And why was he so intent on getting to know her when so short a time ago, he had been absolutely convinced she was out to bring down his company?

She knew those were questions that had been bandied about in some form for centuries by other couples, and she knew she wasn't likely to find answers for them anytime soon. Still, Miranda thought, there was nothing wrong with a healthy, adult curiosity, was there? It had been so long since she'd been attracted to a man beyond a tepid interest. What could possibly be the harm in exploring the possibilities? If he became obnoxious or offensive—as Martians were sometimes wont to do—she'd simply tell him to get lost. And if he turned out to be a gentler, more considerate than usual Martian...well, then she'd be one lucky Venusian, wouldn't she?

As she sipped her red wine and savored the warm, smoky flavor, Miranda decided she'd be a fool not to at least let things progress enough to see how they developed. So whenever she became suspicious that Lucas's intentions might not be what they appeared, she simply tamped her feelings down. She could manage this, she told herself. She wasn't the frail little bird that people often assumed her to be. She could handle Lucas Strathmoor.

But even as she uttered the assurances to herself, something else deep inside her, a feeling Miranda couldn't quite push away, wondered if she might not be kidding herself instead.

When they pulled into her driveway just before eleven o'clock, Miranda started to become a little nervous. It had been so long since she'd been out on a date with a man, and she wasn't sure she could remember what she was supposed to do. What was the protocol in this situation? Technically what they had enjoyed this evening wasn't a date, because they hadn't made prior arrangements, and he hadn't picked her up at her house. It had been a spontaneous decision reached when he had taken it upon himself to show up at her store. But the past few hours had been surprisingly pleasant, she recalled now, once they had gotten past the requisite chit-chat and delved into more meaningful conversation. Certainly having had such a good time constituted some kind of nice capping off of the evening.

What was her obligation? Miranda wondered. Did she invite him in for coffee? A brandy? Sex? No, certainly not that last one, she assured herself in a hurry. As oddly... appealing as she might find the idea.

Stop it, she instructed herself earnestly. Honestly, she was acting like a twelve-year-old girl with a bad case of the boy-crazies. She should just take a deep breath, tell Lucas she had a very nice time and thank him for dinner. That was all that was required, Miranda told herself. Nothing more.

As they strode slowly and silently up the front walk, she repeated those words to herself again. Lucas-I-had-a-very-nice-time-thank-you-for-dinner. That wasn't so hard to say, was it? But when she turned at her front door to utter those words out loud, they got caught somewhere deep in her throat, and all she could do was smile apprehensively at him and feel uncomfortable.

"Aren't you going to invite me in, Miranda?" he asked her in a smooth, thoroughly erotic voice.

Miranda took a calming breath and replied resolutely, "It's late."

He nodded a little absently, as if he were weighing some very important consideration. Then, seemingly resigned to her decision, he muttered quietly, "Well, good night then," and turned to go.

As she watched him slowly depart, Miranda realized he had every intention of leaving her without kissing her good-night, and she felt surprisingly cheated. He couldn't leave without kissing her good-night, could he? Had dating changed since the last time she had partaken of it? Was he supposed to do that? Was it allowed?

Before she could stop herself, Miranda blurted out, "But—"

It was only a tiny word, a three-letter conjunction that was meaningless when used alone the way she had done. And yet, that little word said so much. Miranda knew it. Lucas knew it. His expression was completely telling when he spun around to face her again.

"But?" he prodded quietly.

It would be useless for her to pretend she hadn't meant anything by her objection, Miranda thought. So why not just be honest with him? "But aren't you going to kiss me good-night?" she asked, whispering.

Lucas approached her slowly, then stopped when only scant inches separated their bodies. He studied her face in the sparse moonlight for a moment, then lifted his hand to cup her chin, stroking his thumb over her lower lip. Miranda trembled at the exquisite heat his gesture sent firing through her body, then tilted her head back to gaze into his dark eyes.

"Do you want me to kiss you good-night?" he asked softly.

She nodded almost imperceptibly. "Yes. I do want you . . . to kiss me."

Lucas smiled at her then, a smile that was not smug and victorious, as she might have expected, but gentle and tender and full of promise. Slowly, carefully, he tilted his head forward, pausing for only a very brief moment before touching her mouth softly with his. Gently he rubbed her lips with his, drawing her lower lip into his mouth for only a second to taste it with the tip of his tongue. And then he was pulling away from her, ending the kiss, and Miranda had to cling to the lapels of his jacket to keep her knees from buckling beneath her.

"When will I see you again, Miranda?" he asked quietly, his breathing almost as ragged as her own.

Miranda couldn't respond right away. Their embrace had been little more than a harmless, quiet good-night kiss, but it had left her feeling dizzy and aroused. All she could think was that if this was how he made her feel after a quick peck, there would be nothing left of her but a quivering heap of fallen womanhood after they made love. Because suddenly, certainly, Miranda knew they were going to wind up in bed together. It might be weeks, months or even years away, but somehow it just seemed ordained, destined, that they would become lovers. Oddly, however, the knowledge didn't frighten her a bit.

"How about Friday?" she heard Lucas ask further. "Are you busy?"

Miranda shook her head, forcing words into her mouth. "No, I'm not."

"I've been invited to a cocktail party in Beacon Hill. I wasn't going to go, but..." He curled a finger below Miranda's chin, tipping her head back again so that he could meet her gaze. "Would you like to go with me?"

Almost involuntarily Miranda lifted a hand to thread her fingers through his hair, wanting to pull him close for another kiss. When she realized how forward she was being, however, she forced her hand back down to her side and nodded. "Yes, I'd like that very much."

"I'll pick you up at seven on Friday, will that be all right?"

Miranda took a deep, silent breath, feeling as if she were weighing the most important decision she'd ever made in her life. "Seven will be fine," she finally agreed.

Lucas bent his head forward again and kissed her quickly on the mouth one last time. "Good night, Miranda," he said as he stepped away and began his journey down her front walk to his car for a second time.

"Good night, Lucas," she responded quietly.

It was the second time she had used his given name, he realized, the first being in her backyard three days before. Her voice slicing through the darkness behind him now sounded just as it had then—soft and fragile and almost frightened. Lucas felt something twist painfully in his heart at the gentle way in which she uttered his name. As he took his seat behind the wheel of his car and brought the engine to thundering life, he realized he had Miranda True exactly where he wanted her—attracted to him, wanting him... trusting him.

Everything that had transpired since he'd left her home Sunday afternoon had gone practically as he'd intended. All of it had been elaborately planned and effectively executed—all of it. He had deliberately waited until today to contact Miranda again so that she would have a few days to ponder the intensity of the attraction between them, and perhaps even start to miss him a little bit. And he had consciously chosen to show up at her shop in person instead of making an impersonal phone call, because he'd known it would be more difficult for her to decline his invitation to dinner if she was standing face-to-face with him. And he had asked her out on Friday not only because of the party, but also because it was only two days away and would give her little time to back out of the arrangement. Even his kiss good-night had been orchestrated to turn out the way it had—with Miranda asking *him* to kiss *her*.

It was all moving along nicely and going exactly according to plan, Lucas thought distractedly, with every single piece of the scheme falling precisely into place. He ran a hand restlessly through his hair, grimacing when he tugged one strand a little too hard.

So why then did he suddenly feel as if everything was about to blow apart?

Chapter Five

Friday came far too quickly for Miranda. She awoke feeling nervous about what the evening would hold, couldn't eat breakfast because of something akin to an anxiety attack that gripped her and wouldn't let go, and throughout the morning stumbled into store displays, dropped merchandise on the floor and generally made a mess everywhere she went in the shop. She knew Marcy was trying to be patient with her, but when Miranda came bursting through the back door with a too tall stack of gardening books and slammed into her assistant, who was pouring a cup of herbal tea for one of their regular customers to sample, Marcy finally reached the end of her rope.

"Miranda, what's gotten into you?" the twenty-year-old college student demanded after dabbing the last of the raspberry-chamomile tea from her sweater. "You've been jumpy all day. I almost scalded the heck out of myself back there, not to mention Mrs. Tristan."

"I am so sorry, Marcy," Miranda apologized, lifting a hand to help her assistant with the cleaning of her sweater, knocking over a fixture of herbal remedies as she did so. "Oops," she muttered sheepishly, catching the clawlike apparatus just before it would have hooked on Marcy's sweater.

"See what I mean?" Marcy said, cupping Miranda's wrist gently in her grasp, silently urging her to release the fixture before she could unravel Marcy completely. "You're a hazard to everyone's health today."

"I'm sorry," Miranda apologized again. "It's just that...I mean I...um..."

"What?" Marcy demanded, clearly running out of patience now.

Miranda took a deep breath and on a rush of words announced, "I have a date tonight."

Marcy's eyes widened in disbelief beneath her dark-rimmed glasses. "You?" she whispered in shock. "A date?"

Miranda dropped her fists to her hips in half-felt indignation. "Yes, me. Gee, Marcy, it isn't that incredible, is it? I must have one or two redeeming qualities that a man might find attractive. Think hard."

Marcy shook her head fiercely, sending her red curls flying. "No, that's not what I meant at all. I didn't mean to imply that no one could be interested in you. It's just that I've never really known you to be interested in anyone."

Miranda lifted her chin defensively and smoothed an imagined wrinkle from her ivory suit jacket. "Oh. Okay. Well, that's all right, then."

"Who is it?" Marcy asked in a conspiratorial voice. "Anyone I know?"

"No," Miranda replied, her own voice sounding a little misty as she recalled Lucas Strathmoor's compelling face and incredibly expressive eyes for perhaps the hundredth time that day. "It's someone I met last weekend."

"And you haven't mentioned him to me all week?" Marcy squeaked. "How could you!"

How indeed? Miranda thought. She still couldn't quite get over the feeling that she had dreamed the entire episode—Lucas waiting for her after she locked up the shop, a candle-lit dinner in a very posh restaurant, his soft breath of a kiss good-night... Maybe it had been no more than a dream. He hadn't called her after all; she'd heard nothing from him since Wednesday night to reaffirm their plans for the evening. What if he didn't show up? she worried. What if she got all ready, only to wind up looking like a fool when he didn't come for her?

"I still can't believe it myself, Marcy," she tried to explain to her assistant. "He's like no man I've ever met before, certainly like no one I've ever dated. I've sort of felt like if I talked about him, I'd jinx myself or something. He's...oh, Marcy, I think he might be someone... special."

Marcy nodded knowingly. "You've got it bad, Miranda."

Miranda nodded back. "I know."

"So what are you going to wear?"

"I have no idea. I've tried on everything I own, and nothing seems appropriate."

"What's the occasion?"

"A cocktail party."

"Friends or business associates?"

"I don't know."

"Hmm," Marcy muttered, tapping her chin in deep concentration. "Looks like we've got our work cut out for us."

"We?" Miranda asked.

Marcy nodded with a professional air. "I think we should close up for lunch and run next door to Monique's."

Miranda gazed at her assistant through narrowed eyes. When had the two of them traded places? Normally she was

the one soothing a nervous Marcy about an upcoming date
with a chemistry major or frat guy. And it was usually Miranda who took the younger woman next door to sample
clothes after they closed up the shop at day's end. Now
suddenly Miranda felt like the schoolgirl, giddy and nervous and totally uncertain about how to behave, and Marcy
was the calm, cool, collected one. How had that happened?

"No, Marcy, lunch is our busiest time. Thanks for the
offer, though." With a mischievous grin, Miranda added,
"And thanks for minding the store while I go over to Monique's and check out the selection during lunch."

"Oh, Miranda, you never let me have any fun."

Miranda lifted a hand in fond farewell, retrieved her purse
from the back room and headed quickly toward the door. "I
won't be gone long," she called out cheerfully over her
shoulder. To herself, she added, Only long enough to find
something suitably spectacular for the most fascinating man
I've ever met.

Miranda was ready well before seven that evening. She
had discovered a long-sleeved, butter-yellow cocktail dress
at the boutique that afternoon, a snug-fitting sheath that
outlined her every curve with loving familiarity. Her pale
blond hair was in a French braid and wrapped at the end
with a gold ribbon. A dozen gold bracelets rang softly when
she moved her arms, and gold filigree earrings dangled from
her ears. As she'd prepared herself for the evening ahead,
slowly, gradually, Miranda had begun to feel less like the
clumsy schoolgirl she had been all afternoon, and much
more like the confident woman she wanted to appear.

At six-forty-five, she was a bundle of nerves pacing her
living room, her four cats watching her intently, as if they
sensed her anxious mood and didn't want to cross her. Bix
and Eubie, the two black-and-white toms, simply perched

atop the china cabinet, both of them crouched with their four legs tucked beneath them in their usual manner. But Ella and Billie, the tabby females, moved as close to Miranda as they dared, curled up on the window seat amid ferns, philodendrons and ficus.

On more than one occasion, Miranda's friends had compared her house to a jungle, the entire structure home to thick, lush foliage and prowling feline beasts. There were times when she awoke in the middle of the night, to mysterious unidentifiable clatter and angry feline yowling, when she herself felt the term "jungle" wasn't an entirely inappropriate one.

At five after seven, there was still no sign of Lucas. Miranda told herself not to worry, that he probably had to drive clear across town and Friday night traffic could be monstrous at times. He had said he would be there. Lucas Strathmoor might be a lot of things, she thought, but he wasn't the kind of man who would stand a woman up. At least she hoped he wasn't.

The doorbell finally rang at seven-thirteen. Miranda's heart somersaulted twice before shooting off on a marathon at the grating, tinny sound of it. She took a deep, fortifying breath, smoothed a hand over her dress and hair one final time, cleared her throat discreetly and pulled open the front door.

She had never seen a more handsome man in her life. Lucas stood before her in yet another of what she was beginning to realize must be an impressive collection of dark, exquisitely cut suits. This one defined every solid, muscular inch of him, and the copper-colored necktie knotted at his throat only enhanced the brown flecks in his eyes and the ruddy highlights in his hair. In his left hand he held an enormous bouquet, composed of lilies in every color imaginable.

Lilies—any lilies—were Miranda's favorite flowers. She wondered how he'd known. Then she remembered that he'd checked up on her a week ago, and realized he probably knew more about her than she knew herself. She pushed away the small twinge of annoyance the memory brought with it, and instead reminded herself that things between them had changed since then.

"They're beautiful, Lucas," she said quietly as he held the flowers out for her to take them. "Thank you."

His fingers closed over hers as he transferred the bouquet to her possession, and he replied in his deep rich voice, "You're welcome. But their beauty fades to commonness compared to your own."

Miranda felt herself blushing. She so seldom heard compliments from men, because there simply were no men in her life. Certainly masculine approval wasn't necessary for her survival, but a woman liked to be reassured now and then. Miranda smiled shyly and murmured her thanks, then invited Lucas inside while she put the flowers in a vase.

"I'm sorry I'm late," he said as he followed her inside and closed the door behind himself, ogling her shamelessly as she proceeded down the hall with her back to him. Some dress, he thought with a smile that bordered on leering. Then before he could stop himself, he added silently, Can't wait to get her out of it. "Traffic is unbelievable tonight," he began again, hoping he only imagined the tiny squeak in his voice. "First sign of warm weather, and everybody heads outdoors."

"No problem," he heard Miranda reply from somewhere beyond his vision. "I figured as much. Make yourself comfortable. I'll be right back."

Lucas let his gaze rove curiously over the living room, marveling at what he beheld there. Of course he already knew Miranda had a predilection for plants and growing things, but the inside of her house felt like the great outdoors. The dwindling evening light filtered through a number of windows, mingling with the amber glow of a few lamps she had turned on. Her furnishings were old and lovingly worn, printed pastels in a pattern of flowers that looked as if they predated World War II. The wallpaper, too, was floral and antique-looking, and plants were everywhere. Not just potted houseplants, either—but huge shrubs and trees that nearly reached the ceiling. Over the fireplace was a wreath that must have been three feet in diameter, composed of dried herbs and flowers. Every picture on the wall was a picture of a plant. Lucas inhaled deeply. Her house even smelled like a garden.

It was in complete contrast to his own home. He'd been living in his big house in Cambridge for nearly ten years and still hadn't completely unpacked. His furnishings were sparse at best, nothing beyond what he needed for absolute survival, and he couldn't recall a single decoration on the walls. What color were the walls? he wondered now. White? Ivory? Beige? He couldn't quite remember.

He spent so little time at home, it had seemed unnecessary to go to any trouble with it. There was a couch in the living room, he recalled, a desk and chair, a couple of lamps. The kitchen boasted a table and chairs, and various small appliances that were prerequisites for single living— microwave, coffee maker, that sort of thing. His bedroom was furnished with a bed and a chest of drawers, and another chair. Lucas marveled at the realization that no one would ever guess by the contents of his home that he was a very wealthy man. Some things just took priority over others, that's all, he thought. And his home had simply never been a priority. Instead his business had always come first.

Clearly Miranda would never be content with the meager surroundings to be found in his house. Her home was like a reflection of her life. If he could spend the next fifteen minutes wandering around her living room, Lucas thought, he'd probably get a very good idea of what made Miranda the woman she was. Her bedroom would no doubt be an even better indicator of that. Lucas couldn't help the lascivious thoughts that tumbled into his mind as a result of that realization. He wondered how soon it would be before the opportunity arose for him to get a glimpse into that very room, into that very intimate part of Miranda True.

His scrutiny of the living room and fantasies about Miranda were halted when he realized he was being watched and pondered with equal interest. Four cats had appeared from God knew where, only to circle him on all sides with undisguised animosity. The largest of the creatures, a black beast with a white throat and huge green eyes, opened its mouth to emit a hideous sound that reminded Lucas of a dying police siren. Fortunately Miranda returned then with the flowers arranged expertly in a cranberry-glass vase. He was sure she wouldn't stand by and let him be devoured alive.

When she looked up to observe his predicament, Miranda smiled, and Lucas felt his heart take wing. She was a study in warmth and light, all dressed in yellow and gold. Somehow he knew if he racked his brain for the next million years, he would never be able to name a woman more beautiful than Miranda True. Then he frowned at the avenue his thoughts had taken. This situation with her would only be temporary, he reminded himself. And he couldn't afford to forget the very real possibility that she was still involved with the Lyndons and Panwide.

"I see you've met the kids," Miranda remarked with a quiet laugh.

"You didn't tell me you had four bodyguards," Lucas chastised her playfully.

"They do tend to be a little overprotective at times," she agreed. "But that's only because they know I'm the source of the food that appears in their bowls twice a day."

Lucas nodded, eyeing the big black monster again. "I think it might go deeper than that."

Miranda waved an unconcerned hand at the animal. "Don't worry about Bix. He takes advantage of his size to intimidate. He's really just a big baby."

"Bix?" Lucas asked, his expression clearly curious.

Miranda pointed at the other three and introduced them as well. "Eubie, Billie and Ella."

"So the lady likes jazz," Lucas guessed.

Miranda shook her head. "No, the lady *loves* jazz."

His smile became one of genuine delight. "So do I. We'll have a lot to talk about."

And talk they did, throughout the drive to the party. They discovered a number of things they had in common, and the conversation Miranda had feared would drag and be lackluster was in fact very lively and interesting. She was surprised at how quickly they reached their destination. And once they did, she became nervous at the prospect of meeting Lucas's friends and colleagues.

What if they didn't like her? Miranda worried. What if they didn't approve? What if they thought she didn't belong? She hated herself for letting old fears that should have died long ago resurface with such a vengeance. But a very large part of Miranda was still that young girl who had left Saint Denis with Patrick Lyndon's hurtful words about not belonging in his world still ringing in her ears. She supposed it was inevitable that she would always be a little self-conscious around other people, a little too anxious to please. She only hoped she would be able to leave her worries outside once she and Lucas were mingling with the others inside, and enjoy herself with the man who had preoccupied her thoughts all week.

"Whose party is this?" Miranda asked after Lucas had turned over his keys to the valet and they walked up the steps to the looming brick structure.

"Nelson Paterson," he replied.

Miranda's eyes widened in disbelief. "*The* Nelson Paterson? The millionaire philanthropist?"

Lucas turned to smile at her, taking her hand warmly in his. "The *billionaire* philanthropist."

"Wow."

Miranda tried not to think about what vastly different worlds she and Lucas lived in, and instead focused on how nice it felt to have her fingers affectionately entwined with his. That in turn reminded her that even this small physical contact with him made her nerve endings burst into flame, and inevitably caused her to wonder how it would feel to be even closer to him. She tried to forget that it had been years since she'd been even this close to a man, and tried to forget that this man was far more unsettling than any other she'd ever known.

Tried . . . and failed miserably.

Instead she felt as if she were walking a foot higher in the air than anyone else at the party, and considered herself to be the luckiest woman alive. And from the subtle, curious glances toward Lucas she observed from other women present, Miranda realized she wasn't the only one who thought such a thing. Smug warmth filled her at the knowledge that she was envied. It was something she couldn't remember ever happening to her before, and she decided she rather liked it.

"Champagne?"

She heard the question uttered in Lucas's cognac-warm, velvet-smooth voice as if it were coming to her through fog. Miranda could only manage a single nod, then felt the long-stemmed flute pressed gently into her hand. She started to lift it to her lips for a sip, but Lucas stayed her hand by wrapping his fingers gently around her wrist, coaxing it back down until the rim of her glass clinked softly against his.

"To us," he said quietly, his eyes dark and dreamy and full of unspoken promises.

Miranda's heart pounded in her chest, but she somehow managed a whispered "To us" in agreement.

They each took a single sip, Miranda savoring the effervescent sweetness as it tickled her throat and stomach.

"Come on," Lucas said, lacing his fingers through hers once again to lead her away with a gentle tug. "I want you to meet some friends of mine."

The entire evening passed in something of a blur for Miranda. She met too many people to ever remember their names if quizzed, and was thankful that Lucas remained at her side throughout. He was surprisingly attentive, she thought. Despite being pulled into a number of business-related discussions, he never forgot that Miranda was with him, and always explained the crux and origins of each conversation to her. Not that she understood many of them, but she appreciated the fact that he made an effort to include her.

On the drive home, their discussion was once again lively and covered a range of topics, with Lucas asking Miranda what she'd thought of the party and the people she'd met, and Miranda giving him the honest opinion he'd requested.

"Some of your friends seemed more like enemies if you ask me," she said frankly. "And some of the ones you said were your enemies acted like they were your best friend."

Lucas grinned at her perception. "That's the way it is in the business world sometimes. Everything's a pretense."

Miranda made a face. "I couldn't work that way. I don't see how you stand it."

Lucas shrugged negligently. "It's not so bad if you know the rules."

"You make it all sound like a game."

"In a way, I suppose it is."

"You guys play for pretty high stakes."

"That's what makes it exciting."

Miranda shook her head. "That kind of excitement I can do without."

Lucas glanced over at her in the dark car, his angular face made more so in the green glow of the dashboard lights. For a moment he said nothing, and when he finally did respond, his voice was dangerously low. "What kind of excitement do you prefer, Miranda?"

Oh, boy, Miranda thought, her heart beginning its erratic tattoo once again. She'd set herself up for that one. She knew she should be on her guard where Lucas Strathmoor was concerned, knew he was way out of her league. Nevertheless, she'd had a good time with him tonight, had found it easy to relax and enjoy herself. He'd been attentive and considerate throughout the evening, and she had begun to think he was exactly what she'd told Marcy Dolan he was— special.

"Oh, you know," she said on a weak whisper in response to his question. "The usual stuff. Roller coasters, scary old movies, life in general."

Lucas nodded silently, then turned his attention back to the road. Miranda watched him as he drove, noting the way his fingers curled over the steering wheel while his other hand palmed the gear shift. Once again she found herself wondering what it would be like to feel his fingers skimming down along her spine or gently cupping her breast. The image made her grow warm, and she crossed her arms over her abdomen to halt the spread of such an intense heat.

"Are you cold?" he asked immediately, reaching forward to turn on the car's heater. When he did so, his hand brushed against Miranda's arm and made the fire inside her leap that much higher.

"No," she replied quickly. Too quickly, she realized when Lucas turned to gaze at her with a speculative smile. "I'm—" she cleared her throat discreetly "—I'm not cold."

"Oh," he said softly, his smile growing broader as he spoke. "I see. Are you too hot then? Should I turn on the air conditioner instead to cool you off?"

By the way he let his voice trail off, Miranda knew he was tempted to add something like, *Or shall I think of some other way to put out the fire?* Instead of promoting their flirtation to new heights, she simply ended it by saying, "No thank you. I'm fine."

Lucas bit his lip—a gesture Miranda found extremely erotic, much to her dismay—and replaced his hand on the gear shift. They stuck to harmless topics for discussion during the remainder of the drive home, and Miranda was relieved that he let the subject of her body temperature drop as quickly as she had.

This time Miranda wasn't reluctant about inviting Lucas in for a leisurely glass of wine to be enjoyed over quiet conversation. The evening was unusually warm for April, so she suggested they take their drinks outside to enjoy them. It was a clear night, the sky dotted with hundreds of tiny crystal stars, the moon a mere sliver of silver overhead. Crickets that had been chirping in fierce chorus suddenly silenced at the sound of the screen door creaking open and shut, then slowly picked up their song bit by bit once again. There was still just a touch of winter in the air, but the aroma of approaching spring was heavy. It was the kind of night Miranda loved—peaceful and full of possibilities.

She sat on the swing and put it into leisurely motion with her toes while Lucas took up a casual stance leaning against a pillar to stare out at the yard. For long moments neither spoke, only enjoyed the comfortable silence and reflections of the evening they had just shared together. Finally Lucas was the one to put an end to the quiet.

"What did you think of Richard Barclay?"

The question surprised Miranda. Of everything she might have expected Lucas to say at that moment, the mention of someone she scarcely remembered from the party was possibly last on the list.

"Which one was he?" she asked, hoping her puzzlement at his query wasn't evident in her tone of voice.

"Bald guy. Bright orange necktie."

Miranda smiled. She remembered him quite well. His tie had been hideous. And he had been one of the edgiest people she had ever met. "He was awfully nervous when you went up to introduce me to him."

Lucas's head snapped around, and Miranda thought he seemed almost angry about something. She decided it must just be a trick of the moonlight.

"You thought he seemed nervous?"

Miranda wasn't sure where this conversation was headed, but it seemed harmless enough, so she replied, "Yes, clearly. Didn't you think so?"

In silhouette, she saw Lucas lift his shoulders in a negligent shrug. "Yeah, maybe. I guess so."

"He seems kind of frightened of you," Miranda offered further. "Although it couldn't be too bad, because I heard him jokingly say something to that other guy about how partial you are to cookies."

In the darkness it was difficult to see, but Miranda could almost feel Lucas become as stiff, cold and unyielding as a block of ice. "What guy?" he asked quietly.

"The white-haired guy with the big, bushy mustache," she said, wondering again where this conversation was going.

"What *exactly* did Richard say to him?"

Confused, Miranda replied, "Just that you really like Mama Mangione's cookies."

Lucas said nothing right away but seemed to be lost in thought. When he spoke again, his voice sounded strained and angry. "What did the white-haired guy say?"

"Nothing major," Miranda was quick to assure him. "He just kind of laughed and said that if you didn't back off from them, they were going to make you sick."

Lucas was furious. More furious than he'd ever been in his life. And there was no way he could let Miranda see that. What she had just told him confirmed something he had been suspecting, but which he had hoped and prayed wasn't the case at all. Richard Barclay was one of Lucas's employees, and there had been reason to believe he might just be the leak in the company Lucas had been searching for.

The man Richard had been speaking to was Barry MacNeil, CEO of National Bakeries, who happened to manufacture Mama Mangione's Cookies, and whose company was also, incidentally, the next on Lucas's acquisition list. However, he hadn't intended on anyone at National Bakeries finding out about that until he had made significant inroads into their company. With his innocent-sounding comment, Richard had informed MacNeil that Lucas intended to go after them. Now they knew he was coming. Now they'd be on their guard. Now Lucas was going to have his work cut out for him in trying to buy up stock in their company.

He had never felt more betrayed. It was one thing to suspect someone of wrongdoing, but to have it confirmed this way... Yet he knew he should also feel relieved. Although now he'd be forced to skip over National Bakeries on his list and move to the company after it, he had one less thing to worry about. Tomorrow he'd fire Richard Barclay, and that particular leak would be plugged. Lucas had Miranda to thank for that. And she didn't even realize the enormous service she'd just performed for him.

And that wasn't the first important insight she'd offered him this evening, either. Lucas had taken her to this party specifically because a number of Panwide shareholders were going to be present—people who'd been reluctant to sell

their stock to Lucas. On the drive back to her house, he had
quizzed Miranda shamelessly about those people, asking her
opinion on everything from the clothes they'd been wearing to the way they'd reacted to seemingly harmless questions he'd posed. Miranda had replied without reservation—
just as he'd known she would because of his realization that
she was nothing if not completely straightforward—and her
insights had offered him more than a few things to think
about.

Some of her responses had either reconfirmed suspicions
he already had about people, or had caused him to form new
ones. Other things she'd pointed out had put some of his
fears to rest. During the course of the evening, Lucas had
come to realize that Miranda's observations were remarkably astute. All in all, he found her input to be invaluable
counsel. And now she'd just provided him with even more
substantial information about Richard Barclay and his
unethical behavior.

But there was no way Lucas could let her know the significance of what she was doing for him. If Miranda discovered that the reason he had invited her to the party had
less to do with wanting to get to know her as a person and
more to do with wanting her to ferret out information from
Panwide shareholders, she'd be furious. And, Lucas had to
admit, she'd have a very good reason.

However, he was gradually beginning to wonder if maybe
his intentions were as cut and dried now as they'd been when
he formed his plan last week after leaving Miranda's house.
No, he hadn't intended on getting to know Miranda True as
a person this evening, but he had nonetheless. Through their
conversations he'd discovered she was in no way the shallow, flaky woman he'd suspected her of being when he first
discovered she was a palmist. Instead Miranda had turned
out to be an intelligent, savvy woman with remarkably pro-
gressive ideas, shrewd business sense and a surprisingly so-

phisticated sense of humor. Lucas had enjoyed himself immensely this evening. And Miranda was the one completely responsible for that.

He took a thoughtful sip of his wine and gazed at her through the darkness. Even though the moon was a mere thread of bent silver, light danced in her hair as if *she* were the one so luminous. There was something about Miranda that put Lucas at ease, made him feel calm. He should be enraged about discovering Richard Barclay's duplicity, should be embittered that someone close to him would stoop so low. Instead he almost felt as if the other man's action was completely inconsequential. So what if Lucas wouldn't be able to acquire National Bakeries? Was it the end of his world? The collapse of a nation? The death of modern civilization as he knew it?

No, of course not. It was a shock to his system and a wrench thrown into the works, certainly, but it was nothing from which he couldn't bounce back. Richard Barclay was simply a man of weak and greedy character if he had to resort to something like this. But Lucas would get over it.

In the same way Miranda True will get over your weak and greedy action? a voice inside him piped up then, unbidden. *Really, in what way is the charade you're playing with her any different than what Richard Barclay did to you?*

Entirely different, Lucas tried to assure himself. The two deeds were in no way similar. Richard Barclay was spying for the competition. Lucas was merely investigating his own competition. But when he wasn't quite able to convince himself that he and Richard Barclay were two totally separate kinds of animals, Lucas simply pushed the thought away in an effort to silence the annoying little voice.

"What are you thinking about?"

The question came to Lucas softly through the darkness, sounding sweet and innocent and full of genuine concern. "What?" he replied absently.

"You've been so quiet for the past few minutes," Miranda remarked. "Is something wrong?"

In response, Lucas moved to join her on the porch swing, seating himself close enough to enjoy her presence, but not enough to make her uncomfortable.

"No, nothing is wrong," he told her. "I've just had a lot on my mind lately."

Lucas studied Miranda intently as she took another sip of her wine, marveling again at how beautiful she was. Miranda True must have men knocking down her door, he thought. Despite having planned the outcome, he had still been surprised that she'd been free this evening when she'd agreed to go out with him two nights ago. There were probably very few weekend evenings that she spent by herself. Why Patrick Lyndon had let her get away twelve years ago was a mystery Lucas couldn't begin to fathom. Obviously the young man hadn't known a good thing when he saw it.

If Lucas had met Miranda when he was a much younger, much more idealistic man, he would no doubt have fallen in love at first sight, snatched her up and married her on the spot, then would have spent the rest of his life being utterly devoted to her. Of course, at that age, Lucas had still been working as a mechanic and about to drop out of college, and at that age Miranda was working as a cook's assistant. Two such people would have been cursed to spend the rest of their lives in middle-class America, struggling to make ends meet and worrying incessantly about their children's activities. There would have been orthodontist's bills and music lessons and baseball uniforms to buy, summer camp and college tuition that would have been completely beyond their reach. There would have been so many sacrifices they'd be forced to make in order to simply survive.

Of course, married to someone like Miranda, he'd never have to be alone again. With children, he'd have something of himself to carry on in the world long after he was gone. Being a part of a loud, boisterous family might be kind of fun in its own way. In fact, now that Lucas thought of it, maybe that wasn't such a bad way to live after all. He'd never married because he'd never had the time, had never met a woman he thought he could tolerate for the rest of his life, or who would be able to tolerate him for the rest of hers. Instead he'd spent the past twenty years trying to be something better than lower middle-class, because he'd seen what a toll that kind of life had taken on his father.

Nate Strathmoor was only sixty years old, but his health was worse than most octogenarians. His back was stooped, his lungs were full of fluid, and arthritis had gnarled his hands and joints until they were nearly useless. Lucas had provided his father with a big house on the beach with all the amenities, a live-in nurse, and a Caribbean cruise every winter. But that was all money had been able to buy for Nate. As rich as Lucas might ever become, he would never be able to buy back his father's health—health that had gradually deteriorated because the old man had worked too hard and neglected himself too much. All Lucas could do now was make Nate Strathmoor's life as easy and enjoyable as possible. He only hoped his father had a lot of years left.

"You're still being very quiet."

Miranda's subtle accusation was punctuated with a light smile, and Lucas felt his brooding thoughts evaporate like so much fog. The crickets around them had quieted to an irregular hum, and the swing creaked and moaned softly as they pushed it slowly back and forth. Inside the house, Bix stood silhouetted against the screen door, emitting that irritating, rusty groan that Lucas had heard earlier.

Lucas smiled at Miranda in return. "Sounds like some-one is jealous," he said softly.

Miranda chuckled quietly. "Hungry is probably more like it. Why would Bix be jealous of you? You have to feed yourself and pick up after yourself and worry about bills and politics and societal woes. You have to wake up every morning knowing you won't be able to sleep again until that evening, when Bix can collapse in any sunny spot in the house whenever he wants. A cat's life, Lucas, is the best life."

"Maybe so," Lucas agreed with a seductive smile. "But I'm the one sitting out here in the moonlight with you, and he's the one cooped up inside."

His softly uttered analysis of the situation made Mir-anda feel warm all over, and she lifted her gaze from where she had fixed it on her glass of wine and met his eyes for the first time since they'd arrived back at her house. He was going to kiss her, she realized suddenly, almost dreamily. And at the moment, she couldn't think of anything she would enjoy more.

"That's just like a man," she said quietly, involuntarily leaning toward Lucas as she spoke. "Competing with an-other male for the affections of the female."

Lucas began to lean in slowly, too, his voice as low and full of promise as Miranda's. "Is that what this is? Com-petition for your affection?"

She nodded, still smiling, her head only a hairbreadth away from his.

"Who's winning?" Lucas wanted to know.

Miranda laughed, a deep, quiet sound she scarcely rec-ognized as her own. She couldn't remember the last time she had flirted so shamelessly with a man. Nor could she re-member a time when she'd had so much fun doing it. Fi-nally she replied softly, "The jury's still out."

Lucas reached over and lifted Miranda's glass of wine from her grasp, setting it down on the porch beside his. "Let me see if maybe I can sway the verdict," he whispered on a breath of air before leaning forward to caress her lips lightly with his.

It was a wonderful kiss, Miranda thought, as Lucas nibbled gently at her lips. This time she had no misgivings about entwining her fingers in his hair, and she lost herself in the way the silky strands curled around her fingers as if inviting her to stay. When Lucas emitted a quiet sound of surrender at her touch, Miranda pulled him closer, kissing him back with more assurance and insistence than she thought she was capable of feeling.

At her unspoken invitation, Lucas, too, deepened their kiss, outlining her lips with the tip of his tongue before slipping between them to taste her. Miranda felt her heart go wild, crashing against her rib cage as if trying to break free. She met Lucas's curious strokes with a few of her own, their tongues clinging and dancing as if finding fulfillment for the first time.

When Lucas dropped a hand to her waist, pulling her body closer to his, Miranda eagerly complied, pressing herself as close to him as she could, luxuriating in the hard, solid strength she encountered. Her fingers dropped from his hair to encircle his upper arms, then spread open across his muscular back. For long moments they only held each other, embracing, exploring, tasting and touching. Finally, when Miranda feared she would go too far if she didn't stop now, she pulled gently away, her breathing ragged and raspy, her thoughts fuzzy and faint.

"Lucas, I…" Her voice trailed off when she realized she had absolutely no idea what she intended to say.

Lucas took her hands in his, and lifted them to his lips, then placed a feathery kiss on each of her palms. "You what?"

Miranda shook her head wordlessly, unwilling to tell him that he affected her more deeply than anyone else she'd ever met in her life, that he was like no man she could have ever imagined.

"I'm sorry," he apologized. "I shouldn't have pushed you that hard, I—"

"No," Miranda interrupted. "That wasn't it at all." She dropped her head because the fire that leaped and flickered in his eyes was too much for her to bear. The knowledge that he was as eager as she was to make love right here and now made her face flush with heat. "I mean…" She took a deep breath and looked him squarely in the eye once again. "It's not like I tried to discourage you."

Lucas smiled a little sadly. "But you are now."

Miranda shrugged helplessly. "I have to."

Lucas nodded in silent understanding, cupped her face with his hand, and kissed her softly, chastely, one last time. "I understand, Miranda."

"Do you? Do you really?" she whispered. Because I'm not sure I do, she added silently to herself.

"Yes," he assured her, "surprisingly enough, I do."

And he did, Lucas realized. If Miranda True had been any other woman, he might have resented her putting an end to something they were clearly both enjoying. But her need to back off was indeed perfectly understandable somehow. And, Lucas found to his surprise, it was also rather promising.

"Can I see you again soon?" he asked her, stroking her cheek softly with the back of his knuckles one last time before dropping his hand back into his lap.

Miranda nodded. "If you want to."

"I want to," he told her immediately.

"Would you … would you like to come over for dinner one night next week?"

Lucas's first instinct was to say yes, absolutely, what day? what time?—but then he reminded himself that such a personal, one-on-one encounter with Miranda would in no way allow him to use her powers of perception the way he had intended. And once again he was forced to remind himself that those powers were the only reason he *did* want to see more of Miranda True.

"I have a better idea," he heard himself say, a pang of what he denied was guilt stabbing at his heart. With no small amount of effort, he managed to ignore the irritating twinge. "A dinner party a friend of mine is throwing. Thursday night?"

Miranda tried to brush off her disappointment that he would rather accompany her to a crowded party than to spend time with her in the quieter, more intimate surroundings of her house. Instead she agreed. "All right. What time?"

"Six o'clock?"

"I'll be ready."

Lucas curved his palm over Miranda's jaw one last time, leaned forward and kissed her softly on the forehead, then on her cheek, then pressed his lips gently, tenderly, against her own. "I'll see you Thursday," he vowed quietly.

And with that he was gone, faded into the darkness like a wondrous dream. Miranda sat alone on her porch swing for a long time, remembering the gentle touch of his fingertips on her heated flesh, recalling the intimate potency of his kiss, and thrilling at the knowledge that such a magnificent man would want to see her again. A tiny, tiny shiver of apprehension ran along the length of her spine at the realization, and Miranda curled her arms around her abdomen in an effort to ward it off. There was no reason she should be suspicious of Lucas, she assured herself. No reason at all.

So why did she have the impression that his promise to see her again next week seemed more like a contrivance? And why couldn't she quite shake the feeling that Lucas Strath-moor wasn't what he seemed?

Miranda shook off her worry as nothing more than a leftover adolescent sense of inadequacy, thinking she should be ashamed of herself for having so little self-confidence. Why shouldn't a man like Lucas be attracted to her? She had a lot to offer any man.

Retrieving the two glasses from the porch, Miranda tipped hers back to swallow the last of her wine and rose to return to the house. As soon as the screen door clicked shut behind her, she heard Bix howl in his rusty, feline voice, accompanied by a chorus of demands from the other cats. It was crazy, she knew, but for a moment, their insistent meowing almost made them sound as if they were trying to warn her about something.

She sighed and shook her head hopelessly as she opened a can of food to divide between them. It was one thing to talk to one's cats, Miranda thought idly, nothing unusual for most cat owners. However, she really was missing out on too much sleep if she was beginning to think her cats knew something about Lucas that she didn't know herself.

Lack of sleep, Miranda thought again, as she turned out the lights, locked up her house and headed upstairs for bed. That must be the reason for all her strange feelings this evening. Tomorrow she could think a bit more clearly about all this. Tomorrow she was sure all her niggling little anxieties about Lucas would be put to rest. A small smile curled her lips as she realized further that tomorrow would mean only five days were left before she saw him again.

Chapter Six

The evening Miranda enjoyed at the dinner party with Lucas was almost a carbon copy of the one she'd enjoyed with him at the cocktail party the week before. At the end of the night, they sat on the porch swing talking, and after a soft, gentle, mind-scrambling kiss good-night, Lucas invited her to another party the following week, then slipped away into the darkness.

In fact, for four more weeks straight, they repeated this scenario, with Miranda attending some kind of gathering of Lucas's friends and colleagues—a reception for a visiting entourage of European businessmen, the opening of an art gallery, the dedication of a new office building downtown, and another cocktail party. Every time Miranda invited him to her house for dinner, or suggested they attend a movie or the theater or any of the other numerous events normally available in Boston in the springtime, Lucas offered her a reason why he couldn't make it, then suggested a party instead.

She tried to excuse his reluctance to see her alone as a result of shyness or nervousness around her. Then she remembered that Lucas Strathmoor was quite possibly the boldest man she'd ever encountered. She recalled how forward he'd been with her the very first evening they'd met, and on the following afternoon when he'd come storming into her life and into her house. With no small amount of heated amazement, she also remembered that his hands were the hands of an eager and very experienced lover, and she realized there was no way she'd ever convince herself that the man had a bashful bone in his body.

It wasn't that Miranda felt Lucas was trying to hide anything from her. On the contrary, he was always gregarious in their conversations, offering her bits of his past and himself that she found fascinating. In turn, she found herself revealing things about her own life and personal philosophy that she had spoken of to no one before. Their discussions were always animated and never lacked subject matter, covering every topic from cars to carrots. Gradually Miranda came to know Lucas very well, and allowed him to get closer to her than anyone had been in a long, long time. She enjoyed his company enormously. But she couldn't understand why he wouldn't spend time with her alone.

He did begin to call her during the week, though, between the times they saw each other. So often at night, Miranda would lie in bed in her nightgown with the telephone receiver cradled under her ear, wishing Lucas was in the bed beside her instead of at the other end of a cable. Then she would fall asleep with his softly murmured good-night still lingering in her mind, and would experience the most vividly erotic dreams she'd ever entertained, waking in a damp sweat with the sheets tangled around her, her heart pounding furiously behind her rib cage, her entire body on fire with need. He seemed to be interested in her, she'd think morosely on those occasions. So why wasn't he lying there beside her?

Lucas Strathmoor was an enigma, she decided six weeks after her first date with him, as they were driving home from the cocktail party thrown by one of his friends. But he was an enigma she was determined to solve. She glanced over at his handsome profile, loving the way the wind rushed in through the open window and tossed his black hair onto his forehead, loving how his fingers lingered on the wheel with infinite care. It occurred to her then that she was slowly coming to love nearly everything about this man.

At one time she had thought him nothing but ruthless, power-hungry and self-centered. But over the past several weeks, she had begun to see that those qualities—although present in his character to some degree—were greatly overshadowed by other, less aggressive traits. She had come to realize that the Lucas Strathmoor she'd met initially had been a man on the defensive, a man who had feared his company and his livelihood were threatened, and who had been striking back to protect it. And during their more recent excursions together, she had witnessed his intelligence, inquisitiveness and sense of humor. Not only did he listen to and seem to respect her views, but she had also noted long ago that he often questioned her further in order to clarify his understanding of her point.

Miranda had also observed his ability to be gentle, and his capacity for tenderness. She experienced it every time he sat with her on the porch swing and kissed her good-night. Lucas truly seemed to care for her. It was something that contributed greatly to her confusion about his reluctance to get closer to her.

Tonight, she decided, she would get to the bottom of it. Tonight would not end as unsatisfactorily as the nights preceding it in the past weeks. Lucas Strathmoor was like no man she had ever met, and she had responded to him more quickly, more intensely than she ever had to anyone else, including Patrick Lyndon. Miranda sighed at the realization. The sizzling sensations Lucas roused in her just by sitting this close to him in the car put her girlish affection for Patrick to shame. Without even making love to her, Lucas made Miranda feel like a woman. The consideration he showed her, the way he held and kissed her, the fact that he could converse with her so easily and readily, all made her feel as if he held her in some special regard.

Yes, tonight, Miranda decided, she would either discover exactly what his feelings for her involved, or she would completely embarrass herself trying.

Lucas pulled the car to a stop in Miranda's driveway, thinking that lately he looked forward to coming to her house with more enthusiasm than he'd ever felt for going to his own. The light above her garage cast a warm yellow glow over the car, and a lamp burning in the living room window shone in welcome. The outside of Miranda's house was every bit as inviting as the inside, looking like something from a Norman Rockwell painting, complete with a huge sweeping elm tree in the front yard, and a white picket fence affectionately enclosing it.

Any respectable bachelor would run screaming in horror from such a domestic scene. But Lucas found to his surprise that he liked it. Despite the fact that he'd grown up in a crumbling apartment building planted center-court in the urban sprawl of an industrial community, the coziness of Miranda's little cottage in the suburbs reminded him a lot of his childhood. His parents may not have had much money, but they'd made sure he was showered with attention and affection, had seen to it that the three of them formed a strong family unit. They'd made certain Lucas knew he was loved. Somehow, he was sure that was precisely the case with Miranda True, as well—she would never run out of love.

It was something he hadn't truly realized until he'd spent a good deal of time with her. And it was why he hadn't allowed himself to spend any more time with her than he absolutely had to. The quiet moments they enjoyed chatting on her porch swing at evening's end were difficult enough to keep harmless. Every time he went out with Miranda, Lucas reminded himself that he was only with her for the observations she could offer him about other people. And every time they went out, he got from her exactly what he'd said he wanted.

Without realizing it, Miranda had gleaned a lot of information from other people, and her unwitting analysis of their reactions had provided Lucas with a wealth of information to consider about his potential prospects that might not have occurred to him otherwise. Over the past six weeks, he had succeeded in fully acquiring two companies with a minimal fuss by sneaking up on those that might otherwise have given him fits had he gone about buying them outright. And he had begun stalking three more that he might not have thought worth his time had Miranda not pointed out—unaware of what she was doing, naturally—that all were viable prospects. He was quietly raiding one of them already, and had plans to go after another one next week.

Lucas knew he had promised himself he would only use Miranda's perceptive talents to win Panwide, and he had become victorious in that little problem almost immediately after undertaking his plan to use her. The Lyndons of Saint Denis now owned only five percent of the company they had called their own for a century and a half, and Lucas owned controlling interest at sixty-seven percent. He was now the man in charge of Panwide Textiles, Incorporated. All thanks to some of Miranda's unknowing observations about one of the shareholders—observations Lucas had worked to his advantage in convincing the man to sell his stock in the company to Lucas.

But unwilling to end his liaison with the intriguing Miranda True just yet, Lucas had asked her out a second time. And that second time she had again, without realizing it, provided him with some extremely important insights that had aided in his acquiring a distillery he wouldn't even have thought of going after. Lucas justified his use of her talents that time by reminding himself that the observation Miranda made had been offered freely, with no prompting from him. He'd be crazy not to use it.

At the end of that night, Lucas had found himself asking Miranda out again for the following week, telling himself it was because he'd enjoyed her company, but deep down knowing it was with the hope that she would once again offer him a snippet of information he might be able to use. And she had. So he'd asked her out again, once more assuring himself it was only because she was an agreeable escort. And again, she had made an observation that had led to Lucas's reevaluation of a situation, a reevaluation that then led to his raiding of another company. So he'd asked Miranda out again. And again. And every time, she had performed with amazingly accurate results.

And all the while Lucas had reassured himself by repeatedly reminding himself that Miranda was a woman who had offered these insights and observations freely and readily to his casually asked questions, and never once had he been forced to use ulterior means to extract the information from her. He enjoyed being with her—that much was true. And if he happened to profit financially from her company because of her carelessly offered comments, without having to extort information, well . . . what was wrong with that?

Now as he sat in her driveway, trying to reassure himself with that line of logic again, Lucas was having some problems. Because somewhere along the way, that line of logic had ceased to be convincing. Somewhere along the way, his plan had become something other than a game to be enjoyed by himself and, to a lesser, unknowing degree, by Miranda. And somewhere along the way, Lucas had begun to worry about the outcome of his actions.

He felt her eyes on him in the dim light and turned to meet her gaze. He tried to smile at her, tried to come up with something clever and affectionate to say. Almost involuntarily he lifted his hand to brush his curled fingers over her cheek, and felt the satiny skin grow warm beneath his touch. He wondered if she'd respond that quickly, that heatedly, on other parts of her body. Maybe tonight... He stopped himself before his thoughts could go too far. He couldn't afford to make love to Miranda feeling the way he did now. There was too much confusion, too much uncertainty surrounding his feelings for her. Simply put, Lucas didn't know exactly what was going on between them anymore.

"You're coming in, aren't you?" Miranda asked quietly.

Lucas nodded silently, and unfolded his big body from the car, then strode around it to open her door and help her out. The June night was warm and pleasant, sprinkled with the sweet scent of the flowers that grew throughout Miranda's yard. As she rose from the car, the fragrance of her perfume, a spicy concoction Lucas was sure had been mixed with the expressed intention of driving men to madness, joined the aroma of the night. Her short-sleeved flowered dress was perfectly in tune with the garden setting surrounding them, and he skimmed his knuckles along the length of her bare arm before lacing his fingers with her own.

Silently they strode to the house, and Lucas waited while Miranda unlocked·her front door. She was wearing new shoes that she'd told him had been bothering her feet all night, so he was not surprised that the moment she was inside, she slipped them off and dropped them by the hall closet.

"Sorry," she apologized sheepishly. "But my feet are killing me."

Lucas smiled at her. "All that dancing we did. I don't mind getting more comfortable myself." And with that he shrugged out of his pearl gray suit jacket and hung it on the closet doorknob, then loosened his necktie and unbuttoned the top two buttons of his shirt.

As Lucas preceded her down the hall toward the kitchen—their usual nightly routine—Miranda watched fascinated as he rolled up the sleeves of his ivory shirt to reveal the solid, muscular forearms beneath. Inevitably her mind began to wander toward thoughts of how his bare skin would feel next to her own, and she felt her heart kick up that unsteady rhythm she was beginning to find so familiar. Miranda wet her lips, took a deep breath, and told her libido to behave itself.

It was strange, yet somehow comforting, how well acquainted Lucas had become with her house, she thought. The downstairs part, anyway. He still hadn't seen her bedroom upstairs, but perhaps tonight she might be able to lure him there. Miranda put that erratic thought on hold as Lucas went to the cabinet over the sink and pulled down two wineglasses, plucked the corkscrew from the drawer beside the stove, then went to the wine rack and chose a bottle of Beaujolais. They chatted amiably about the evening's events as he pulled the cork from the bottle and splashed a generous portion of ruby red into each of the glasses.

Three of the cats had come running at the prospect of people in the kitchen who might feed them, and now twined themselves around table legs and human ankles as they meowed for attention. But Bix remained ominously absent.

"I don't think your big cat likes me," Lucas said as he handed Miranda a glass of wine. "He seems to avoid me at all costs."

As if summoned by Lucas's assessment of his character, Bix came barreling out of nowhere with a ferocious cry just as Lucas was releasing the glass into Miranda's hand. The sudden appearance of the cat startled both of them, and the glass went tumbling from their grasp to shatter in a spray of red and crystal on the white tile floor. Bix disappeared as quickly as he'd arrived, followed by the other three cats who had been frightened by the chaotic din. For a moment Miranda and Lucas only stared at each other dumbfounded, then they both began to laugh at the same time.

"See?" Lucas said through his chuckles. "Your cat doesn't want me to get anywhere near you."

"That's not true," Miranda tried to reassure him. "He probably just saw a spider or something."

Lucas began to laugh again at the prospect that such a large, seemingly fearless animal would be spooked by a bug, then scooped Miranda into his arms with a flourish.

She gasped at the suddenness of his action, wrapping her arms around his neck to keep from falling. "What are you doing?" she asked him breathlessly.

Miranda wasn't sure, but she thought Lucas held her a little closer as he replied, "The glass. You're not wearing any shoes. I don't want you to cut yourself while I clean this up."

He set her down on the nearest raised surface, which in this case happened to be the kitchen table. They made a number of cat jokes while Lucas cleaned up the spilled wine and broken glass, laughing and giggling like two teenagers. Finally, when the last of the mess had disappeared from the floor, Lucas came to stand in front of Miranda, reaching out to pluck her down from the table. However, when he settled his hands securely on her hips, instead of pulling her down from her perch, he pulled her closer to him. Suddenly he paused, and his face seemed to lose some of the light humor they had shared.

Miranda wasn't quite sure when or how the change took place. She only knew that one minute she was sitting on the kitchen table where Lucas had set her to keep her from stepping on the broken glass, and the next moment he had insinuated himself between her thighs, with his hands planted firmly on her hips. His eyes were dark with wanting, the deep brown and gray blending into a stormy color that spoke of a passion long unassuaged. Before she had time to say anything, Lucas was leaning forward, pulling her hips more intimately into the cradle of his thighs as he did so, taking her lips with his.

It was a nice kiss, Miranda thought fondly, as he plied her mouth with his. It began as a soft, gentle caress of her lips, then his tongue flicked over the corners of her mouth, urging her to open up to him. She obeyed willingly, then went a little mad at the feel of his tongue filling her mouth. He tasted her deeply over and over again, all the while rubbing his pelvis insistently against hers in a rhythm to mimic the motions of his mouth. With one hand braced against her fanny, Lucas let the other roam up over her rib cage, pausing when he met the lower curve of her breast.

It was the most intimate touch he had offered her, and Miranda welcomed it as heartily as a slumbering flower welcomes the morning sun. Her breath came in ragged gusts as he cupped his hand over the soft mound and gently kneaded her tender flesh. When he raked his thumb across the taut peak, she cried out. Lucas smiled at the sound, a dangerous, feral smile, and removed his hand long enough to unfasten every button of her dress that climbed in a vertical line up her torso. The skin between her breasts was flushed and warm, extremely sensitive to his touch because of the intimate entwining of their bodies. When he leaned forward to place a quiet kiss over her heart, Miranda shuddered, sighed and tangled her fingers in his hair to pull him closer.

As if in complete understanding of her unspoken demand, Lucas pushed the fabric of her dress aside to expose the cream-colored brassiere beneath. Her breasts were straining against the delicate confection of lace, and he couldn't keep himself from leaning down to taste her through the silky soft scrap of lingerie. His tongue flicked over her three, four, five times before he drew her breast as fully into his mouth as he could manage. Then, unable to stand even that small barrier any longer, Lucas shoved at the flowered fabric of the dress until it was off her shoulders and over her arms, then reached behind her to unfasten her brassiere.

It floated to the floor in a discarded cloud of lace, and Lucas took a moment to gaze at the prize he had won. Miranda was so beautiful, more perfect than anything he'd ever seen in his life. With a ragged gasp he lowered his head once again, cradling her heavy breast in one hand as he went back to his ministrations, circling her with his tongue, mouthing her, tugging at her, nipping gently with his teeth until she thought she would go mad.

As he continued to taste her, Miranda insistently pulled him closer, then began to struggle with the fastenings of his shirt. Her fingers fumbled with his necktie but finally loosened the knot and pulled it free. Then she deftly unbuttoned his shirt and pushed it off his shoulders, marveling at what she found beneath it. His skin was like satin steel, masking a strength that was solid and warm, barely hinting at the heat and hardness she knew was to come.

Wherever Miranda touched Lucas, his body came alive, the muscles in his back bunching and flexing as she skimmed her fingertips over each one. When she brought her hands around to tangle her fingers in the dark hair sprayed across his chest, Lucas bit off a moan of pleasure. Miranda dipped her hands lower then, raking her fingernails over the washboard ruggedness of his torso, halting only when she reached the barrier of his trousers. With one hand, she deftly unhooked his belt and yanked the length of leather free, while with the other she unfastened the button at his waist.

Lucas caught her hand in his then, holding it away from his body as he gasped for breath. When he looked up to meet her gaze, his eyes were filled with a desire like none Miranda had ever seen. After a moment fraught with tension, when he seemed to be weighing the most important decision in the world, Lucas slowly, so slowly, settled Miranda's hand over the surging strength she had so deliriously sought, closing his eyes and biting his lip as she cupped him more fully. She, too, was nearly overcome by the frantic heat and solid vitality she encountered, but she had only a moment to ponder it, because then Lucas began to go exploring once again.

Dreamily Miranda felt his hands drop to her knees, lifting her legs to wrap them around his waist. When she circled him tightly to bring him closer, he skimmed both of his hands up her thighs, pushing up the skirt of her dress oh so slowly as he ventured farther.

Miranda emitted a wild little cry at the pressure of his fingers on her bare skin. Where had all this passion come from? she wondered vaguely. What had caused this raging fire? It was as if they had both been tamping down their desires for six weeks and were simply unable to halt their release now. Miranda had never felt such a heat, such an incandescence, inside her before, and knew that Lucas was responsible. All she wanted was to be closer to him, as close as a woman could be to a man, and in her urgency, pushed her body more demandingly against his as she stroked that hard, masculine part of him.

Lucas responded with a muffled groan, edging his fingers higher up her legs, then higher still. When he finally came into contact with the silky fabric of her panties, he paused at the thin barrier to consider his options. Miranda gasped when he flattened the pad of his big hand over the soft fabric protecting the most intimate part of her, crying out loud as he pressed his fingers firmly against her.

Upon feeling her heat, her readiness for him, Lucas pulled his mouth away from her breast, his gaze boring into hers in silent question. Whatever reply he found there seemed to reaffirm his intentions. His eyes never leaving hers, Lucas slipped his hand beneath the satin barrier, nudging her body backward on the table to stroke her gently with his thumb.

His gesture caused Miranda to become lost in a silver haze of pleasure. She had never felt so exquisite, so sexy, so…so free…in her life. As he continued to press his fingers against her, caressing, stroking, journeying deeper, she knew she was lost to this man. And when she felt him pulling her panties down her legs, she knew she wanted nothing more than to become one with Lucas Strathmoor.

"Lucas," she said raggedly, gasping for breath. "Please…"

He, too, seemed to be on the verge of delirium, but smiled wickedly when he replied, "Please what? Please don't? Please stop? Or please…do this to me forever."

"Yes." Miranda nodded feverishly. "And please, please make love to me."

It was all the invitation Lucas needed. Freeing himself from his trousers, unable to stand the torture of touching Miranda without having her any longer, he thrust himself deep inside her waiting warmth. For a moment, he could only stand still, glorying in the exquisite pleasure of the union, marveling that nothing had ever felt this good in his life. Then slowly, gradually, he unsheathed himself, only to plunge deeper still. Miranda cried out at the action, then felt herself tipping backward onto the table. Quickly she righted herself, wrapping her arms around his shoulders with all the strength she could manage. As she fastened her legs tightly around Lucas's waist once again, he circled her ankles fiercely with his hands and began to make love to her with a ferocity that demanded response.

And respond she did. With every foray Lucas made, Miranda met him equally, until their rhythm built to a frenzied pace. Faster and faster they went, higher and higher they climbed, until neither was quite sure who or where they were. Lucas pounded into Miranda with a ferocity she would never have guessed him capable of possessing, and she pulled him closer as if she'd never get enough. Finally he gripped her hips with bruising strength and buried himself as deeply inside her as he could, exploding like a supernova. Their cries split the heavy air churning between them, giving voice to the absolute joy they experienced in their culmination.

Slowly their heart rates began to quieten, but neither moved from the position in which they found themselves. Lucas spread his palms open against Miranda's sweat-dampened back, raking his hands over the moisture to cup her shoulder blades. He wanted to make love to her again right now, he realized, shocked. He'd never had the desire so immediately, so soon after making love, but with Miranda, it was a demand almost frightening in its intensity. Before his body betrayed his need, he pulled himself slowly from within her, cradling her shoulders in his hands to pull her immediately back into his arms.

As he held her close, rubbing his hands up and down her heated, slick skin, Lucas felt alive, really alive, for the first time in years. He was confused and uncertain about what had just happened between him and Miranda—about the speed and intensity of his reactions, and the eagerness of her own response—and he was afraid to speak lest he blurt out

some clichéd avowal of affection. He only knew one thing
at that moment—he had absolutely no intention of ever letting Miranda go.

He continued to hold her for a long time, willing his body
to calm down and his breathing to return to normal. "Are
you all right?" he finally whispered roughly, not altogether
certain whether he was talking to Miranda or to himself.

She was trembling, he realized, awed that her reaction to
what they had just shared would mirror his own. As he
continued to hold her in his arms, he understood that Miranda had been affected as profoundly by what had just
happened as he.

He felt her nod, but she said nothing, only clung to him
in much the same way he did her. They were both only half-
naked, the dress bunched around Miranda's waist and Lucas's unfastened trousers both blatant reminders that they
had been so utterly consumed by passion that they hadn't
even bothered to fully undress. Nothing like this had ever
happened to Lucas before.

Miranda, too, was amazed by her behavior. She felt wan-
ton and dangerous, and ready to make love again. Lucas
had roused feelings and responses in her she would have
sworn she was incapable of offering, had brought to life
parts of her body she didn't think capable of sensation. And
now as she clung to him with her heart pounding wildly and
her lungs groping for breath, she didn't know what to do.
She had never made love this wildly, this impetuously, before. She was sitting on her kitchen table, for goodness'
sake. How was one supposed to snuggle and drift off into
sweet dreams in such a position?

"Lucas, I—"

"Miranda, this—"

They spoke at once and ceased at once, then both began
to chuckle. Miranda pulled herself only far enough away

from his embrace so that she could look into his eyes, and she smiled at the genuine affection she saw burning there.

"You first," she said softly.

"No, you first," he replied.

She took a deep breath and willed her voice to be even and matter-of-fact as she spoke. "I've never had an experience quite like this before, and . . . and I'm not quite sure how to act."

His smile told her that he was entertaining thoughts similar to her own, and his nod only confirmed her suspicions. "Nothing like this has ever happened to me, either."

And it hadn't. Lucas still wasn't sure what had made him lose control the way he had. But as he'd knelt on the floor cleaning up the spilled wine, he'd been acutely aware of Miranda carelessly swinging her bare legs only inches from his head, and when he'd risen to help her down from the table, he'd been enveloped by the tangy scent of her once again. Suddenly it was as if his body had a will of its own, and he had been helpless to stop himself from kissing her, holding her, making love to her. Now as they held each other, exhausted and spent, he was amazed to discover that even this explosive union hadn't come close to satisfying his need for her. Vaguely he wondered if he would ever get enough of making love to Miranda True.

"Can I stay the night?" he asked her quietly.

Miranda's heart began to pump even more furiously at his roughly uttered question. His eyes showed his eagerness, and his chest rose and fell in ragged gasps for breath that rivaled her own. "Wh-why would you want to?" she stammered softly, already knowing the answer, but wanting to hear him voice it nonetheless.

For a moment Lucas didn't answer, only gazed into her eyes as if he'd found a treasure he'd been seeking for years. Finally he lifted his hands to cup her face in his palms, and leaned forward to place a brief, chaste kiss on her lips.

"Because I want to make love to you again," he told her simply. "In your bed, with all the care and tenderness I wasn't able to manage this time. I want to wake up beside you in the morning and make love to you again, and I want to spend all day making sure that you're satisfied."

Miranda blinked, feeling as if she were spinning out of control into a wild vortex at the center of the universe. Where had this man come from? she wondered, her thoughts fuzzy and bordering on incoherent. Lucas Strathmoor was a man who could have any woman he wanted, yet some unknown force had been generous enough to give him to her. Miranda still couldn't believe the amazingly fortunate set of circumstances that had brought the two of them together. Clearly the fates had gone out of their way to orchestrate this union. And who was Miranda to interfere with fate?

"The shop is closed tomorrow..." she began, her voice drifting off at the realization. "And I...oh, Lucas, I'd love for you to stay the night."

Lucas released a breath he'd been unaware of holding, and only then did he realize how much he had feared her possible refusal. Without another word, he tightened one arm around Miranda's shoulders, then hitched the other under her knees. She wrapped her own arms lovingly around his neck. Lifting her carefully from the table, he carried her to the stairs off the kitchen he assumed would lead up to her bedroom, because he knew it wasn't on the first floor.

As he made the slow journey up the winding staircase, Lucas marveled at how small and nearly weightless was the woman in his arms. Miranda seemed more innocent and vulnerable than she'd seemed before, and something twisted painfully in his heart when he realized how much he had come to care for her. He chastised himself for ever thinking her anything other than what she so clearly was, and felt ashamed of himself for ever hatching his plan to use her perceptive talents to gain a corporate advantage. If she ever found out what he had done . . .

But she wouldn't find out, he promised himself. Because he was never going to use her that way again. From here on out, he and Miranda would be like any other lovers. They would spend time getting to know each other better—go someplace other than parties and business gatherings, talk about the most intimate things people could discuss. They would make love until they were too exhausted to go any further, then they'd rest and make love some more. Maybe they could even get away for a week together at his house on the Cape. All Lucas knew now was that he wanted Miranda to be a part of his life in every way he could manage.

When his foot hit the top step, he glanced up to find that Miranda's upstairs was half the size of her downstairs, one large room that she had turned into a bedroom with a sitting area at the opposite end. Like the rest of the house, this room was filled with floral prints and living plants, a small boudoir lamp glowing amber by the bed and offering the only light. As if fearful of breaking her, Lucas set Miranda on the bed as gently as if she were a priceless piece of crystal. But when he moved to pull away from her, she reached up for him and pulled him down to the bed beside her.

"Don't go," she murmured softly, tangling her fingers insistently in his hair.

Lucas smiled at her, a smile full of intimate promise. "I was only going to get undressed," he told her with a quiet chuckle.

Miranda smiled back, her eyes warm and liquid in the soft yellow light of the lamp. "Let me do it."

Lucas felt his body catch fire at her offer, her voice low and throaty and utterly erotic. He lay down beside her again, trying to stay in control as her fingers roved hungrily over him. When he could no longer tolerate not touching her, his hands snaked out to the flowered fabric still bunched around her waist, and he finished unfastening the tiny buttons until he could pull the dress from beneath her and toss it onto the floor beside the remainder of his own clothing. Then the two of them lay naked beside each other, and suddenly they had all the time in the world.

They spent the rest of the night trying to satisfy each other, succeeding instead in driving each other into an ever-deepening desire. Only when the dawn began to creep over the horizon did they finally slip into a peaceful sleep, their dreams entwined, their hearts pressed together, their bodies nestled intimately against each other.

The last thought Lucas entertained before easing into unconsciousness was that he'd never felt more at peace in his life. Then slumber claimed him with all its soothing innocence, and in his dreams he saw himself with Miranda, beneath a sweeping elm tree, and protected by a fortress vaguely reminiscent of a white picket fence.

When Miranda awoke on Sunday, it was to find the sun hanging high in the sky, splashing through the bedroom window in a streak of white to warm their naked bodies. At some point during the night they must have become hot and pushed the bedclothes to the foot of the bed. Miranda smiled shyly and snuggled closer to the hard masculine body beside her. She could remember several points during the night when the two of them had grown so warm they had nearly burst into flame.

Lucas still slept peacefully beside her, so Miranda lay still in the morning light, amazed at her situation. She was being held tenderly, lovingly, by a pair of strong, muscular arms, her legs entwined intimately with his. Last night had been the most wonderful she could ever remember, surpassing anything she had known before. Of course, she had seen by the lines on his hands six weeks ago that Lucas Strathmoor would be a magnificent, very physical lover, but last night had far exceeded anything she might have imagined. True to his Martian predisposition, and just as she had told him that night at Grace Devon's party, Lucas had indeed been very ardent in his romantic pursuit. And he did indeed have a very passionate disposition.

Miranda couldn't prevent the satisfied sigh she expelled at the memories warming her brain, nor the catlike stretch that lengthened her body as a result. She ached in places she never would have thought could be affected by lovemaking. But they were pleasant, almost enjoyable aches, brought about by her own curiosity and Lucas's more than eager attempts to satisfy that inquisitiveness. She wasn't sure she'd ever reach a time when she would be fully satisfied, however—she would always want more of Lucas.

He stirred beside her then, rubbing his hands along her arms before pulling her body closer to his. Tucking her head into the hollow created between his chin and shoulder, he wrapped his arms around her waist and squeezed gently.

"Good morning," he said softly, his voice low and slumber-rusty.

"Good morning," she replied as softly, circling his waist with her arms to hug him back.

"How did you sleep?"

Miranda smiled contentedly and closed her eyes. "I had some pretty interesting dreams."

She could feel his chest rise and fall in quiet laughter. "Yeah, me, too."

For a moment they remained silent, then Lucas curled his fingers below Miranda's chin and tilted her face back so that he could meet her gaze. His eyes reflected an emotion she wasn't quite able to identify, but before she could say a word, he leaned down and pressed his lips gently against her own. It was a kiss of quiet greeting and intimate memory, a kiss that told Miranda he was happy he had stayed the night. But it told her nothing of the future, of what lay ahead, and somewhere deep inside her soul, a little part of her trembled with apprehension.

"Are you cold?" Lucas asked as he pulled away, reaching for the sheet to drag it up over their exposed bodies.

Miranda shook her head but did feel a bit chilled. She didn't know why—the room was warm—but something had made her shiver. She nestled closer to the warmth afforded by Lucas's big body, and gradually the coldness began to dissipate. When she felt his fingers brushing against her cheek, Miranda lifted her head from its resting place against his chest, then she reached for his hand and kissed it lightly before inspecting it more closely. As she studied the lines etched on his palm, she began to smile a little cryptically.

"What?" Lucas asked when he noted her expression.

"I do believe that your mount of Venus is even more pronounced now than it was before," she told him with a wicked grin.

"Oh, it is not," he insisted. "You're just making that up."

Miranda shook her head in silent denial. "No, I'm certain it's changed. And see this little line here?" She pointed to a tiny groove among many that fanned away from the base of his thumb.

Lucas nodded. "Yes. What about it?"

"I don't think that line was there before." Her smile became mischievous. "I think that line represents me."

"Miranda, there are a million lines right there—"

"Each one representative of a woman you've made love to," she informed him with surprising calm.

Lucas paused before continuing, gazing down at the lines she had indicated. He began to count them silently, but ceased before the final total. "I have *not* made love to that many women," he assured her. "And anyway, how can you tell which ones were there before? Lines do not form on the human hand in one night."

"I know, but it's been six weeks since I studied your palm. It's changed."

Lucas was clearly skeptical. "Uh-huh, I see. And in what way might it have changed?"

Miranda bent her head to inspect his hand further, her expression intensely puzzled. "I'm not sure," she admitted. "But there's something different here. Or maybe something I missed or misinterpreted before. Your hand doesn't reflect as aggressive and overbearing a nature as it did before." When she glanced up at him again, her face was open and unconcerned. "Of course, I didn't get much sleep last night," she added blithely, "so I may just be blathering on like an idiot because of exhaustion."

Lucas smiled the smile of a predator about to pounce. "Well, let's see if I can't get your blood going. A little morning exercise never hurt anybody. And I know a great aerobic workout we can do together."

Miranda wrinkled her nose playfully. "I've never much been one for organized exercise. It can get pretty boring."

"Not this one," Lucas assured her as he dropped his hand to her naked thigh. "You'll enjoy this one. I promise."

And Miranda did. Immeasurably.

Chapter Seven

Despite having finally made love with Lucas Strathmoor, the week that followed for Miranda differed little from the ones that had preceded it since first meeting him. When he had left Sunday afternoon, it was with his usual invitation to join him for a gathering of friends and colleagues the following weekend, this particular event a fund-raiser for a local politician. He had called on Wednesday night to re-affirm their plans for Friday, and now as Miranda stood before her bedroom mirror, putting the finishing touches on her hair, she could almost convince herself that making love with Lucas last week had been nothing more than a dream.

Almost.

Then she would recall every moment they had spent together—the way he had touched and kissed her, the soft caresses of his body against hers that had built steadily into a fierce, demanding insistence, the way he had claimed her over and over again in a frenzy of need, and the explosion of emotion that had preceded the quiet, gradual slowing of her heartbeat until she had drifted off to sleep in his arms. Such memories would be more than sufficient in reminding Miranda that what had happened last weekend had not been a dream. Her skin still grew hot and flushed at the memories.

At the sound of the doorbell's metallic rasp in the hallway below her, Miranda jumped. How could she still be nervous around Lucas after all they had experienced together? Why did her heart still pound like an out-of-tune kettledrum at the simple realization that she would be spending an evening with him? Perhaps it was because she remembered how their last evening together had turned out, she thought. And because of the very real chance that such an outcome would be the result of the evening ahead as well.

At least this time she would be prepared, she thought. Last weekend, their lovemaking had resulted from such a spontaneous, surprising need, that neither of them had even considered the possible consequences of their actions. And although she had been reassured Monday morning that she wasn't pregnant, Miranda intended to make sure she took precautions against the possibility on future occasions.

When she tugged open her front door, she was offered yet another reason for her nervousness. Lucas was wearing a tuxedo, a black-and-white creation that seemed sewn by the gods to bring every solid muscle into achingly arousing appearance. As he had on that first evening, he extended a bouquet of lilies, and Miranda lifted them gingerly to her nose to inhale their sweet, heady aroma.

"Thank you," she said softly, meeting his gaze shyly.

How strange, she thought, that they could act the same way as before, after having made such wild, reckless love together. There was indeed a strange new intimacy between them, but Miranda knew it wasn't something that would prohibit their talking to each other or smiling at each other, or teasing each other as they always did before. Curiously she thought it might make those things even easier now.

"You're welcome," Lucas told her quietly as he stepped inside.

Wearing a gown of some nearly transparent material that fell away from her shoulders in a soft cascade of pale peach, Miranda looked more beautiful than he could ever recall her looking before. And that was saying something, because Lucas had seen Miranda looking pretty damned beautiful in the past several weeks. Last weekend alone, he had thought he would never see anything lovelier than Miranda True succumbing to the passion that had burned unsated inside her for years. It had been an image that haunted him all week long, a memory that had virtually prohibited him from getting any work done. All Lucas had been able to think about was the way she reacted to his caresses, and the incredible responses she'd roused in him with her touch. His thoughts had been completely wrapped up in the prospect of making love to Miranda again.

It was why Lucas had forced himself to keep his distance from her all week. Every day he had lifted the phone with the intention of asking her out or inviting himself over, and every day he'd spent the better part of the afternoon talking himself out of doing it. He'd almost called off their date for tonight, because he just wasn't sure anymore what was happening between the two of them or how their relationship had come so far, so fast. He wanted time to think about things, wanted time to reevaluate the situation. However, more than either of those, he'd come to realize, he wanted to spend more time with the alluring Miranda True.

"I'll put these in some water, and then we can go," she said softly, bringing Lucas back to the matter at hand.

Then we can go, he repeated to himself as he watched her walk away. They could go to yet another gathering of people about whom he couldn't care less, when all they really

wanted was to be alone someplace far removed from the
crowds of Boston. Maybe they could call it a night early, he
thought with an uncharacteristic indifference to his professional obligations. Just make a quick appearance for Sen-
ator Miles and then go out for a quick bite before returning
home. And then maybe they could spend the rest of the
night making up for their separation of the past five days.
How had they made it to Friday without being able to hold
and touch each other every day that week? he marveled. He
doubted they'd ever be able to do that again.

Miranda returned with the lilies arranged in the same vase
she had used before, placing them with infinite care in the
center of the steamer trunk she substituted for a coffee table, just as she had before. But everything else was different this time, Lucas thought. Maybe they were going
through the same motions as before, but the emotions involved had changed considerably.

Miranda rearranged the flowers with quick, jerky movements, then straightened to glance at Lucas hastily before
dropping her gaze to the floor. When she offered him that
one brief look, he noted that her eyes were brighter than
usual, her cheeks flushed a becoming shade of pink. He
further observed that she stood with her fingers tangled together in front of her, biting her lip a little anxiously. His
curiosity became amazement when he realized that Miranda was nervous.

Lucas crossed the short distance between the front door
and the steamer trunk with quick measured strides, until he
stood no more than an inch away from Miranda. Then he
curled his index finger below her chin, tipping her head back
in an effort to make her meet his gaze.

"Miranda, does what we did last weekend…do I…make
you feel embarrassed?" he asked her quietly. He wasn't sure
if he could stand it if she told him yes. He wanted Miranda
to feel as freed and uninhibited by their actions as he did.

Miranda shook her head slowly. "Not embarrassed," she corrected him gently. "But shy, maybe. Yes, what's happened . . . and you . . . make me feel a little shy."

"Why?"

With an almost imperceptible shrug, she replied carefully, "I...it's just that..." She took a deep breath and tried again. "I've never known a man like you before, Lucas. You're so different from most people I meet—ambitious, charismatic, focused, assertive . . ."

"You're all those things, too, Miranda," he reminded her.

"But not to the extend that you are. What I mean is, you're a man who knows what he wants and sets out to get it without ever questioning the outcome—you're simply that confident of your abilities."

"And you're not?"

"No, I'm not," she replied honestly. "I never have been. That's why I'm still a little intimidated by you. There's a part of me that still wonders why you're here—with me— and not with some successful executive or intellectual genius or wealthy jet-setter."

Lucas didn't know what to say. *She* was intimidated by *him?* How could that be when he was still so utterly thrown by Miranda? *He* was the one who should be scared to death of their situation, because he was the one who had completely lost control of it. Somewhere along the line, Miranda had sent him spinning dizzily into territory he'd never explored before. When he looked into her eyes, he felt himself drowning. The melody of her voice made all other sounds disappear. And making love with her... Good God, making love with her had been indescribable. When the two of them were together, it was as if the rest of the world simply faded away to nothingness, because none of it was important except for what they created together.

Lucas had never experienced such a total reaction to another human being. Stumbling onto Miranda True had been like finding a piece of himself that had been missing for years. And now that he was complete, he never wanted to lose her.

"I don't want to be with a successful executive or an intellectual genius or a wealthy jet-setter," he said softly. "Not unless any of those people happen to be you. I only want to be with you, Miranda. No one else."

The words were out of his mouth before Lucas realized what he was saying. However, once uttered, he couldn't deny their truth. Suddenly he realized he *didn't* want to be with anyone else but Miranda. And suddenly he became a little intimidated, too.

Because he wasn't quite sure whether it was Miranda or himself who needed reassuring right now, Lucas remained silent after that. He picked up her pale peach wrap from the arm of the sofa and draped it over her shoulders, then led her out to the car. The drive toward town was quiet, their conversation nowhere near as avid as it usually was, and Lucas found his mind wandering far from the situation at hand.

"Let's skip this fund-raiser tonight," he said suddenly, impulsively, uncertain why he made the suggestion. Hell, Parker Levinson of Levinson Electronics was going to be at this gathering tonight, Lucas reminded himself, and he had wanted to gauge Miranda's reaction to him—Levinson Electronics was a company about to go under that Lucas had been thinking about going after. But for some reason, Parker Levinson suddenly seemed like the most insignificant mote of dust on the planet. And for some reason, Lucas couldn't care less whether Levinson Electronics was within his reach. All he wanted at the moment was to be with Miranda, alone somewhere, away from everybody and everything that might distract them. Somewhere with a beach, perhaps. And a bright yellow sun to warm their naked bodies.

"Can you get away from the shop this weekend?" he asked Miranda, feeling a little reckless and spontaneous.

Her expression indicated she was more than a little puzzled, but she replied, "Sure, I guess so. Sundays, we're closed anyway. And I think Marcy could handle things alone with two of the part-timers tomorrow. Why?"

"What about your cats?"

"My neighbor Mrs. Ransdell usually feeds them for me if I go out of town. Why?" Miranda repeated meaningfully.

Lucas said nothing in response, only smiled when he realized they were just over a mile away from the exit for the Southeast Expressway. Instead of remaining on I-93, which would have taken them to their destination, Lucas exited onto State Road 3. Miranda eyed him warily for a few moments, then she began to smile, too.

"Where are we going?" she asked him mildly as soon as they had left the city limits.

"Cape Cod."

"Cape Cod?" Miranda asked. "But you said this party was in Brookline."

"Oh, there's a party in Brookline all right," Lucas agreed. "But there's an even better one on the Cape tonight."

"But you said the one in Brookline was so important."

Lucas glanced over at Miranda in the darkness, his eyes glittering with an unknown fire. "The one on the Cape is a hell of a lot more important."

Miranda lowered her voice when she spoke again, as if telling him something he didn't already know. "But it's such a long drive. It will be awfully late when we get home."

Lucas's eyes never left the road as he replied, "No, it won't. It will be early. Early Monday morning."

"But we didn't pack anything," she protested halfheartedly. "No toiletries, no clothes..."

"I keep the house stocked with the basics, and we can stop at the grocery store before we get there to grab some supplies. As for clothes, well . . . it will be a casual weekend. We won't need much."

"The house?" Miranda asked lamely, trying to focus on one thing at a time, deciding to worry later about what a "casual" weekend with Lucas might involve.

"My house. I have a house in Yarmouth."

"And that's where we're going?" she asked quietly, surprisingly calm about the entire situation. "Your house?"

Lucas nodded, then turned to meet her gaze fully. "If that's all right with you."

Miranda's heart hammered hard in her chest when she realized he meant for the two of them to spend the weekend together—alone. Away from his friends and colleagues and any organized situation that would prevent them from acting on their impulses. She knew if she told him to turn the car around and take her home Lucas would, with no ill feeling toward her decision. The fact of the matter was, though, turning around to go home was the last thing Miranda wanted to do.

"I . . . it's fine with me," she said softly.

They arrived at Lucas's house, a rambling old Victorian sitting on a small rise just above the beach, at a little before eight. In the dark, Miranda couldn't detect much about its exterior, but Lucas had told her during their drive that his house had been recently renovated, with fresh paint inside and out, and much of the original hardware, which he'd discovered boxed up in the basement, restored to its original splendor.

It shouldn't have come as unexpected to Miranda that Lucas had done much of the renovation work himself—he did after all have a history of working with his hands. Yet for some reason, she had found it surprising that he would have taken on the labor himself—in many ways, he seemed like the kind of man who wanted to put his past behind him. It heartened her to know that he still took pleasure in physical tasks. She herself found enormous pleasure in getting her hands dirty during hard, physical work, and in the knowledge that she'd done the job well. The fact that at least some part of Lucas still enjoyed that, too, was something else they shared.

As he led her to the front door, Miranda marveled once again that she had allowed herself to be lured into a weekend away from home without even packing a suitcase. And she was especially unprepared this evening. In anticipation of her evening with Lucas, she had donned a brand-new formal gown and fragile high heels, and was carrying a tiny, beaded clutch large enough to hold only a comb, keys, credit cards, compact, lipstick and vial of perfume. She had spent over half an hour sweeping her hair up off her neck to coil it into an elegant French twist. Now the shoes dangled from her fingertips, the gown's hem was filling with sand and the ocean breeze had tugged free a number of unruly strands of hair.

Miranda had rather thought they might go out for a late dinner at some posh restaurant after the party, but instead they had stopped for groceries at a small market a few miles up the road. She had telephoned Mrs. Ransdell from the grocery store, apologizing for her last-minute petition, and had been reassured by the other woman that the cats would be well cared for until Monday morning. She and Lucas had purchased peanut butter, jelly, bread, tuna fish, mayonnaise—all the essentials for a weekend stay at the beach—pretending not to notice the curious looks they received from the few other people shopping for groceries. Now as Lucas jockeyed the bags from hand to hand while fumbling with his front door key, the incongruity of their situation finally hit Miranda and she began to laugh.

"What's so funny?" he asked as he pushed the front door open.

Miranda followed him in, still giggling as she watched him switch on lights, wandering along behind him through the house and up the stairs as he opened windows to allow in the fresh ocean breeze.

"Look at us," she said through her laughter. "We left tonight thinking we would be attending some socially upright, politically correct affair in Brookline, and instead we wind up on the Cape with absolutely nothing that we'll need. Your tuxedo, although very, very nice, isn't exactly *toute la rage* in these parts."

As they made their way down the stairs and through the hallway toward the kitchen, Lucas retorted brilliantly, "Oh, yeah?"

Miranda idly inspected the house as she wandered through it behind him, taking in the casual elegance of neutral colors and functional furnishings, the gleam of hardwood floors covered by dhurrie rugs, and the paintings of coastal scenes that hung on the walls. When she entered the kitchen, she saw that it, too, was as large and spacious as the other rooms, in a color scheme similar to what she had already viewed.

She watched him stow their meager foodstuffs in a cabinet over the stove, then recalled that he had responded to her comment with a very clever retort that deserved an equally clever reply.

"Yeah," she said with a smile.

Lucas spun around to face her, his expression full of intent. "Then maybe you'll just have to help me out of it, won't you?" he murmured in a sultry voice.

Miranda inhaled a deep, slow breath, willing her heart to cease its erratic thumping. There was nothing she would have liked more at that moment than to help Lucas out of his clothes. It was something she'd fantasized about on a number of occasions this week.

"Would you like a glass of wine?" he asked.

His question was uttered in a casual and matter-of-fact voice, and for a moment, Miranda wasn't sure if he'd made his suggestion that she undress him or not. "Yes, I'd love one," she told him, feeling a little off balance.

Lucas went to another cabinet and opened it to reveal a well-stocked wine rack. He plucked a few bottles out, one at a time, glancing at their labels until he found one he must have decided was acceptable. Miranda watched intently as he inserted the corkscrew and yanked the cork from the bottle with a crisp pop, loving the way his fingers and hands were so certain and confident in the task. After he splashed some of the pale ruby wine into two glasses, he handed one to Miranda, lifting his own to her in a silent toast before placing it against his lips for an idle sip. She did likewise, relishing the strong, woody flavor that greeted her tongue.

"It's delicious," she told him as the wine left a warm trail from her throat to her stomach.

"I've been waiting for a special occasion to open it," Lucas told her. "Tonight seemed appropriate."

That look was back in his eyes again, Miranda thought. That heated, predatory glimmer of promise that so thoroughly unbalanced her. She knew she was setting herself up for trouble with her next question, but she could no more prevent herself from asking it than she could keep her heart from beating.

"What's so special about tonight?" she murmured with a shallow sigh.

Lucas didn't answer right away. Instead he took another sip of his wine, slowly closing the distance between them as he did so, to stand immediately in front of her. Miranda tilted her head back to meet his gaze, marveling at the fires burning in his eyes. It was almost as if she could feel their heat burning her up as well. Unable to help herself, she lifted her hand to cup his rough jaw, then let her fingers delve into the dark hair at his temple, journeying farther until they found the sensitive nape of his neck. Lucas closed his eyes and took a deep breath, as if trying to stay calm.

"You want to know what's so special about tonight?" He turned Miranda's question back onto her.

When Lucas opened his eyes again, the fires were dancing brighter than she'd ever seen them before. Miranda swallowed with some difficulty and nodded silently.

"Tonight, Miranda, I'm going to make love to you."

She felt her knees beginning to melt away beneath her, and it was only through a supreme effort of will that Miranda forced herself to remain standing. "And why should tonight be more special than last weekend?" she asked him in a near whisper.

Lucas wound his arm around her waist, pulling her close. "Miranda, nothing could be more special than last weekend was," he assured her. "But we were at your house then, playing by your rules. Tonight we're at my house. Tonight we play by my rules."

The fire in his eyes leaped higher as he spoke, and Miranda felt her own temperature start to rise. "And why are your rules so different?" she asked after a difficult swallow, her voice barely audible now.

Lucas's lips turned up into a smile that was rife with wicked promise. "I only have one rule, Miranda—there *are* no rules. In my house, anything goes."

Her heart thundered behind her ribs as if heralding the arrival of the most violent of storms. Miranda recalled how wild and reckless, how incredibly physical Lucas had been in his lovemaking last weekend. She thought of how many rules he'd broken then, and wondered how many more there could be to break. She was so naive where men were concerned, she realized a little fearfully. How could she be sure this wasn't just some game with him? How could she be certain his feelings mirrored her own?

Trust was the immediate answer. Miranda would simply have to trust him.

Lucas took her hand and led her silently to the living room, where he went to the stereo and turned on something low and sweet and smooth. The subtle strains of a saxophone mingled with a softly cadenced piano tune, a combination that made Miranda want to indulge in a slow, sensual dance. As if fully understanding her unvoiced request, Lucas set his wine on top of a stereo speaker and opened his arms.

"Dance with me," he petitioned softly.

Miranda smiled, then placed her own glass on the coffee table. "I'd love to."

They walked toward each other and met at a spot on the rug that was perfect for an intimate dance. As they swayed slowly to the softly playing music, Lucas pulled Miranda closer to him, oblivious to the fact that they were already about as close as two people could be without being joined together. Her body was smooth and solid against him, and she smelled of something dark and rich and reminiscent of a sultry summer night. He dropped one hand from her shoulder to spread it open over her back, then skimmed it downward, down more, down further still, until his palm rested against the small of her back and his fingers dipped over the soft swell of her derriere.

Miranda nestled against him at the action, a gesture Lucas interpreted to mean that she wanted to be as intimately entwined as he did. Inching his hand lower still, he fully cupped the lower curve of her bottom, pulling her more snugly into the cradle of his thighs. When he heard her catch her breath, he realized she could detect how aroused he had become, and felt his heart race wildly out of control. Knowing it would be dangerous to escalate the stakes, but wanting to touch as much of Miranda as their position would allow, he squeezed her buttocks gently and rubbed himself against her more insistently, stifling a groan at the raging heat that spiraled through him as a result.

Miranda wasn't so successful in remaining quiet. She bit off a gasp just as it erupted from the back of her throat, and Lucas smiled at the stirrings of arousal he detected in that one little sound. He continued to press her body against his as he dropped his other hand from her shoulder to splay it open across her back, but instead of journeying down with it this time, he began to make a casual circuit around Miranda's rib cage. One slow song on the stereo faded into another as he brushed his fingers along the side of her breast, wanting to rejoice out loud when Miranda turned to give him freer access. He brought his hand to a halt where it curved below the weight of one breast, his thumb and index finger forming a U to support it. He could feel Miranda's heartbeat go wild beside his thumb, and he pulled his head away from hers to gaze into her eyes.

She watched him through heavy lids, her lips parted slightly in what could be curiosity, trepidation or desire. Hoping it was the last, Lucas dropped his gaze to her breast, lifting his thumb to brush it over the peak, and smiling at the immediate response she offered the caress. When he cupped her fully in his palm, Miranda groaned out loud, pushing herself forward to bring his touch closer. Lucas stroked her with his thumb again, and she closed her eyes, tilting her head to the side as she touched the tip of her tongue to the corner of her mouth.

It was a silent request, but one Lucas would never refuse. He dipped his head to Miranda's, kissing her temple, then her cheek, then her neck. When he lifted his head again, it was to find her watching him with eyes that were dark and filled with desire. Without thought, Lucas lowered his mouth to Miranda's, limning her lips with his tongue before kissing her deeply. She tasted wonderful, the smoky traces of wine mingling with an essence that was uniquely hers. Lucas couldn't get enough of her, reaching for more with every stroke of his tongue.

As he kissed her, his fingers crept up the column of her neck toward her hair. He wanted to feel the silky strands cascading against his skin, but realized to his dismay that her hair was still wound up in the elaborate twist she had arranged for their evening out. One by one, he pulled pins and combs from Miranda's hair, letting them drop carelessly to the rug, gradually freeing the shafts of pale gold until they draped around his hands for him to wind possessively around his fingers. Then, after filling both hands with gold, he cupped the back of her head in his palms so that he could kiss her more deeply still.

Over and over his mouth claimed hers, until Miranda wasn't sure where she ended and Lucas began. When she felt her knees begin to buckle beneath her as desire overcame her, she gripped his shoulders fiercely, marveling at the hard strength that rippled below her fingertips. Sliding her hands over his shoulders and around to his back, Miranda felt her pulse go wild. His body was so hard, so perfect, so unbelievably sexy. She wanted to see more of it. She wanted to see all of it.

Struggling with his bow tie, Miranda finally managed to free it, then went to work on the studs of his shirt. One by one, they fell free, tumbling to the floor in an irregular series of thumps and clicks and clacks. When Lucas realized what she was doing, he sought to aid her in any way he could, shrugging out of his jacket to toss it onto the couch. His gesture caused them both to cease in their eager motions long enough to meet each other's gaze.

"Miranda, are we doing what I think we're doing?" Lucas asked her softly.

She laughed a little nervously in response. "Well, we're certainly not dancing anymore, are we?"

"Not any socially acceptable dance, no," Lucas agreed, with a sexy smile.

"How do we always manage to get ourselves into these situations without even trying?" Miranda knew she was stalling, but they had become so overwhelmed by their passions, she felt the need to do something to slow them down.

"Who says we're not trying?"

A hot flame flickered to life in Miranda's midsection at the sound of Lucas's voice, so deep and low and dangerous, and when her eyes met his, she knew they reflected the heat and desire she saw burning brightly in his own. Before she could say anything in response, Lucas spoke again.

"I, for one, have been able to think of little else but making love to you ever since you opened your front door. Why do you think I suggested we spend the weekend at my house?" he asked further. "Why do you think I virtually kidnapped you to bring you here?"

Miranda shrugged slightly. "Maybe you have an impetuous nature?"

Lucas shook his head slowly. "No, I don't. That's what's so scary about all this. I've never done anything spontaneous in my life. Not until tonight." He pressed his forehead against Miranda's, cupping her chin in his hands to stroke his thumbs tenderly over her cheekbones. "You...you make me do things I never planned on doing. I won't pretend to understand what's happening between us. All I know is that I can't stop thinking about you. Ever since I met you, I've been completely preoccupied with thoughts of making love with you."

Miranda took a deep breath before asking, "Then why did it take you so long to get around to doing it?"

A tiny pain twisted Lucas's heart at her quietly uttered question. Because he hadn't wanted to make things more complicated between them, that's why, he thought. When he'd first conceived of his plan to use Miranda True, he had been completely willing, and even looking forward, to luring her into his bed. But on that first date, he'd learned a few things about her as a person. He'd seen how trusting she was, how vulnerable she could be. He'd discovered that he liked her. Liked her very much. And then he'd realized that he was no longer so certain exactly what his intentions toward Miranda involved. He hadn't wanted to take things between them any further until he knew for sure what was going on.

Now as he gazed into the guileless blue eyes of Miranda True, all Lucas could do was call himself every kind of heel and wish there was some way he could turn back the clock to start things all over with her. Because he'd finally begun to understand what was going on between them. And tonight he knew for sure. Tonight he'd been alarmed to discover that he honestly cared for Miranda. He wasn't sure exactly when it had happened, or how, but this evening he had realized suddenly and without question that she had become important to him. Important enough that he wished he'd never dragged her into this stupid, sorry scheme of his. Important enough to make him promise himself he would never use her talents for his own financial gain again. Important enough to scare the hell out of him when he pondered the way things had progressed between them.

And important enough to make him pray to every god available that she never, ever, found out about his thoughtless, insensitive behavior of the past several weeks.

"What took me so long?" he repeated Miranda's question quietly to himself. "I wanted to be sure you cared for me as much as I care for you."

Miranda smiled at him, a shaky, nervous smile that reassured Lucas the way nothing else could. "Oh, Lucas, how could you have ever doubted?"

"Didn't you once tell me that Martians tend to overlook the feelings of others?"

Miranda nodded. "They do tend to do that."

"Well, this is one Martian who won't make that mistake again. I'm a new man, a new Martian," he said with a quiet chuckle.

Miranda laughed, too. "And just what's responsible for bringing on this rebirth?"

"You," Lucas replied immediately. "You are."

Miranda said nothing, but her eyes told Lucas everything he needed to know.

He thought long and hard before putting voice to the other startling revelations whirling through his mind. Finally he met her gaze with an intent scrutiny of his own and told her, "Miranda, I've never said this to anyone before, but . . . I think I might be falling in love with you."

"Oh, Lucas," she whispered, circling his waist tightly with her arms in a fierce hug. "I love you, too."

Her response was so quick, so genuine, so honest, that Lucas had to tamp down a fear he felt flickering to life in the back of his brain. Miranda loved him. He had presented himself to her in such a way as to make her love him. But if she knew the truth, if she found out why he had originally nurtured their relationship, would she still feel the same way? Did he even want her to love him? And was he really falling in love with her? How could he know when he'd never experienced such an emotion before? The question brought an unruly knot to his stomach and a slicing pain to his head.

Lucas reminded himself that he'd never been in love in his life and demanded to know why he should think he was succumbing to such a malady now. So Miranda True was a beautiful, fascinating woman who made him feel wonderful inside, he thought. What made him think that was love? Why not just a more advanced stage of desire than what he was used to? He wasn't even sure he knew *how* to love someone that way—intimately, sexually, completely. Why had he told Miranda he might be falling in love with her? What had he gotten himself into?

Lucas wasn't all that surprised to find that there were no answers to follow up his questions. He pushed his troubling thoughts away and tried instead to reassure himself that he no longer had to worry about the consequences of his actions. Miranda loved him. And he was sorry for ever using her the way he had. That was all that mattered now. Everything was going to be just fine. Things could progress as normally as they did for other couples who found themselves in potentially romantic situations.

As long as Miranda *never* found out what he had done, Lucas reminded himself brutally. As long as she remained forever oblivious to the fact that he had originally viewed her as little more than a means to an end and had used her so blatantly and carelessly—used her perceptive talents to gain wealth and success.

But there was no way she would ever find that out, right? Lucas asked himself. He'd told no one of his plan, of his activities, except for Simon Lawler. And Lawler was the most tight-lipped human being on earth. It was why Lucas kept him on the payroll. As long as he and Simon were the only ones who knew, Miranda would never find out what he had done. He had nothing to worry about, Lucas assured himself. Nothing at all.

But Lucas was worried. Worried that what might be the best thing that had ever happened to him would blow up in his face because of a few thoughtless, ill-planned actions. Before his anxieties could get the better of him, he swept Miranda into his arms and strode quickly to the stairs at the other side of the living room. He had to be certain she wouldn't leave him before he had a chance to make her understand unequivocally how important she had become to him. And if it meant he had to make love to her from now until eternity to achieve that certainty, he would do it.

"Lucas, what are you doing?" Miranda gasped as he lifted her into his arms.

"I'm going to make you mine," he whispered as he took the stairs two at a time. His lips were right beside her ear, and his words came in soft bursts of warmth as he continued. "And I'm going to give myself to you. I'm going to bury myself so deep inside you that neither one of us will be sure which part belongs to whom. I want us so confused by passion that we'll never be able to do anything alone again. I want you surrounding me, embracing me, loving me as much as I intend to love you. Do you understand, Miranda?"

She nodded quickly, unable to find her voice. Suddenly Lucas was so intense, so insistent, so demanding. And suddenly she realized she had a few demands of her own.

"What about my wants, Lucas?" Miranda asked him quietly as they entered his bedroom.

The scent of the ocean was strong and pungent on the salty breeze that raced through the window, and the roar of the surf promised a distant storm was growing nearer. Lucas lay Miranda gently on his bed, then took a few steps back to finish unbuttoning his shirt and go to work on his belt. At her softly voiced question, he ceased in his motions, however, snapping his head up to meet her gaze. His dark hair fell down over his forehead, gilded with silver by the moonlight. His eyes were bright beacons of desire, ever changing in the darkness.

In response, Lucas said nothing, but after a brief pause in his actions, slowly shrugged out of his shirt, wadding it up fiercely before tossing it without concern into a chair near the foot of the bed. As he continued to gaze at Miranda wordlessly, he methodically unzipped his trousers, the quiet rasping of metal almost deafening in the otherwise silent room. A great fist grabbed hold of her stomach and squeezed hard when she realized he meant to completely undress for her, and she watched, mesmerized, as he did just that.

Miranda hadn't taken the time last week to really look at Lucas's naked form. They had been too eager to make love, too anxious to quench the fires burning them up inside, for her to have been leisurely about anything.

Now she took the time. And she saw that he was... she took a deep, ragged breath and exhaled it slowly... magnificent.

Even in the pale moonlight, Miranda could see that his skin was kissed with just a slight tan—one that completely covered his body—and she realized he had probably already made a few trips to his beach house this year, and that he obviously sunbathed in the nude. A thrill of anticipation shivered down her spine at the recollection that he was so thoroughly uninhibited, something she herself would never be. A thick dark scattering of hair spiraled across his expansive chest, arrowing down his torso to his waist, where it narrowed to a thin line before flaring out again at the juncture of his thighs.

Miranda blushed furiously and dropped her head when she realized she was scrutinizing the most masculine part of him, but her sudden bashfulness was less a result of recognizing the intimacy of her gaze, and more a consequence of her realization that he was so ready for her—and her absolute wonder that she had been able to accommodate such a large man in her slender body. The differences in their physiques were incredible, she thought, yet they were so perfectly suited to each other.

"Look at me," she heard Lucas say when she glanced away from him. "You say you have wants, too, Miranda. If you want to look at me, then look."

She did as he instructed, raising her head again to let her gaze rove hungrily over every inch of him. Muscles bunched and roped through his sinewy arms and legs, rising and falling and winding and curling when Lucas began to walk slowly toward her. He moved like some kind of nocturnal animal, she thought, with stealth, grace and infinite care. He paused at the foot of the bed, standing over her as if trying to decide which part of her to nibble first. Miranda sat stock-still with her legs tucked into a curl beside her and her palms flat against the bedspread, her heart pounding with need. Lucas leaned forward and placed his own hands on the mattress, lifted one knee and then the other, and began to crawl slowly, and with much intent, across the king-size bed toward her.

Miranda parted her lips to utter a halfhearted cry of protest, but no sound emerged. Still Lucas moved toward her, inch by slow inch, until his hands were splayed on either side of her, and his body hovered over hers. She filled her lungs with the scent of him—a spicy fragrance enhanced by the ocean breeze, and touched with a hint of something else that Miranda had come to know as inherently Lucas. Forcing herself to look up and meet his gaze, she found him studying her with eyes as dark and dangerous as the night enclosing them, eyes that promised her sensual pleasures unlike any she had ever known before.

Once again Lucas began to move slowly forward, and Miranda reflexively tried to scramble backward on the bed. When she bumped against the headboard and realized she could go no farther, she tried to turn and scoot back the way she'd come. Upon realizing that such an escape was impossible because it was thoroughly barred by the naked man who had joined her on the bed, Miranda halted, then turned to face up to her pursuer. Immediately Lucas was upon her, smiling with feral intent as he brought his big body over hers, causing her to lean backward lest she be seared by his heat. As Miranda struggled to breathe evenly, Lucas lowered his face to hers, rubbing his rough cheek against the soft skin of her jaw before pushing aside a fistful of her hair and ducking down to place a row of fever-inducing kisses along her neck and collarbone.

There was something distinctly erotic about being fully clothed with a naked man, Miranda decided as Lucas feathered kisses over her heated skin. She swept her hands down his back and over his taut buttocks, down to his hard thighs and back up again. Everywhere she touched him, her hands and fingers encountered the silk-enclosed steel of his muscles and skin, and the rest of her body felt cheated for not being able to enjoy the same pleasure. The gown she had thought so lovely when she'd purchased it was now nothing but an annoyance she wanted fiercely to discard, but when she reached to unfasten the zipper hidden by a side seam, Lucas wrapped his fingers around her wrist and stilled her hand.

"Not yet," he instructed her quietly. "I'll take care of that when the time comes."

"But—"

"What else do you want, Miranda?" he interrupted her softly as he cupped his other hand over her shoulder, pushing aside the pale peach fabric so that he could taste a tiny freckle he found there. "Anything you want—name it, it's yours."

Miranda could barely think clearly, let alone speak aloud any demands she might have. It occurred to her vaguely that Lucas Strathmoor had already met and exceeded every want or need she would possibly ever have in this lifetime, so she simply shook her head silently and reached out for him.

"You," she murmured in a voice she scarcely recognized as her own. "I only want you, Lucas."

His smile was full of promise when he replied quietly, "Then you shall have me, Miranda True."

And with that he lowered his head and kissed her deeply, exploring the dark recesses of her mouth as if for the first time. Outside, rain began to patter softly against the house, surrounding them with a sound that reminded Miranda curiously of sizzling bacon. After that, all thought left her as she felt his fingers circling her ankles, skimming up along her bare legs and pushing aside her gown as he went. Lucas continued to kiss her until the fabric was bunched around her waist in a circle of pale peach, and then he pulled away from her. For a brief moment, he met her gaze silently, then he bent to place a chaste kiss over the soft skin revealed between her navel and the ivory silk of her panties.

Miranda bit off a moan at the exquisite sensations the touch of his warm mouth wreaked, rolling her head back against the mattress when she felt his fingers settling snugly against her inner thighs. She thought vaguely that she should do something about removing her panties, but Lucas was apparently unconcerned by their presence. She felt his tongue tasting her through the silky fabric, touching her in a way no man had ever touched her before. Miranda gasped at the intimacy of his caress, tangling her fingers in his hair as she jerked her hips instinctively forward.

"Oh, Lucas," she whispered hoarsely. "Please..."

Miranda wasn't sure if she was asking him to stop or to carry her farther away on her tide of passion, but Lucas made the decision for her. When she lifted her hips toward him again, he gripped her panties and tugged them down her legs, tossing them carelessly over his shoulder to discard them on the floor, before returning to his ministrations once again. Miranda felt herself sinking into a dark, hot place aeons away from her normal existence, luxuriating in physical sensations she never would have guessed she could enjoy. Deeper and deeper Lucas carried her, until all she could do was feel. Only when her body began to shudder with exquisite delight did he put an end to his onslaught, pulling himself up over her body to gaze down at her with a savage hunger.

"You want me, Miranda?" Lucas ground out as if barely able to control himself. "Then here I am, all of me. Just for you."

He plunged himself inside her with a mighty thrust, causing them both to cry out at the sheer heat and headiness of the action. After only a moment's pause, he began to unsheath himself, only to hurtle himself deep inside her again just before pulling out. After that, Lucas instigated a steady rhythm that built from slow and measured to fast and completely uncontrolled. Over and over he claimed her body with his, until they were both nearly delirious with fever and heat. Something inside Miranda tightened like an overwrought spring, coiling smaller and smaller until it burst into a blaze of sensation. At the same time Miranda succumbed to her white-hot emotions, Lucas lost control of his own feelings, exploding inside her with unrestrained fury.

When Miranda cried out at the volatile culmination of their joining, Lucas quieted the sound by taking her mouth in a deep, ferocious kiss. Gradually their heart rates slowed, and their ragged gasps for breath steadied. When he pulled away from her only enough to gaze down into her eyes, it was to find her staring at him with undisguised awe for what had just transpired between them.

"Wow," Miranda whispered.

Lucas nodded his agreement. "Wow."

It was only then that he realized he had been so overcome with his need to be inside Miranda that he hadn't even finished undressing her, and he kissed her cheek softly in apology.

"I'm sorry," he said quietly. "I didn't mean to lose control that way."

Miranda gazed at him lovingly, and her words were low and thick with passion when she spoke. "Lucas, what just happened was heavenly. How can you possibly think of saying you're sorry for it?"

"I didn't even undress you all the way," he explained. "It could have been better for you."

Miranda chuckled seductively. "Oh, no, it couldn't."

"But—"

"Listen," she began as she tangled her fingers possessively in his hair, her eyes sparkling with mischief. "If you're so concerned about it, then we'll just have to do it again, and this time you can undress me."

Lucas smiled. "Oh, boy," he said as he reached for the zipper at the side of her dress. "This is going to be fun."

Miranda lifted her arms over her head languidly, knowing the feeling of complete satisfaction that filled her would be short-lived. Just as she suspected, in no time at all, Lucas was wreaking sweet havoc on her body again, and she was filled with a new kind of need, one he was quick to answer.

Outside, the night grew darker, the rain fell harder, and the ocean roared against the beach. The last thing Miranda recalled thinking about before falling into a restless sleep a few hours before dawn was that she loved Lucas Strathmoor with all her heart, and never, ever, wanted to be apart from him again.

Chapter Eight

The weekend they spent at Lucas's beach house was the most extravagant, exquisite, explosive Miranda had ever known. And the four weeks that followed were the most wonderful she had ever spent. Summer was without question her favorite time of the year, the days long and hot and languid, every moment she could manage filled with working in her gardens and stocking her shop with merchandise. She prepared herbs for teas and spices for seasonings, dried flowers for wreaths and potpourri, distilled and extracted oils from a number of other plants for healing remedies and cleansers. And although her experimental herbs had failed once again, everything else in Miranda's garden burst into eager bloom, and her yard came alive with activity.

Where her days were filled by her shop and her gardens, Miranda's evenings were filled by Lucas. It became a ritual for him to meet her after work and take her home, often staying to eat dinner or when he couldn't tolerate another meatless meal, taking Miranda out to eat. It wasn't that he didn't *like* her almond-cauliflower quiche or spinach-broccoli lasagna, he assured her. It was just that a lifelong meat-and-potatoes man such as himself was hard-pressed to change his habits at this late date. Miranda simply nodded with a silent smile at his assurances, knowing full well that Martians were notorious meat eaters, and harbored him no ill will because of the practice.

And after dinner, Lucas spent nearly every night at Miranda's house making love with her. The first few times they were scarcely able to finish dinner without lunging for each other; they almost never made it up to Miranda's bedroom in time, and instead wound up making love on the kitchen floor or the living room sofa. Once they managed to struggle halfway up the stairs, but weren't able to tolerate being so close without being united, and succumbed to their desires just above the stairwell landing. Miranda's cats made themselves ominously absent on such occasions, as if fully aware that such strange human behavior required privacy.

Eventually, though, Miranda and Lucas were able to pass the evening in companionable calmness, quietly talking about the day's events or watching old-movie festivals on TV. At times, Miranda would read aloud to Lucas, as he lay on the couch with his head in her lap, his eyes closed as he listened to her softly cadenced voice describing an island of treasure or the heart of darkness.

Many were the nights when Miranda drifted off to sleep in her bed beside Lucas, cradled in his strong arms and snuggled against his solid body, surprised at how familiar the two of them had become. She had discovered things about him that no one else knew, and in turn had revealed things about herself to him that she had never acknowledged to anyone. There were times when she almost thought she could tell what he was thinking, knew how he was going to finish a sentence or what he was going to suggest they do that evening. In many ways, they were like an old, married couple, Miranda thought, two halves of one whole that had come together to find that they were perfectly complementary in every way. And her feelings of love only enhanced the complete confidence she placed in him.

By the end of four weeks, Lucas and Miranda had become a couple. And by the end of four weeks, Miranda knew without doubt that she had fallen hopelessly, irrevocably in love.

And for that reason, she didn't mind at all when Lucas asked her to attend another party with him. She had reached a point in her feelings where it no longer concerned her that Lucas would want or need to spend time with people other than herself. That was what love was all about, she realized. Being completely secure in her affection for Lucas, and trusting fully that he also cared for her.

It was something she had never quite known with Patrick Lyndon. Throughout her two-year relationship with him, she had always experienced an undercurrent of fear that Patrick would do something to betray her, or would ultimately abandon her—a fear that in fact had finally been realized.

With Lucas, however, Miranda experienced no such worries or misgivings. She trusted him. He had told her he loved her, and she fully believed him. There was no reason for her not to. She felt it in the way he held her and made love to her, in the way he spoke to her and laughed with her. And although Miranda suspected he hadn't quite reached the "hopelessly in love" stage that she herself now rejoiced in, she had no doubt that he would. Venusians were simply much quicker to give in to their emotions than Martians were, she thought. Eventually Lucas's love for her would run as deep and wild as hers did for him. She knew it with all her heart.

Trust. That was what had made all the difference between her past relationship with Patrick and the current one she enjoyed with Lucas. Miranda trusted in Lucas implicitly—in his intentions, and in his affections.

"I'm sorry to have to drag you to one of these parties again," he told her that night as she gathered her purse and shawl and prepared to leave.

"I don't mind," she assured him. "I think it will be fun. We haven't really done anything with other people for weeks—"

"We've had other things on our minds," he interrupted her, his eyes flashing with fire.

Miranda felt her skin grow warm beneath her strapless black cocktail dress. "Yes, well, that's true," she mumbled quietly. "But we can't live on...on..."

Lucas grinned lasciviously. "Sex?" he supplied for her in a lazy drawl.

Even after all the times they'd been together, his smooth, sensual, erotic voice could still make Miranda's heart triphammer wildly. "Yes. We can't live on...sex...alone."

"Maybe not," he agreed. "But we've been giving it our best shot, haven't we?"

Miranda felt herself blushing and quickly ducked her head lest Lucas see how much he continued to unsettle and distract her, even after everything they had shared together. "But I still think it's about time we got out and started enjoying the company of others again," she said tactfully. "Not that it hasn't been a thoroughly...delightful best shot, mind you," she hastened to add as she continued to stare furiously at the floor.

Lucas couldn't help the mischievous grin he felt curling up the corners of his mouth. "Yes, it has been delightful, hasn't it?"

Surprisingly delightful, he thought as he followed Miranda to the car. The past several weeks with her had far exceeded anything else he'd ever experienced with another human being. Never had his preoccupation with, and affection for, a woman so thoroughly invaded everything else in his life. Wherever he went, Miranda was with him, and thoughts of her permeated every project he undertook. Simply put, Lucas couldn't stop thinking about her. And he'd been amazed to discover that such a realization didn't bother him at all.

In fact, oddly enough, it almost comforted him in a way. Lucas didn't pretend to understand the strange emotions that had been roiling and simmering inside him since meeting Miranda True, but he knew it would be ridiculous to try to deny them. He readily admitted that she had long ago become special to him, and that what he felt for her was in no way similar to feelings he'd ever harbored for anyone else. There were times when he lay in bed at night with her nestled close beside him, tangling his fingers in her pale gold hair, and marveling that he had even managed to fall in love with her.

But such reflections, he reminded himself, were pointless. After all, the two of them were too entirely different from each other to ever be capable of maintaining a long-term relationship. Even Miranda had said that Martians and Venusians don't normally make a good match. Certainly nothing permanent could ever come of their time together, he'd tell himself.

Or could it?

It was a question Lucas had found himself asking frequently, but one which he had yet to answer sufficiently. And now as he and Miranda pulled up in front of a looming brick town house in Cambridge, the question troubled him again. This time, however, Lucas didn't waste time searching for an answer. There were too many other things cluttering up his mind.

"So whose party are we attending this evening?" Miranda asked as they made their way up the stairs to the front door.

Lucas withdrew a key ring from the inside pocket of his dark blue suit and inserted one of the keys into the lock beneath the doorknob. "Mine," he said simply.

Miranda's eyes widened in surprise. "This is your house?"

He nodded, pushing the door inward before indicating she should precede him. "My party, my house. You go to these things often enough, eventually you have to have one of your own to pay back everyone else's hospitality. Tonight it's my turn."

Miranda entered almost reluctantly, feeling strangely out of place in his house. Although Lucas had told her where he lived, she had never seen his house before, inside or out. And viewing it for the first time now, when they had enjoyed so much together and should know everything about each other, she was simply reminded how very little she did in fact know of Lucas's life outside her own experiences with him. Miranda hadn't honestly given much thought to the fact that lately they spent all of their free time together at her house instead of his, thinking theirs was just an arrangement of convenience—her shop was closer to her house than his, and since Lucas picked her up and took her home, it made little sense to drive all the way to Cambridge every night, only to wind up driving across town again at evening's end.

But now that Miranda gave some thought to the situation, it did seem strange. Lucas could have had a wife and six children stashed here, for all she knew. Then she reminded herself that surely someone in his social circle would have told her before now if such was the case.

Still, the fact that she was just now stepping inside Lucas's house made her feel funny. Suddenly she wondered if he had something to hide, if there was some ulterior reason why he had never invited her over before. They had become so close, so intimately involved. Yet while Lucas had thoroughly invaded her life, had touched and colored every aspect of her existence, Miranda hadn't left a mark on his at all. There were bits and pieces of him to be found everywhere in her house—his toiletries had become mingled familiarly with hers in her bathroom medicine cabinet, his favorite snacks had mysteriously appeared in her pantry, and only yesterday she'd come across a T-shirt he had discarded and left behind one Saturday when he'd grown too warm working with her in the garden.

But what was there to be found here in Lucas's house that was even remotely related to her? Miranda wondered, as she looked around. Absolutely nothing. The walls were white, the furnishings neutral, functional and nondescript . . . and in no way touched by her influence. In fact, she noted further, curiously there was little here to remind her of Lucas, either. The house looked like something from a realtor's catalog, a model to be considered for its possibilities and potential. Beyond that, however, it was vacant.

"Let me take your shawl," Lucas said from behind her.

Miranda started a little, nearly having forgotten he was there, and the silent gesture caused her shawl to drop from her shoulders and into his hands.

"Is something wrong?" he asked.

Miranda turned to face him, plastering on what she hoped was a convincingly cheerful smile. "No, of course not. I was just thinking about how strange it was that I haven't been to your house before now."

"I would have invited you over sooner, Miranda, but I'm rarely home myself," Lucas explained.

That's because you're always over at my house, she wanted to tell him. *What's the real reason you haven't asked me over before now?* But the words remained firmly entrenched in Miranda's mind, and she only nodded in unfelt understanding.

"The guests won't be arriving for about a half hour," he told her further, "but my assistant, Simon Lawler, is around here somewhere. I'd like for you to meet him."

It was the equivalent of introducing Miranda to his parents, Lucas thought. For some odd reason, he actually felt a little nervous about the outcome of the introduction. Certainly he wasn't concerned about whether or not Simon would approve of Miranda—how could anyone find fault with her? But Lucas had become friends with the other man over the years, despite that rather blurry line connecting them as employer and employee, and it somehow seemed appropriate that Simon and Miranda should meet and get along well. Lucas handed her shawl to one of the servers who had come rented with the catering company, then guided her toward the study.

Simon leaned against the bar in all his blond glory, sipping his drink with what Lucas was certain was feigned casualness. He smiled grimly. Simon Lawler was one of those men that most people noted with an element of caution, because they could never quite discern what he was thinking. Lucas probably knew Simon better than anyone else did, but he was by no means overly familiar with him. The two had met while they were still in college, and Lucas knew little of the other man's history prior to that.

They had worked together virtually since receiving their business degrees, combining their talents to acquire a substantial collection of suffering businesses, which they'd succeeded in turning around and reselling for considerable profit. Simon contributed to the arrangement his remarkable business savvy and particularly ruthless ambition, while Lucas provided a charming personality and a number of contacts to finance their endeavors. It was a situation that had worked well over the years, and one that would undoubtedly continue to bring prosperity. Because regardless of, and above all else, the two men were friends. And that wasn't likely to change.

"Simon, this is Miranda True," Lucas introduced them. "Miranda, this is my business associate, Simon Lawler."

Simon straightened some, setting his drink down on the bar to extend his hand in greeting. "So you're Miranda," he said, in a voice Lucas recognized as the one he used to lull people into a false sense of security before striking. "I've heard a lot about you."

Miranda took his hand gingerly in her own, tipping her head back to meet Simon's gaze. Lucas was surprised by a tremor of jealousy that shook him when he saw the expression on her face. She found Simon attractive. He could see it in her eyes, in the way she parted her lips. For one insane, outrageous moment, Lucas wanted to strangle his friend for being the kind of man Miranda would like. Then he told himself to calm down and stop behaving like a mistrusting fool. So Miranda found another man attractive, Lucas thought. That didn't mean she was going to go running into Simon's arms and abandon him, did it? Of course not. Falling in love with Miranda hadn't made Lucas stop noticing other attractive women, had it? So why should Miranda stop looking at other men?

Then Lucas realized how he had just reassured himself and paused to quickly rewind his brain. *Falling in love with Miranda,* he repeated to himself. Was that true? he wondered again. Had he really fallen in love with her? And if so, what was he going to do about it?

"I'm sorry, Mr. Lawler, you have me at a disadvantage," Lucas heard Miranda reply to Simon's greeting. "Lucas hasn't mentioned you to me before."

Simon glanced over at Lucas with a knowing grin. "That's because he never mixes business with pleasure."

Miranda nodded, but said nothing, trying to hide her surprise at such a statement. She hadn't been under such an impression at all, recalling that the first few times she and Lucas went out, it was always to some function claiming a number of his business associates. In fact, it had only been since their weekend together at his beach house that he'd been able to fully put aside his work concerns and enjoy their private time together. But Miranda didn't want to do anything that might disrupt the evening. If Simon Lawler thought Lucas didn't mix business with pleasure, then he probably didn't have a good idea what pleasure was.

Although she found that very difficult to believe. Mr. Lawler was, after all, a very handsome man, with the most compelling green eyes she had ever seen. Still, he wasn't nearly as attractive as the man who had preoccupied her thoughts for nearly three months, and didn't even come close to claiming the qualities she loved most in Lucas. There was something secretive about Simon that set Miranda on edge. As if he possessed some important information she had been denied and he was reveling in that knowledge. She was tempted to turn his hand up in hers to inspect it, knowing the lines on his palm would tell her more about him than he would ever reveal himself. But as she gazed into his cold green eyes, she was suddenly shaken by a feeling of dread and decided she didn't want to know.

Quickly Miranda released Simon's hand, forcing herself not to wipe it off on her dress as she instinctively wanted to do, and mumbled, "It's nice to meet you."

Simon nodded before turning to Lucas to tell him, "You had a call from Paul Cheswick while you were gone. He said it was important."

Lucas's expression when he looked at Miranda indicated impatience and annoyance. "I'm sorry," he told her. "But I really should call him back. We've been playing telephone tag all week, and it's beginning to get on my nerves. I won't be long."

Without waiting for her to reply, Lucas spun around and exited the room, leaving Miranda with her mouth half-open in unuttered protest, and alone with Simon Lawler. Oh, well, she thought. Might as well make the best of it.

"So, Mr. Lawler," she began casually.

"Simon," he corrected her mildly.

"Simon," she began again. "Why is it that I haven't met you before, at one of the many parties Lucas seems to attend?"

Simon smiled at her cryptically and replied mildly, "I'm not much of a party-goer."

Miranda nodded, wracking her brain for some other mundane topic of conversation. "And what is it exactly that you do for Lucas?"

"I'm kind of a silent partner in a number of his projects," he told her carelessly. "Would you like something to drink? Lucas completely restocked the bar for this shindig. You name it. It's here somewhere."

Miranda lifted a curious brow at the swift change of subject, but nodded. "I'll have a gin and tonic, please."

She watched as Simon deftly poured her drink, wondering if he'd been a bartender in his past, his motions were so fluid and certain. When he handed her the drink, he touched his fingertips to her knuckles in a gesture that could only be interpreted as one of a man interested in getting to know a woman better. Miranda narrowed her eyes at him suspiciously. What kind of man would so blatantly come on to a woman his best friend had been seeing on a regular basis for several months? she asked herself. Immediately she realized the answer. A man who was no friend at all.

"Excuse me," she said coolly, making a production of removing the drink—and her hand—from Simon's grasp before taking several steps away.

Turning her back on him in what she hoped he would interpret as a symbolic gesture, Miranda went to the window on the other side of the room and gazed out at the traffic dotting the street below. The moon hung low and yellow in the sky, and for some reason made her feel sad. Before she had a chance to contemplate why, Miranda felt Simon suddenly standing behind her, and the fact that he could move so soundlessly and with such shamelessly predatory intent, put Miranda on edge. Telling herself not to let the man get to her, she remained silent, and simply continued to stare out the window, wishing Lucas would return.

"It's a beautiful night," Simon murmured near her ear.

Miranda snapped her head around and met his gaze levelly. The eyes that met hers indicated unmistakably that Simon Lawler wanted to get more familiar with her, and in a much more personal way than was normally acceptable after such a short time. "Yes, it is," she agreed before stepping away from him again. When Miranda had achieved what she felt was a safe distance, she spoke again, hoping she sounded bolder than she felt. "Mr. Lawler—"

"Simon."

"Mr. Lawler," she repeated emphatically. "Are you . . ." How did one say this tactfully? Miranda wondered. "Are you . . . flirting with me?"

Simon shrugged, seemingly unconcerned that she would suggest such a thing, and took a step toward her. "What if I am?"

Miranda couldn't believe Lucas called this man his friend. "Then I'll have to ask you to stop," she told him as she took another step back.

"Why?"

"Why?" Miranda repeated incredulously. "Because Lucas and I are . . . that is, he . . . I mean, we're . . . and you're supposed to be . . ."

"What?" Simon taunted. "We're all something, Miranda. But you have yet to indicate exactly what."

She drew an impatient breath and expelled it slowly as she gazed at him. With much exasperation, she had to concede that Simon was right. Just exactly what they all were remained a mystery, even to Miranda. Well, not Simon—she knew he was a heel. But what about her and Lucas? They were lovers, she thought, but that was scarcely something one admitted to a virtual stranger, even if that stranger probably already suspected that something of the sort was true.

Miranda admitted to herself that she had no idea how to describe her relationship with Lucas to someone like Simon, but she also decided that there was no reason Simon had to be a witness to her uncertainty. So instead she sipped her drink, hoping she looked nonchalant, and studied a hexagonal shape in the Persian rug below her feet, stubbing it unconsciously with the toe of her shoe.

"If you are flirting with me, Mr. Lawler, then you may save your breath," Miranda told him wearily, glancing up quickly once again. "I'm not interested."

In response to her statement, Simon only lifted his dark blond eyebrows in what could have been surprise, speculation or skepticism, but Miranda didn't even make an effort to understand. If this was some kind of game, or if there was some kind of unspoken little rivalry passing between Simon and Lucas, she wasn't sure she wanted to know the particulars. She was wishing fervently once again that Lucas would return, when he strode casually into the room looking unruffled and unconcerned, approached the bar and poured himself a drink.

"Sorry about that," he apologized to both of them. "Cheswick can be long-winded when he puts his mind to it. But he usually has good news."

Neither Miranda nor Simon asked what the good news might be, and Lucas offered no further information. With a resigned sigh, Miranda told herself not to worry about it, that if the news he'd learned was something important, Lucas would share it with her. But that niggling little feeling of being excluded, the one that had settled onto her shoulders once she entered his house, wouldn't quite allow Miranda to convince herself. She still couldn't understand why Lucas hadn't come to include her in his life as readily as she had welcomed him into hers. And once again Miranda wondered if maybe there was more to Lucas Strathmoor than she had allowed herself to see.

Oh, you're just borrowing trouble, Miranda, she told herself. *Why can't you simply accept the fact that you've finally found someone to love who will love you back?*

Because it seems too good to be true, Miranda replied to her own question. *It just seems too good to be true.*

When her gaze fell on Lucas, it was to find him studying her with a curious, inscrutable expression. He seemed to be lost in concentration, as if the news he'd just received was more important than he'd let on. Miranda wanted to ask him about it, but before she opened her mouth to speak, Lucas turned his attention to Simon, and something—some indefinable expression in his eyes—prevented her from doing so. She got the distinct impression that the two men had something to discuss in private but were too polite to ask her to leave. So in an effort to be accommodating, Miranda resorted to that tried and true age-old women's excuse.

"Pardon me," she said quietly, bringing Lucas's attention back to herself. "Is there someplace where I can... uh...powder my nose?"

She wasn't sure, but she thought Lucas was smiling when he told her, "Upstairs, down the hall, first door on your right."

"Thanks."

"You're welcome."

Miranda was halfway up the stairs when she realized she'd been so rattled by the events of the evening thus far that she had forgotten to bring her purse with her. It wouldn't be particularly convincing if she went to powder her nose without her powder, would it? And it wasn't likely that Lucas kept a ready stock of supplies for his women guests—although there had probably been platoons of them in the past, Miranda thought caustically, before she could stop herself.

Squaring her shoulders, she told herself to stop feeling so inconsequential and unimportant, and spun around to retreat to the living room in order to retrieve her purse. As she approached, she heard Lucas and Simon engaged in avid conversation, and wouldn't have slowed her step, except that one of the words they seemed to be speaking frequently was Miranda.

Naturally curious about what the two men might have to say about her, Miranda paused shamelessly just outside the door to eavesdrop, excusing her breach of etiquette by assuring herself that it might help her put to rest once and for all her fears about where she stood with Lucas. If she could just hear him tell Simon that he cared for her, even in some vague, uncertain way, she could convince herself to stop worrying about his feelings toward her. She knew she probably shouldn't be concerned, and was almost completely certain in her belief that he did actually love her, but the fact that words like *probably* and *almost* continued to crop up when she thought about her relationship with Lucas left Miranda with a tiny sense of uneasiness that simply would not go away.

"Miranda's great, Lucas," Simon said. As he sipped his drink thoughtfully, the ice in his glass shifted and clinked against the cut-crystal tumbler. "Beautiful, articulate...and annoyingly enough, she seems to be very devoted to you."

Lucas snapped his head up at Simon's curious observation, putting aside thoughts of Miranda that had distracted him all night to bring his attention back to the conversation at hand. "What do you mean?"

Simon shrugged negligently. "Just that I, uh, I made a play for her while you were on the phone, and she gave me the brush-off in no uncertain terms."

Lucas shook his head in silent disbelief that his friend still played the game that had originated between them in college. Every time one of them had asked a girl out, the other would make a play for her, just to see if he could rouse a little interest. Lucas couldn't remember which of them had started such an adolescent game, or why it had gone on as long as it did. But it had been years since they'd indulged in it, and the fact that Simon had chosen tonight to revive it put Lucas on edge.

"You came on to Miranda?" he asked the other man.

"Yeah, a little. Just to see how she'd react."

Lucas sighed. "Why her?"

"I just wanted to see if this thing—this...*arrangement*— between the two of you was mutual. I wanted to see if she was only spending her time with you because she was more interested in spending your money," Simon told him. "You can never be too careful."

"Yeah, well don't worry about it, okay?"

"I'm not worried," Simon assured him in a voice that to Lucas sounded dangerously edged. "Not about you, anyway."

An odd tension had suddenly risen full-blown in the room to burn up the air between them, and for the life of him, Lucas couldn't understand where it had come from. All he knew was that one minute he and Simon had been talking about a business prospect the Cheswick conversation had spawned, and the next minute, the two of them were snarling and spitting, looking as if they were ready to lunge for each other's throats.

"Just what the hell is that supposed to mean?" Lucas demanded, slamming his drink down on the bar with such force that a good portion of it sloshed over the rim to spread across the marble surface in a puddle of amber.

Simon mirrored the action, nearly shattering his own glass when he did. "It means I was under the impression that the woman I was going to meet tonight would be some overblown, overdone, clinging vine who had latched on to you because you'd be her meal ticket to all the best restaurants in town. Instead I find that Miranda's a nice kid, Lucas— nothing at all like the vipers you usually date. Seems to me that *you're* the only one who's profiting from this situation. It's nice and convenient for you, isn't it? Having someone like Miranda around who's not only beautiful and passionate, but who can help you out financially as well?"

"You're beginning to get on my nerves, Lawler," Lucas said impatiently. "Don't beat around the bush. Say what's on your mind. But finish this conversation before she gets back."

Simon leaned menacingly forward to get in Lucas's face, biting his lip as if trying to hold back a storm of furious words. Finally he said simply, "I don't like the way you're treating her, Lucas."

And Lucas didn't like where this conversation was going. Nor did he even begin to understand what Simon was talking about. Months ago, when he'd first conceived of his plan to use an unwitting Miranda and her perceptive talents as a kind of... consultant, Lucas had fully explained and outlined the situation to Simon. He'd described his suspicion that Miranda knew more than she was letting on about Panwide, and he'd seen no reason to offer excuses for his intentions. He recalled now that Simon had been unusually reserved in his opinion of such an endeavor. The other man had simply nodded and told Lucas he hoped he knew what he was doing. Since then, the two of them hadn't discussed the situation much, except for Lucas's admission that his suspicions about Miranda working as a corporate spy had been wrong.

Suddenly understanding began to dawn on Lucas. Simon didn't realize how his relationship with Miranda had progressed. He knew Lucas was still seeing Miranda, of course, but must still be under the impression that his only reason for doing so was to get more information from her. Simon didn't realize how Lucas felt about Miranda. He didn't know how much Lucas loved her.

"Simon, you don't understand," Lucas began.

But the other man cut him off. "I mean it's one thing to use someone who's using you in return, Lucas, but I don't see any indication that Miranda's benefiting at all from this little arrangement."

"Simon—"

"You take her to all these parties, milk her for information about people after you leave, then use her innocently offered observations to buy up stock and go after companies. But what does she get in return?"

"Simon, things have changed," Lucas assured him. "It's not like that anymore."

"Are you saying you've stopped using her?" Simon wanted to know.

"Yes."

"You only take her out now because you enjoy her company?"

"Yes."

"And what does she get in return?"

After a moment's pause and a slight shrug, Lucas replied quietly, "Me."

"Some prize," Simon muttered distastefully.

At the moment, Lucas couldn't disagree.

"So I suppose next you'll be telling me you intend to marry her," Simon went on as he reached for his drink again, his tone of voice indicating he'd believe that when he saw it.

"No, I won't be telling you that," Lucas said, feeling defeated and dejected and more than a little depressed. Simon was right. He was certainly no prize. What he'd done to Miranda was reprehensible, regardless of how his intentions toward her had changed. She deserved a man who would honor her from the beginning, a man who didn't quiver back and forth in his emotions for her. A man who could stand up and tell her unequivocally that he loved her, and that his love for her would never waver. A good man, a decent man. A man completely unlike Lucas Strathmoor.

"No, I won't be marrying Miranda True," he said again, taking a deep sip of his drink. "You're right. She's a nice kid. She leads a nice little life in a nice little house with four nice little cats and a nice little garden. She has a nice job in a nice shop, nice friends, nice ambitions. She doesn't belong in our world, Simon. She would be eaten alive and spit out like so much refuse swimming with sharks like us."

"*Would* be?"

The small voice sounded like booming thunder in the otherwise silent room, and both Lucas and Simon turned to see Miranda standing in the doorway, framed by the dying sunlight.

"Sounds to me like I already *have* been."

There was a catch in her voice that pierced Lucas's heart more viciously than a serrated blade. He wondered how long she'd been standing there, wondered how long he and Simon had been arguing. But simply by looking at her face, he knew. Too long. She'd heard everything they'd said.

"Is it true?" Miranda asked him, her voice surprisingly steady, her gaze levelly fixed on his.

Lucas didn't know what to say. "Is what true, Miranda?"

She took a few cautious steps into the living room, wrapping her arms around her abdomen as if trying to hold herself up. Her eyes were huge and haunted-looking, her lips thin and bloodless. "What did Simon mean when he said you milked me for information and used my innocent observations?" As she spoke, Lucas saw Simon slip away as quietly as possible.

"Miranda," Lucas said softly, searching for the right thing to say. Hopelessly he realized there *was* no right thing he could say, nothing that would truly explain his callous behavior. So he simply tried, "You're misunderstanding this."

For a moment she appeared to be thinking about something, and when she spoke again, her words were slow and seemed to be carefully chosen. "I think I remember now. That first day you came to my house…after Grace's party. You told me I was good at reading people. That was why you asked me out, wasn't it?"

"Miranda…"

"That's why you always took me to parties—so that I could meet the people you wanted me to meet. And that's why you always asked me so many questions on the way home."

"Miranda, there was a lot more to it than that—"

"Yeah, I'll say." She shook her head in disbelief. "You've been using me to uncover information about other people, other companies, haven't you?"

Lucas couldn't deny it, but he said nothing to confirm it, either.

"How many did I help you steal, Lucas?"

"Miranda, I didn't *steal* anything," he stated adamantly. "Every one of those companies was bought and paid for."

"How many?" she repeated.

"Miranda, it wasn't like that—"

"Dammit, Lucas, answer me. How many?" Miranda nodded with slow consideration, then seemed to be suddenly struck by a new thought, and her eyes widened in horror. "Oh, God, I even helped you get Panwide, didn't I? I mean, I knew you'd finally seized it from the Lyndons, but I didn't think *I'd* had anything to do with that."

"Why should it bother you that you were instrumental in the downfall of that company?" Lucas wanted to know. "After the way they treated you, I'd think that you'd at least be pleased by your role in *that* situation."

Miranda shook her head again. "You just don't get it, do you, Lucas? You just don't understand about personal loyalty, personal integrity. The Lyndons were good to me at a time when I didn't have much else going for me. No, things between me and Patrick didn't work out, but that doesn't mean I want terrible things to happen to them."

She lifted her hand as if groping, reaching for something, then dropped it to curl around her midsection again. "You see everything in terms of black and white, loss and gain. Well, I've got news for you, Lucas. There are a lot more colors to be found in the world, and a lot more to life than what a person owns. I honestly thought you had come to understand that. I honestly thought you had changed. But now I realize that you are indeed exactly the kind of man I thought you were at first."

"A Martian, right?"

"In every sense of the word." Miranda emitted a single, mirthless chuckle, then unwound one of her arms to run a hand nervously over her hair. "I should have realized. I mean, I *was* kind of suspicious . . . at first. One minute you were accusing me of being a spy, the next you were telling me you wanted to get to know me better, but . . . You really made me think you were telling the truth. You really made me think you were attracted to me. Eventually I even started believing that you…cared…for me. I actually believed you when you told me you loved me."

"Miranda, I do love you," Lucas vowed desperately. "But I'm not the kind of man you deserve."

She took a deep, shaky breath, her entire body trembling as she did so. "Oh, I don't know about that, Lucas. Anyone who's stupid enough to believe that someone like you could be romantically interested in me probably deserves whatever she gets."

"Don't say that."

"But as gullible and naive as I've been, at least I can rest easy in the knowledge that I've been honest. I have a heart."

She walked across the room to the chair where Lucas had placed her belongings. Beside it was a table, and on that table was a potted plant—a peace lily Miranda had given him a few weeks ago. It was the only warm thing in Lucas's house, the only thing that brought a little life into a building where there was none. He watched as Miranda lifted a hand toward it, touching the tip of her finger to the single white bloom that rose high above the green leaves.

"You know, Lucas," she said softly, her mind clearly on something other than the plant. "Even beneath miles of ice and stone, there's a warm place inside the earth. But you…" She glanced up quickly and stared him straight in the eye for the first time since entering the room. "There's not a single part of you that's warm, is there? You're just ice and stone through and through."

A single tear fell from the corner of her eye to slide carelessly down her cheek. Miranda glanced down again as she added, "And the worst part of this isn't that I fell in love with you. I guess I couldn't have helped that. The worst part of it is—" Her voice broke off then, and she inhaled a slow, deep breath to steady it. "I trusted you," she managed to whisper before turning away. "And I really should have known better. I can promise you one thing, though. I'll never make that mistake again.''

With that, she picked up her purse and shawl and began to make her way slowly back out of the room. Her movements were jerky and inelegant, and more than anything in the world, Lucas wanted to sweep her into his arms, carry her up the stairs to his bedroom and make her forget the scene that had just transpired. But he knew that Miranda wouldn't let him get within two feet of her. She looked more fragile and vulnerable now than he'd ever seen her, yet more indomitable than anyone he knew. All he could do was watch silently and helplessly as she strode away from him, all the while wondering how he was going to fix this one.

Chapter Nine

The days that followed were the worst Miranda could ever remember experiencing. Even after her breakup with Patrick Lyndon, she hadn't felt the crippling, inconsolable sensation that her world had come skidding to a halt. With Patrick she had always had her doubts. But with Lucas... With Lucas, she had been so certain that he returned her love. She had trusted that he did. Now, of course, she knew better. Now she realized he had never loved her at all.

Miranda wondered if all men were like that—willing to lead a woman on as long as it served their purpose to do so, only to cast her aside when the game was discovered. She wasn't sure there would ever be a time when she could put her faith fully and confidently in a man again. She was two for two in the trusting-too-readily-only-to-be-led-on department. Not a particularly good record. It had taken the passage of twelve years after Patrick's desertion for Miranda to rebuild her faith enough to allow herself to fall in love with another man, only to wind up betrayed more heartlessly than the first time. After her experience with Lucas, Miranda suspected it would take even longer for her to learn to trust again. She might never be able to do so completely.

On Saturday morning, Miranda called Marcy at the shop to tell her she was sick and wouldn't be coming in. And then to make good on the promise, she wandered through her house like a ghost all day, blindly watching cartoons in her pajamas until noon, nourishing herself with an apple and a glass of water around dinnertime. She told herself she needed that day to bounce back from the shock her system had received. She promised herself the next day would be better.

On Sunday morning, Miranda tried to pull herself out of bed with her usual zeal for the day ahead, but instead of showering quickly and heading straight for her gardens, she dawdled before the bathroom mirror, gazing at her sullen expression and lifeless features, wondering how she could ever have let herself believe that Lucas Strathmoor really loved her. When she finally did stumble into the shower, she turned the water almost completely on hot, suffering the stinging streams of heat as if punishing herself for being so blind to the obvious.

When she opened her medicine cabinet for a comb, only to find so many of Lucas's things mixed in with her own, it was almost Miranda's undoing. The presence in her home of something so intimate as his toiletries was a testament to how comfortable she had become with him, a glaring reminder that she had trusted him so implicitly, she had virtually invited him to live with her. Instead of falling apart, however, Miranda simply took a deep breath, squared her shoulders and plucked the items out one by one to toss them into the wastebasket.

Downstairs in the kitchen, she fared little better. When she opened the refrigerator to retrieve a bottle of juice, her hand fell instead on a bottle of the imported beer that Lucas favored. Behind it were cartons of leftover Chinese food they had hastily consumed before the party Friday night. Again, Miranda tossed everything into the trash, carting it all out to the big can in the garage. She tried unsuccessfully to ignore the little jolts of pain that shot through her at the realization that the final resting place for the remnants of their affair would be the local landfill. Such a resting place was perfectly suitable, she told herself sarcastically. Because everything Lucas had said to her, every touch and caress he'd offered, every plan they'd made together had been nothing but a load of garbage.

For the rest of the day, Miranda dashed through her house armed with cleaning supplies, scouring everything in sight, and discarding any reminder of Lucas. By the time she had finished, the sun hung low and red over the trees, and she had filled three boxes to ship back to Lucas's house. Among the items she had packed inside were articles of his clothing and a few magazines he'd left behind, a near-full bottle of his favorite brandy, videotapes of some W. C. Fields movies he had brought over one night, and a copy of *Winnie-the-Pooh* she had bought for him, having assured him that reading it would completely alter his outlook on life. She had also included the makings for an indoor herb garden they had planned to plant together. Lucas had expressed an interest in seeing how things grew, she recalled with a melancholy shake of her head. Miranda couldn't imagine why, when he was so much better at killing things.

But the more she tried to clear reminders of Lucas away, the more Miranda uncovered that evoked memories of him. Even among her own possessions, in every corner of every room, she knew she could find something that would rouse thoughts in her head and feelings in her heart. Miranda slumped her shoulders in defeat. She wasn't likely to rid herself of reminders of Lucas Strathmoor anytime soon, she realized. He would remain a part of her for a long, long time to come.

She still wasn't quite sure what had caused her more pain—realizing that Lucas had only kept her around because of her ability to help him predict what his business adversaries were thinking and planning, or hearing him state so unequivocally that she didn't belong in his world. Miranda would have thought by now that she could no longer be hurt by such an assertion from another human being, would have thought by now that she felt confident and comfortable enough in the world she had created for herself that she wouldn't want to belong anywhere else. And perhaps, deep down, she didn't. But there was still that little part of her that craved acceptance and felt slighted when she didn't receive it. And that was the part Lucas had wounded when he'd told Simon that she didn't belong in their world.

Miranda wished she hadn't told Lucas she loved him. As she turned off the light and went to bed that night, she pulled the sheets up over her head in an effort to keep the pain and humiliation at bay. But her dreams were filled with everything she'd done wrong. Even in sleep, Miranda felt the hurts.

The following morning, she telephoned a delivery service to come for the boxes of Lucas's belongings, and as she watched an impossibly young-looking teenage boy lift the cartons into his truck and drive away with them, Miranda felt some of the weight on her shoulders lift a little. Unfortunately, though, it didn't quite go away. When she turned to walk back into her house, she tried to tell herself that now everything was precisely as it had been before she'd set eyes on Lucas Strathmoor. Everything except for herself, she realized then. And that would never be the same.

At the shop that morning, her spirits didn't lift at all. Marcy knew as soon as she entered that something was wrong, and tried to get Miranda to talk about it. Instead Miranda offered her assistant a slight shake of her head and a weary expression, told Marcy she'd rather not go into it right now, and retreated to the back room. At lunchtime, Marcy braved entry into Miranda's office with a cup of tea and carry-out vegetable soup from the deli next door, but Miranda had no appetite to consume either. By four o'clock, the traffic in the store had dwindled to a few casual browsers, and Miranda decided to call it a day.

"I'm going on home, Marcy," she said as she gathered some of the paperwork she'd stared at blindly all day and tossed it into her briefcase. "I don't think we're going to be very busy for the next couple of hours. You and Toni should be fine on your own until closing, don't you think?"

Marcy nodded. "Absolutely, no problem. Are you sure you'll be okay? You don't want to maybe go out for a bite later and talk?"

Miranda silently shook her head and snapped her briefcase shut.

"It's Lucas, isn't it?" Marcy asked quietly. "Something's happened."

Marcy had never been one to keep her worries and concerns bottled up, Miranda recalled. She'd been expecting questions from her assistant all day, and would have been surprised if she'd made it out the door this afternoon without having to own up to a few of them.

"Yes, something's happened," she said with a quiet sigh. "But it's nothing I want to talk about, Marcy, okay? Suffice it to say that Lucas and I won't be seeing each other anymore."

Marcy gazed at her with wide, incredulous eyes. "But why not? You guys were great together. You've been positively glowing for the past few months. How could that have changed so suddenly?"

Miranda hefted up her briefcase as if it were the heaviest, most onerous weight she had to bear. "I thought we were great together, too," she said quietly, trying to get past Marcy before the tears she felt threatening began to fall. "But one of us . . . one of us turned out to be not so great. One of us wasn't what he professed to be."

Before Marcy could ask anything more, Miranda fled the shop and hastened to hail a cab. She couldn't handle riding the bus today. There would be too many eyes to avoid. All she wanted was to be safe at home, alone with her cats and a pint of chocolate chocolate-chip ice cream.

Home alone, she repeated to herself sadly. Somehow the phrase had a feeling of permanence like nothing else Miranda had ever known.

Monday night found Lucas seated in his library, his necktie loosened and hanging askew, an uncorked bottle of brandy on the table beside him. He'd slugged back a good portion of it without even bothering to get a glass from the bar, something he hadn't done since college. For some reason he felt little like a self-respecting, business-minded executive tonight, and more like the uncertain, uncouth slob of his youth. He gazed almost unseeingly at the three boxes thrown open on the floor before him, wishing Miranda could have waited at least a little while before returning his things to him.

Then he would have had an excuse to go over to her house and see her.

His own house offered him little comfort, if any at all. Until he'd arrived home that afternoon to find the three boxes waiting for him, there had been nothing of Miranda here except for the peace lily on the table beside him. And that had provided him with no reassurance, either, because every time he'd looked at it, he'd heard her voice accusing him of being nothing but ice and stone through and through. It was the last thing Lucas had wanted or needed to be reminded of.

And now, thanks to Miranda's quick and efficient discarding of his belongings, he had even more to remind him that he'd treated her so callously and with such complete disregard for her feelings. Now he had a copy of a children's classic he'd laughed off when she'd assured him it was a must-read for every adult. He had two T-shirts that were redolent with the scent of a rose sachet, because they had lain in her dresser drawer beside some of her most intriguing lingerie. And he had that damned herb garden they had planned to grow together. Why had she sent that? he wondered. Why hadn't she kept it for herself?

Because it probably reminded her of you, you jerk, Lucas thought in reply to his own question. *And why would she want to be reminded of that?*

Lucas lifted the bottle of brandy and filled his mouth with the warm, smoky-tasting liquor, relishing the fiery heat that burned down his throat and around his heart when he swallowed it. He'd really gotten himself in deep this time, he thought. Somehow he'd managed to let himself fall in love with Miranda True, only to chase her away before convincing her she was the best thing that had ever happened to him.

He knew he shouldn't be surprised by how much he regretted hurting her, nor by how guilty he felt as a result. He knew he shouldn't be surprised at how much he missed her now. But Lucas was frankly amazed by the scope and depth of the emotions he had experienced since Miranda's departure from his home Friday night. He'd never felt so...so empty in his life. Over the weeks they had spent together, Miranda had become something to him no one else had ever been before. She had become *important* to Lucas—more important than success, more important than wealth, more important than anything else in the world. He loved her. It shocked him still to realize it. There had to be some way he could put things back as they'd been before, some way to make Miranda understand how much he loved her and that he couldn't live without her.

Suddenly Lucas realized the enormity of the challenge facing him. Winning Miranda back would be the biggest challenge of his life. It would be a battle unlike any he had ever fought, a raid to end all raids. And in the raid on Miranda's heart, the prize would be infinitely more rewarding than money or success. In this case, the prize would be love—Miranda's love. And Lucas vowed to do whatever was necessary to win it back.

As he stared at his belongings scattered on the floor before him, he began to formulate his plan.

"Miranda, you better come out front. I don't think you're going to believe what's going on out there."

Miranda glanced up over her glasses at Marcy, who stood framed by the office door. In addition to her usual loose-fitting, brightly colored clothes, her assistant was wearing a wide, suspiciously satisfied smile.

"What is it?" Miranda asked cautiously, not altogether certain she wanted to know.

"You've got to see this," Marcy assured her, with a lift of her auburn eyebrows.

"I'm in the middle of payroll right now, Marcy. Can't it wait? You do want to get paid this week, don't you?"

Marcy's grin grew broader. "At this point, Miranda, my paycheck is going to be totally anticlimactic. I have *never* seen anything like what they're doing to your store. You've got to come out here and experience it for yourself."

Her curiosity sufficiently piqued, Miranda sighed impatiently, removed her glasses to set them down beside her pencil, then rose slowly from her desk. She took her time in smoothing out her sleeveless lavender dress. There was no reason Marcy had to detect how successful she'd been in rattling her into response, Miranda thought. Tucking a strand of blond hair carelessly behind her ear, she followed her assistant to the front of the store.

Miranda caught her breath at the sight that greeted her. Everywhere she looked—on the counter, on display cases, on every fixture imaginable—were huge bouquets of lilies. Every variety of lily she could name, every color of lily she could imagine, was represented by the dozen. Before she could say a word, the front door opened and a uniformed deliveryman entered carrying more, setting another massive bouquet on the floor when he saw nowhere else to put it.

"There are six florists' vans out there," Marcy said as another man in a different uniform with another bunch of flowers came in. He was followed by yet another. "Six of them. And they've carried in about four arrangements each so far."

"Good heavens," Miranda whispered.

Already the store had become redolent with the sweet aroma of the flowers, and she closed her eyes to inhale deeply their fresh, heavy fragrance. She didn't need to wonder who had sent the flowers or why, but she approached the nearest of the bouquets anyway, reaching almost reluctantly for the small white envelope nestled among the blooms. With trembling fingers, she opened it, extracting a tiny card barely large enough to contain Lucas's scrawling handwriting. Miranda bit her lip nervously and rubbed at the furrows that formed on her forehead when she read the sentiment inscribed there.

Forgive me.

That was all he'd written. No signature, no excuses, no attempts to explain, nothing but his expressed desire that she forgive him his transgressions. Miranda went to another arrangement of flowers and plucked the card from the greenery. Again those two little words leaped out at her, tugging at something deep inside her that refused to back down.

But how could she forgive him? she asked herself. How could she forgive a man who had so thoughtlessly and heartlessly let her believe he loved her in an effort to profit from the trust she had placed in him? Because that's precisely what he had done, Miranda reminded herself. She couldn't have been clearer in making her feelings for him known. There was no way he could have mistaken her emotions as anything other than honest, deeply felt love. Yet knowing that, he'd done nothing to discourage her affections. Instead he had nurtured her love for him by leading her to believe he cared for her, too, and had exploited that love to make his job a little easier. Forgive him? she asked herself. Not because he brought her some flowers. Not in a million years.

"Take them back out," she told one of the deliverymen as he entered with yet another huge arrangement.

Immediately he stopped to gape at her, clearly amazed that she would reject so generous a gift. "I beg your pardon?" he asked politely.

When two of the other deliverymen entered behind him, she turned to them as well. "Take them all back out. There's a nursing home less than a mile up the road on the same side of the street we're on. Saint Rita's. Take them all up there and distribute them so that everyone can enjoy them. I can't have this clutter messing up my shop."

"But, Miranda . . ." Marcy began to object.

"Excuse me, Marcy," she replied curtly. "I have a lot of work to do in back. Please see that my wishes are carried out, all right?"

Marcy shook her head at Miranda in obvious disappointment. "If you insist."

"I do."

Miranda spun around so quickly that she almost lost her balance and made her way as hastily to the back of the store as she could. As she stumbled blindly down the hall toward her office, she prayed silently that she would reach it before completely losing her composure. She would not cry, she promised herself as she slammed the door behind her and let her body sag wearily against it, her breathing ragged and uneven. She hadn't cried after she and Patrick had parted ways, and she certainly wasn't going to waste tears over the loss of a man like Lucas Strathmoor.

He thought he could buy her forgiveness with a purchase of something beautiful, she thought. A gaudy display of his extravagance. Well, he was wrong. Forgiveness came through actions and deeds, not as a result of who spent the most money. Forgiveness would come to Lucas Strathmoor only when he did something to convince Miranda he deserved it.

That evening when the bus deposited Miranda two blocks from her house, she made the short journey home on foot slowly. Lucas's flowers had been followed up with the arrival of several dozen boxes of her favorite cookies, and later still by the delivery of hundreds of helium balloons. All had come accompanied by cards with the same simple two-word request the lilies had borne—Forgive me. Miranda had reacted precisely as she did with the flowers and had told Marcy to arrange to have them sent to a local children's hospital instead.

Miranda shook her head slowly in wonder now as she walked. She would give Lucas an A for effort, she allowed, that much at least she was willing to do. But she couldn't understand his persistence, didn't know why her forgiveness would mean so much to him. She would admit now that she had probably been somewhat overly melodramatic in denouncing Lucas as nothing but ice and stone through and through. Certainly there must be some part of him that was warm, she thought, because no one could make love as tenderly and considerately as he had unless there was some emotion involved.

But that emotion hadn't been love, Miranda reminded herself, regardless of whether or not he had said it was. And it should be easy enough for Lucas to get on with his life without her. He wasn't the kind of man to make profuse apologies for his actions, even if those actions had been wrong. The fact that he had gone to such trouble and expense in an effort to win Miranda over puzzled her. Why did it matter to him whether or not she forgave him? Unless of course he wanted her to come back because he needed her skills once again, needed her to help him seize control of another company he'd set his sights on, needed her to help him put some other poor unsuspecting business owner out on the street.

Miranda rounded a final corner, and only the sight of her house in the distance kept her anger from escalating to dangerous proportions. It was well past the dinner hour, but the sun, which had yet to set, still bathed the little frame cottage in glowing yellow warmth. Off in the distance, a dog barked, and the warm evening breeze rustled through the trees above her. For a brief, solitary moment, Miranda felt a settling sense of tranquility, and she sighed deeply. She would get through this, she promised herself. It wouldn't be easy, and it wouldn't be quick, but she would get over Lucas Strathmoor.

However, it wouldn't be anytime soon, she thought, when she drew nearer to her house and saw him seated with galling familiarity on her porch swing. As if she needed to feel more betrayed than she already did, she noted that her cat, Ella, had curled up in his lap, and that Billie had situated her ample fuzzy body comfortably beside him.

Without breaking stride or offering him any indication of how much his presence there unsettled her, Miranda approached her house, withdrew her keys and shifted her briefcase to her other hand as she ascended the three steps leading to her front porch.

"Slumming, Mr. Strathmoor?" she asked coolly as she inserted her key into the lock with an anxious scrape.

Lucas stroked the cat in his lap with a lengthy caress, then curled his knuckle to rub it under Ella's chin. Something caught at Miranda's heart to see him treating the animal so gently, so tenderly. She could still remember the way his fingers felt skimming over her own body, the way his soft touches made her nerve endings burst into flame. Ella turned her striped face to greet the rubbing fingers more aggressively, the loud thrumming of her purr an indication of how much she enjoyed Lucas's attentions. It was insane, Miranda knew, but for a moment she was actually jealous of her cat.

"You refused my gifts," he said, choosing to ignore her statement.

Miranda didn't ask him how he knew that. She should have realized he would be aware of what she had done. "Yes," she said quietly.

He lifted his head to meet her gaze, and Miranda turned her attention back to the key.

"Why?" he asked her.

Only after she'd pushed her front door open and had one foot safely inside the house did she turn to gaze at Lucas fully from around the screen door. "Because I make it a policy never to accept gifts from strangers."

"But I'm not a stranger, Miranda," he pointed out.

She paused only the briefest of moments before stepping completely inside her house. When the outer door latched softly behind her, she stared at him through the screen and replied, "Oh yes, you are."

Lucas lifted a protesting Ella from his lap to settle her beside her slumbering sister, then slowly approached the front door. However, he didn't enter without invitation as he had that first afternoon so many weeks ago. Instead he remained outside looking in at Miranda, his hands shoved deeply into the pockets of his trousers, his necktie rumpled and twisted, his expression worried.

"Will you at least give me an opportunity to explain?" he asked.

"There's nothing to explain, Lucas. You lied to me. You asked me out pretending to have a romantic interest in me, then you manipulated me into revealing my opinion of people and situations, which you then applied to your own hunches in order to put people out of business."

"Miranda, there was a hell of a lot more to it than that, and you know it."

But Miranda hastened to continue before Lucas could rattle her enough to make her lose her train of thought. "Now I don't claim to understand exactly what's involved in this corporate raiding thing that you do, but considering the number of parties we attended and the length of time we...*dated*...I imagine I helped you gain quite a lot for yourself, didn't I? I probably helped you take a lot of companies and saved you quite a bit of money. I suppose in a way I was even something of a career consultant, wasn't I?''

No longer able to meet the dark, stormy depths of Lucas's eyes when her next thought occurred to her, Miranda dropped her gaze and swallowed with some difficulty before going on. ''And even better for you, in addition to all that, I provided you with a nice little sexual diversion on the side. Of course, during all this, I never realized what you were doing, what your intentions were, so I never charged you a fee. But then if I had, what would *that* have made me, do you think?''

Lucas remained silent as she rambled on, fully understanding that she had a lot of anger she needed to vent. He tried to ignore how her blue eyes seemed larger and more expressive than usual, and tamped down his urge to tangle his fingers in her silky hair. He simply stood stock-still at Miranda's front door and let her go on with her speech as long as she wanted, because he knew that when she was finished, he had a little speech of his own to make.

''Do you deny it?'' she asked him, still gazing down at the floor.

Lucas drew in an impatient breath before responding. ''Do I deny leading you on at first?'' he clarified. ''No, I don't deny that. It was a pretty despicable thing to do, and I don't suppose there's anything I could say that would provide a sufficient apology. But will you please come outside or let me come in so that I can explain? Talking to you through the door is . . . uncomfortable.''

Actually Lucas just wanted the opportunity to touch Miranda again. He wanted to be close to her, wanted to inhale the sweet floral fragrance that surrounded her, and weave his fingers through the long shafts of her pale gold hair. He wanted to make love to her. And the fact that he might never be able to do any of those things again filled him with something akin to terror. He held his breath as he awaited her decision. Finally she pushed the screen door forward with an ominous creak and stepped back to allow him inside.

Lucas smiled his thanks as he entered. The house inside was even warmer than the summer day outside, and he yanked his tie completely free to unfasten the top button of his shirt. "Why don't you get an air conditioner?" he asked absently as he rolled up his sleeves to the elbow.

"I don't like air-conditioning," Miranda told him softly, watching his careless actions with an expression that bordered on worry. "I don't like having to close the windows when there's so much going on outside. I don't want to miss anything. Would you like something cool to drink?"

"Please."

She nodded silently, went to the window to switch on a fan, then retreated to the kitchen. Lucas took a seat on the sofa, positioning himself to get as much relief as he could from the breeze the fan provided. He closed his eyes and listened to the steady, reassuring hum as the blades spun faster, willing his heart to mimic the easy rhythm. When he opened his eyes again, Miranda stood before him in her sleek lavender dress, looking as tall and cool as the two glasses of iced tea she held in her hands. She set one of the green glasses on the coffee table before him, and Lucas watched as if mesmerized the beads of condensed water sliding down the side to pool in a perfect circle at the base. He raked his thumb up the side, relishing the coldness beneath his fingers, unwilling to meet Miranda's eyes just yet. The last time he had gazed at them, there had been too much pain there for him to bear.

The ice in her glass shifted and clinked as Miranda sat in a chair opposite—and well away from—him, and Lucas tried to ignore the stab of something hot that pierced his heart at her obvious reluctance to be close to him physically.

"You said you wanted to explain," she said quietly. "I'm waiting."

Lucas slugged back a generous swallow of his tea before he began, savoring the sweet, minty flavor as if it would be the last time he quenched his thirst. Finally he found the words he had spent the weekend searching for, and gazed at Miranda levelly.

"When I first met you, I had absolutely no idea what kind of woman you were. I'm used to dealing with people who don't want to deal with me. In my line of work, deception is rule number one of every situation. It was nothing personal, Miranda. I don't trust anybody when I first meet them. I usually still don't trust them even after I've known them for a while."

"I trusted you."

Lucas dropped his gaze back down to his glass. "I know. And that only made it worse when I finally did realize what kind of woman you are—trusting, forthright... someone with a lot of integrity. I'd never known anyone like you, Miranda. You came as something of a shock to my system."

"Why did you do it, Lucas? Why did you use me that way?"

He stood abruptly and began to move restlessly about the room, feeling like a caged animal who longed to break free. "Because I was at the end of my rope where Panwide was concerned," he told her. "Look, I know it's a lame excuse now, but you have to understand my frame of mind at that point. I was so close to getting that company. All I needed was an angle of some kind. And when I realized you could provide me with that angle..." He shrugged hopelessly.

"Unfortunately that was all I saw. I never took your feelings into consideration until it was too late. And for that I'm sorry."

"Just for that?" Miranda asked him.

Lucas whipped around at the quietly uttered question, worried by the tone of voice she'd used in asking it. "What do you mean?"

"Sounds to me like you're only sorry because things went beyond your control," she said. "You haven't said a word about your behavior. You don't seem sorry at all that you wound up with all those companies as a result of deception and manipulation. You're only sorry that my feelings got stepped on in the bargain."

"Isn't that why you're mad at me?" he asked her.

Miranda couldn't believe what she was hearing. "Of course I'm mad at you for that. But I'm even angrier that you don't seem to be bothered by the fact that you profited from all this." Now Miranda rose, too, and she began to pace. "I thought when you said you wanted to explain that you would at least express some regret that you had acquired those companies through false pretenses. But that doesn't bother you at all, does it? You only feel guilty because you started to care for the person you set out to exploit."

"Isn't that enough?"

Miranda shook her head. "No, it isn't. I understand that you're sorry for the way you treated me, Lucas. I even believe that you do care for me to some degree. Otherwise you wouldn't be here trying to apologize. But there's still a ruthless, ambitious streak in you a mile wide if you don't see how wrong you were in the way you went about buying those companies. And even if I could find it within myself to forgive you for deceiving me, I could never forgive you for turning a profit by that deception."

"Miranda, you still don't understand—"

"Oh, I think I understand perfectly. You're the one who doesn't seem capable of comprehending the coldheartedness of your actions." She went to the screen door and pushed it outward. "I think you should go."

"But you still haven't let me explain."

"There's nothing left to explain."

Lucas stared at her in disbelief. She was going to let it end this way? She was just going to push him away without so much as a fond farewell? "Are you telling me it's over between us?" he asked quietly, not wanting to hear her reply.

Miranda's eyebrows drew down beneath a furrowed forehead, and she sighed heavily before answering with a silent nod.

"You won't give me a chance to redeem myself?"

"I don't think you want to redeem yourself, Lucas," she told him softly.

Lucas wasn't sure what Miranda was implying by her comment, but he could see by the expression on her face that she was as disappointed by the way things had turned out between them as he was. She didn't want to see him leave any more than he wanted to go. But their conversation was beginning to seem pointless. She was obviously unwilling to listen to any further explanation from him, and frankly, Lucas wasn't sure how to make her understand. But somehow he would win Miranda back. He would just have to try a little harder.

Lucas exhaled deeply, but didn't say anything further to try convincing her to let him stay. Instead he slowly crossed the living room toward her, pausing before he passed through the front door. Miranda stared down at the floor again, clearly reluctant to meet his gaze. So Lucas stood firmly rooted where he was and stared at her until she finally looked up at him. The moment she did, he leaned down and pressed his mouth gently against hers, kissing her not with the fierce demand his libido insisted upon, but with a subtle hope he felt from the heart. The moment he felt her starting to kiss him back, Lucas pulled quietly away.

"This isn't over, Miranda," he assured her softly. "Not by a long shot."

And with that he was gone, leaving Miranda feeling dazed and a little fuzzy, and thoroughly uncertain about what had just happened between them.

Chapter Ten

Several weeks passed, and Miranda heard not a word from Lucas. The hot summer Boston nights had never bothered her before, but for the first time since leaving Saint Denis, she began to give serious consideration to buying an air conditioner. Suddenly her nights were unbearably hot—too stifling, too uncomfortable, too comfortless for anyone to be able to sleep. So Miranda lay awake in her bed night after night, thinking about Lucas and everything that had passed between them, wondering if she could have done something to prevent herself from falling in love with him.

And every night, she decided that there was nothing she could have done differently. Things had happened as naturally and normally as any other love relationship progressed, she thought. Except that in this case, one participant had thoroughly misled the other. Miranda wished with all her heart that she could go back to the beginning—back to that very first night at Grace Devon's party—and start all over again.

Why hadn't she paid more attention to the lines on Lucas's hands? she demanded of herself now, as she lay awake on yet another hot summer night. It was perhaps the hundredth time that she had asked herself the question since ending her relationship with Lucas. Miranda rolled over restlessly in her bed and punched her pillow into a tight ball before pounding it down flat again. Why hadn't she reminded herself of his Martian's potential for ruthlessness and the disregard of other people's feelings that went along with it? Why hadn't she remembered that her own Venusian tendency toward ready trust would make her a completely inappropriate mate for a man like Lucas Strathmoor? Why hadn't she just offered him a politely uttered no the first time he'd asked her out?

Probably because she'd fallen hopelessly for him the moment she laid eyes on him, Miranda thought morosely. Probably because the second he had opened his mouth to tell her in his maddeningly sexy voice that she seemed soft to him, she had been completely lost.

The fan in the window hummed quietly as it directed a warm breeze over the bed, and Miranda closed her eyes, trying to focus on the soothing sound in an effort to lull herself to sleep. But such an escape was impossible. Immediately her eyes snapped open again, and she gazed blindly into the darkness of her bedroom.

"Boy, it's hot tonight," Miranda muttered as she kicked her sheet to the foot of the bed.

A series of disgruntled, disembodied meows erupted around her in reply to her distress.

"Sorry," she apologized.

As the cats settled silently back into their easy slumber, Miranda envied them their feline ability to sleep undisturbed, unburdened of human worries. She would get over

Lucas Strathmoor, she promised herself yet again. She would. But as she closed her eyes, she was assaulted by memories of how tenderly he had made love to her, and how eagerly she had responded to his touch. She remembered exactly how deeply her love for Lucas ran, and she knew her assurances to herself were meaningless.

She knew she would achieve some serenity in time. But a part of her would never get over the way he had betrayed her trust. She would never be able to put her faith in another person entirely again. In that respect, Lucas would always haunt her. She would just have to do the best she could. But would the best be enough?

As she drifted off into an uneasy slumber, Miranda began to dream. They were dreams filled with visions of quiet lovemaking and melancholy laughter—the final remnants of her affair with a stranger.

Business at the shop the following day was slow, even for a summer Friday. During the colder months, Fridays were usually among the busiest days of the week for Miranda's shop, but during the summer, because Boston was so close to so many vacation spots, Fridays—and Saturdays—tended to drag. Everyone with regular Monday-to-Friday hours who could afford it left the city for the weekend, heading for the Cape or to coastal destinations north. From May to October, Miranda was lucky to keep a steady stream of people coming into the shop on Fridays and Saturdays. And apparently this week would be no different.

Therefore she was surprised to see Grace Devon enter the shop late that afternoon. Of all people, Grace seemed to be the type who would escape to a tall, breezy house on the Cape every Friday. Yet it was almost dinnertime, and the other woman was dressed in a conservative navy suit, clearly still very much involved in her workday. Miranda had seen her on a number of occasions since working her dinner party last spring, always at functions she was attending with Lucas. Grace had been outgoing, warm and very friendly on each of those occasions, never disguising the fact that she thought Miranda and Lucas made a wonderful couple.

However, Miranda hadn't seen her since her relationship with Lucas had come to an end, and she wasn't sure how to act toward Grace now. Grace and Lucas were very close, Miranda knew, so she must be aware of how things had crumbled between the two lovers. But Grace was smiling when she waved at her from the other side of the room and didn't seem to harbor any concern for what had happened.

"There you are, Miranda," she said as she approached the back of the shop where Miranda was restocking an assortment of organically grown teas. "I just came from a meeting with my attorney. His office is less than a block away, and since I haven't seen you in weeks, I thought I'd drop in to say hello. How have you been?"

Miranda wasn't sure how to respond. "I . . . I'm fine, Grace. How have you been?"

"As well as can be expected, I suppose. Have you heard from Lucas lately?"

Maybe Grace didn't know, Miranda thought. Maybe she hadn't seen Lucas for a while, either. "Not since . . . not for several weeks," she hedged.

"Not since the two of you had your little disagreement, is that it?" Grace asked.

Obviously Grace had heard, Miranda thought. But equally obvious was the fact that she hadn't heard correctly. "It wasn't such a little disagreement, Grace. I don't know what Lucas told you—"

"Actually, he's told me nothing. But he's been moping around and being temperamental as hell lately, so I gauged something of the sort had happened. When I finally cornered him and demanded to know the particulars, he simply said the two of you weren't seeing each other anymore."

So Lucas had finally given up, Miranda realized. She knew she shouldn't be surprised but rather relieved that he wasn't going to pursue her anymore. Still a part of her had been holding on to the last words he had spoken to her, his promise that what had happened between them wasn't over yet—not by a long shot. However, it appeared now that his impassioned avowal had been as meaningless and unfelt as the rest of their relationship. He no more wanted to reestablish contact than she did.

"No, we aren't," Miranda agreed.

"Why not?" Grace's pointed question was in no way discreet or apologetic. She clearly demanded to know what had gone wrong.

"Grace..." Miranda began, hoping to end the discussion before it got started.

"I know, I know," Grace interrupted. "It's none of my business. But Lucas is almost like a son to me. I hate seeing him hurting as much as I would hate to see Peter, Jr., feeling that miserable."

"Lucas is hurting?" The question was out of Miranda's mouth before she realized she was even thinking it, and she only hoped her tone of voice didn't hint at the anguish she felt.

"He's like the proverbial mighty lion with a thorn stuck in his paw."

Miranda felt herself deflate a little. "If I recall correctly in that story, the thorn caused a small enough wound. The pain easily ended by simply removing it."

"Removing it has only made it worse in this case, Miranda."

Miranda studied Grace's expression closely. "What do you mean?"

Grace expelled an efficient, satisfied breath and crossed her arms over her waist. "Why don't you and I go to dinner and talk about it?"

"I'm not sure there's anything to talk about, Grace. This thing between Lucas and me—"

"Isn't going to go away anytime soon," Grace finished for her. "Trust me. I know about these things. Peter and I went through more than our share of trouble way back in ancient times when we were dating. Now, I know this wonderful little place just outside of town that you will absolutely love. The wine selection is marvelous, and the beef…" Grace smacked her lips as if recalling the most delicious meal she'd ever had. "Simply delectable."

"I'm a vegetarian, Grace."

"Oh, I'm sure you'll find something on the menu that will . . . meet with your satisfaction," the other woman said with a cryptic smile. "We'll take my car. I'll drive."

"But—"

But Grace would hear no excuses. "Come on, grab your purse."

"The shop," Miranda tried again. "I don't close for another hour and a half."

"Close early today. You deserve it. And no offense, Miranda," Grace added in a tactful bonus, "but you don't really seem to be doing a booming business at the moment."

With the exception of a number of plants, the two women were the only actual live creatures occupying the shop at present.

"Well, I guess you're right about that," Miranda conceded. "All right. Dinner sounds good. What's the name of the restaurant?"

Grace seemed to falter for a moment, then said quickly, "I'm not going to tell you. I want it to be a surprise."

Miranda surrendered to the other woman's exuberance then and smiled genuinely for the first time in weeks. "All right, Grace, whatever you say. It'll be nice to have dinner out again. I get tired of cooking for myself."

Grace smiled back, a smile that was full of smug satisfaction. "Well, maybe you won't have to this weekend."

"What?" Miranda called out over her shoulder as she went to retrieve her purse from her office in back.

"Nothing," Grace replied breezily when she returned. "Just thinking about the weekend ahead."

There was something a little unsettling about the situation, Miranda felt. Still, she had agreed to go, so she turned on the alarm and locked up the shop. Grace linked their arms together and led Miranda to where she had parked her car at the end of the block. For just the briefest of moments, and for some crazy reason, Miranda couldn't help thinking about lambs on their way to the slaughter.

"Just where is this restaurant, Grace?" Miranda asked some time later, as the two of them passed the exit for Hyannis. "When you said, 'Just outside of town,' I thought you meant just outside of town. We've been on the road for over an hour."

"It won't be much longer now."

Ever since Grace had turned her car onto Route 3, Miranda had been plagued by feelings of déjà vu, inevitably remembering the last time she had ventured along this road. In fact, not too far past Hyannis lay Yarmouth, she recalled, and Yarmouth was where Lucas's beach house stood. The suspicion that had hovered unchecked in the back of her brain sped to the forefront at the realization, and she not so suddenly began to wonder about Grace's motives.

"We aren't going to a restaurant, are we, Grace?" Miranda asked with surprising calm.

Grace shook her head. "No."

"We're going to Lucas's house, aren't we?"

Grace nodded. "Yes."

"He put you up to kidnapping me, didn't he?"

"Actually, this part was my idea," Grace confessed, her gaze never straying from the road ahead. Miranda wasn't sure whether it was because she was such a conscientious driver or because she was feeling guilty about having misled her.

"Well, I'd appreciate it if you would turn the car around at the next exit and take me back to Boston," she said as politely as she could.

"Oh, Miranda, just give him a chance," Grace pleaded.

"I did give him a chance," Miranda said softly. "But he and I are . . . we're just not suited to each other."

Grace glanced over quickly then, and met Miranda's gaze directly before returning her attention to the road once again. "No two people have ever been more suited than you and Lucas are. Just give it one more try."

"Grace, I can't."

"Of course you can."

"Will you please get off at the next exit?" Miranda asked again.

Grace smiled. "Certainly. That's the exit we want anyway."

Miranda looked up in time to see that it was indeed the same exit she and Lucas had taken when he had driven the two of them to his house. Inevitably her thoughts returned to that weekend of early summer, remembered how spontaneous and reckless they had been in detouring on the way to a party in their evening clothes so that they could spend some time alone uninterrupted. They had walked along the beach in their formal wear, collecting seashells and starfish at midnight, had talked for hours about their pasts, their presents and their futures. They had made love more tenderly and with more care than Miranda would have thought possible for two people with such passionate dispositions as theirs. And Miranda, at least, had fallen completely in love.

Now she was expected to return to that place, feeling betrayed, manipulated and misled, and would be forced to relive every wonderful moment of it only to recognize how hollow the experience had actually been. What Grace was doing now would rob Miranda of her treasured reminiscences of that weekend, and in their place she would be left with unwanted memories of an awkward confrontation with Lucas she simply did not want to experience.

When she opened her mouth to voice her objections again, she realized any further protest would be useless. Grace had pulled her sporty, vintage Jaguar coupe into the dusty, gravel-strewn driveway of Lucas's house, and Lucas was out in the yard watching them pull up. Miranda noted with no small amount of surprise that he was in the middle of doing some gardening work—planting several rows of multicolored limp petunias and pansies along the walkway. She smiled sadly. Didn't he realize it was much too late in the year to be putting out flowers?

"Grace!" he called out as he approached the car, lifting a hand in greeting, the delighted smile on his face at odds with the faint, weary-looking purple crescents below each eye.

Miranda held her breath as he approached, watching his movements closely. It was the first time she had seen him in several weeks, and she noted a number of significant changes in him. He moved more slowly than she remembered, seeming nowhere near as enthusiastic or aggressive as he'd been before. He was dressed as he'd always been when he was spending the weekend at her house, in dirt-streaked khaki shorts and an aged Boston University T-shirt that was wet with perspiration all the way down the front. He looked nothing like the forbidding Mr. Strathmoor Miranda had met at Grace's party last spring, and everything like the Lucas who had become such an intimate part of her home life—the Lucas with whom she had so desperately fallen in love.

When he drew nearer and realized the other occupant of the car was Miranda, he paused for a moment, his mouth silently forming her name as he quickly detoured to the passenger side door. Immediately he dropped to a squatting position and rested his arms over the open window, as if he wanted to prevent her from rolling it up should she try.

"What are you doing here?" he asked quietly, his gray eyes dancing with a fire Miranda wasn't quite able to ignore.

At the sound of his voice, so soft and sexy and familiar, Miranda nearly burst into delirious tears. It was a voice she hadn't heard in a long time, the voice that had always followed their lovemaking—concerned, quiet . . . loving.

"I guess you'd know the answer to that better than I would," she told him.

Lucas arched his eyebrows in confusion, then he looked past Miranda toward Grace.

"Look, I know you just asked me to talk to her," Grace said apologetically, "but there was nothing I could say that would get her out here on her own, so I . . ."

"She kidnapped me," Miranda finished for her.

Lucas bit his lip, and when he glanced back at her, Miranda could tell he was trying not to smile. "You did what?" he asked, returning his attention to Grace.

"She kidnapped me," Miranda repeated.

"Actually, it wasn't quite as . . . as *illegal* . . . as Miranda makes it sound," Grace defended herself.

"That's true," Miranda agreed, reluctantly meeting Lucas's gaze once again. "She didn't pull a gun on me or club me on the back of the head with a blackjack, and I did get into the car of my own free will. But it was under the pretense of going to dinner, not to your house."

"I'll fix you dinner," he offered. "I can even do something vegetarian, I promise."

A quick series of trilling chirps caused them all to look down at the beeper on the dashboard. Grace picked it up with a quietly uttered, "Oh, dear," and asked Lucas if she could use his phone. He nodded, and as Grace exited her side of the car, Lucas opened Miranda's door to help her out. For a moment, she remained firmly planted in her seat, unwilling to face Lucas without the metal barrier of the car door between them. Finally she admitted she was being silly. Besides, she decided, the thought of stretching her legs after a long journey by car was very appealing.

God, she looked beautiful, Lucas thought as Miranda extended one ivory-silk-covered leg toward the ground. He quickly came around the door to take her hand in his, tightening his grip when she tried to tug it free. She was dressed all in white—a white sleeveless shirt, body-hugging white skirt, with her pale gold hair tied back with a sheer white scarf. Her eyes were bluer than he remembered, shadowed beneath by evidence of sleepless nights. He wondered if she had been lying awake in her bed at night as he had, plagued by memories of their time together. When he realized there was a very good chance that she had been, Lucas began to feel a little better. Maybe, just maybe, he still had a chance with Miranda True.

He tangled his fingers with hers as he pulled her forward and around the car door, helpless to stop himself when he continued the action until he held her in his arms. Miranda lifted her free hand to double it against his chest in a half-hearted fist, but she didn't pull away from him. Lucas held her gaze with his, trying to think of something to say that would chase away the hurt and haunted emotions he saw lingering in her eyes.

But all that emerged when he did speak was a softly murmured, "I've missed you."

"Lucas, please don't," Miranda said softly. "We've said all we have to say to each other."

"No, we haven't."

He wasn't sure, but he thought he felt Miranda releasing her fist to briefly spread her hand open over his heart before curling her fingers closed once again. "What's left to go over?" she asked him.

Lucas was about to reply when Grace came barreling out of his house, her legs moving nearly as quickly as her mouth.

"Oh, boy, I have *got* to go," she said as she hurried past them. "Morris has really done it this time. I *told* him not to touch his ears in front of the representative from the Sicilian company. They always misinterpret the gesture as an insult, you know—apparently over there it means something like, 'You should be wearing earrings,' or some other thing. But Morris is just getting over an ear infection, and I guess they're still pretty irritated...

"Anyway, he's just called to say he's on his way to the airport because the Sicilian reps are leaving in a huff, and that they keep going on and on about family ties that bind or something. Now *Morris* is afraid he's going to wake up beside a horse's head, and the *Sicilians*—who are perfectly delightful people, and in no way connected, I assure you— are very offended, *I'm* upset, and... I really have to go."

By this time Grace was seated behind the wheel of her car and had ground the engine to roaring life. "I'll call you later," she threw over her shoulder as she shifted into reverse.

"But, Grace," Miranda began to object halfheartedly. Unfortunately her words were directed toward a swiftly departing sports car. She turned to look at Lucas, who still held her in his arms, and shook her head hopelessly. All she could say was, "My purse was still in the car."

Lucas only smiled and pulled her closer.

"My cats..."

"You'll call Mrs. Ransdell," he told her.

"What if she's not home?" Miranda asked plaintively.

"Then Grace can look after your cats. She owes you that much, anyway." Lucas neglected to add that Grace had a notorious distaste for cats. However, she was at least honorable and tenderhearted enough that she wouldn't let the defenseless little creatures go hungry. Then Lucas recalled that Bix was anything but defenseless, and nearly laughed out loud as he envisioned a standoff between the big tomcat and the indomitable Grace Devon.

"Why do I always find myself stranded here with nothing but the clothes on my back?" Miranda asked him with a resigned sigh.

Lucas tilted his head to place a chaste kiss at Miranda's temple. "I have everything you need here," he told her softly.

Miranda freed herself from his embrace and took several steps away. "Oh, I bet you do," she said. "I bet you planned this weekend down to the last detail, didn't you?"

Lucas sighed impatiently. "I assure you I had nothing to do with this, Miranda. I admit I asked Grace to check in on you, to see how you were faring and maybe offer a few words in my defense to get you talking to me again. But this kidnapping business was entirely of her planning and execution. However," he added, taking a predatory step toward her, "that doesn't mean I'm not going to make the most of the situation. I'd be a fool if I let an opportunity like this one get away from me."

Miranda studied him sadly. "That's what I am to you, too, aren't I, Lucas? Just another opportunity."

Lucas stopped when he was as close to her as he could get. He lifted a hand to curl it around her nape, then reached up to tug free the scarf that bound her hair. As the silky shafts tumbled unfettered around his hand, Lucas wound a thick strand of gold around his index finger. When his eyes met hers, they were dark and sad and compelling. "The first time I met you, Miranda, I confess that you meant nothing more to me than an opportunity. But not anymore. You've become..."

"What?"

He hesitated, as if reconsidering what he was about to tell her. Finally he said softly, "You've become everything to me."

Miranda's heart kicked up double time at his roughly uttered declaration, but she willed herself to remain unmoved. "Lucas, please, don't start—"

"Don't start what?" he demanded. "Look, you're stuck here with me until Grace gets back, and I'm going to do whatever it takes to make you change your mind about me."

Miranda tried to ignore the second part of Lucas's statement for the time being, and instead honed in on the implication behind the first part. "What do you mean I'm stuck here until Grace gets back?"

"My car is in town at Mack's."

"Who's Mack?"

"The local mechanic," Lucas told her with a smile. "I've got one of those temperamental foreign sports cars, you know. Blows a gasket with just the slightest provocation."

Miranda narrowed her eyes warily. "I thought you used to work as a mechanic in your father's garage. Can't you fix your own car?"

Lucas's smile faltered only the tiniest bit. "Uh... yeah. I can. But Mack really enjoys working on it, so when the inconvenient hunk of metal goes out when I'm here, I let him do the repairs."

"Oh, I wouldn't call that inconvenient," Miranda said suspiciously as she moved away from Lucas again. "I'd call car trouble a pretty pertinent necessity for the weekend you have planned."

Lucas settled his hands on his hips with an impatient sigh. Miranda tried not to notice how the gesture pulled taut the fabric of his shirt and shorts to define parts of Lucas she had been having far too much trouble forgetting. "Miranda, I didn't plan this."

"You're a Martian, Lucas," she reminded him unnecessarily. "You never do anything without planning it."

He smiled and shook his head. "Believe what you want. It's all immaterial, anyway."

"Why?"

Lucas began to approach Miranda again, with slow, measured steps that were perfectly in sync with the predatory gleam in his eyes. "Because the fact remains that you're stranded here alone with me until Grace decides to come back for you or Mack finishes working on my car." He paused before her, never touching her, but his gaze held hers fixed and firm. "And that could be days, Miranda, because Mack works at his own leisurely pace, and God only knows what Grace is up to."

Miranda swallowed with some difficulty, trying to steady the erratic pace her pulse had adopted. "I could call a cab," she said softly.

"And pay him with what? You left your purse in Grace's car, remember?" Lucas reminded her.

"Wouldn't you lend me the money?"

A low, raspy chuckle rose from the back of Lucas's throat. "What do you think?"

I think I'm in trouble, Miranda wanted to say. "I think I'm stuck here for a while."

Lucas nodded with much satisfaction. "What would you like for dinner?"

If someone had told her when she first met him that Lucas Strathmoor could whip up a very nice baked lentil casserole and a mouth-watering spinach soufflé, Miranda would have doubled over in hysterical laughter. Now as she studied him over the rim of her wineglass, she couldn't help but marvel at his culinary ability.

"I've been practicing," he told her, as if he had interpreted perfectly what she was thinking about.

"Why?" she asked him pointedly. "You didn't like anything I cooked for you that was vegetarian."

"I never said that."

"You never had to."

Lucas had the decency to look sheepish. "Maybe I just never opened my mind enough to let myself enjoy your cooking."

Miranda couldn't help smiling at his seemingly genuine embarrassment. "Maybe not." She replaced her wineglass on the table, and Lucas was quick to refill it. "Does this mean you've given up meat?" she asked further.

"No," Lucas was quick to reply. "You'll never convince me there's anything more satisfying than prime rib cooked medium rare or a nice thick halibut steak dripping with dill butter." He topped off his own glass of wine. "However, I'm willing to concede that there are other foods to enjoy as well. I'm keeping my mind open to all the possibilities."

And so should you. Miranda was sure that's what Lucas was trying to imply. She rolled the stem of her wineglass slowly back and forth between her thumb and index finger, watching the ruby liquid quiver and spiral with the circular motion. "Maybe I should . . ." she murmured thoughtfully aloud, before she could stop herself.

"Maybe you should what?" Lucas asked.

Miranda snapped out of her musings and shook her head slightly in an effort to chase away the cobwebs. "Maybe I should turn in," she finished hastily. "It's getting late."

"It's nine-thirty," Lucas informed her with a quick glance at his watch. "The night is still extremely young. And you have to help me clean up this mess. I always helped you clean up when you cooked for me.''

It was yet another reminder to Miranda of how much fun she and Lucas had always had together. As she watched him clear away the dishes, she had to admit that she was enjoying herself now, too. Lucas was being wonderful—attentive, considerate, moving at a pace that didn't overwhelm or threaten her. She could almost let herself believe that whatever differences there were left unsettled between them were insignificant, fixable ones. Clearly Lucas wanted their relationship to continue along the same lines as it had been, and he was making every effort to prove to Miranda that he had not returned to the self-centered, thoughtless man he'd been when she met him. He was planting flowers in his yard. He had cooked her a vegetarian meal. What else did she need for proof that he was trying to make amends?

How about some indication that he was sorry for having manipulated and exploited her for occupational gain? Miranda asked herself. How about some sign that he had changed his professional habits as well as his personal ones? She still hadn't seen anything to suggest he had adopted a new outlook in that respect. As far as Miranda could tell, Lucas still harbored no regrets about having turned a profit by taking advantage of her, nor could she be certain that he had any qualms about doing something similar should another opportunity present itself.

And he had never spoken to Miranda of any long-term future the two of them might share. Just what were his motives right now? she wondered. Even if she could find it in her heart to forgive his behavior of the past, could she ever honestly, truly trust him in the future?

"I'm tired," Miranda told him, taking comfort in the fact that it was the truth. "Considering the situation—my being here against my will—essentially—I don't think it's unreasonable that you should clean up the kitchen by yourself. It's been a long day, and I have a lot on my mind."

Lucas nodded his understanding, a hopeful smile playing about his lips. "Can we assume that *I'm* one of those things you have on your mind?"

Miranda realized they'd both know she was lying if she denied it, so she replied softly, "Yes. We can assume that."

"Good."

Before Lucas could say anything further that might confuse her even more, Miranda pushed herself away from the table and stood. She had been hoping she could make an imperious, stoically silent exit, but then she remembered she had come here completely unprepared for spending the night.

"Do you...do you have something I could sleep in?" she asked with some difficulty. The mere idea of wearing anything that belonged to Lucas bothered her. Even the thought of being surrounded by his clothing made her feel as if he had somehow taken possession of her. She could sleep in the buff, of course, Miranda told herself, but the prospect of being naked under the same roof with Lucas caused her even more distress.

Lucas grinned at her lasciviously. "You know, if I were a lesser man, I'd tell you, 'Gosh, no. I'm sorry but I don't. You'll just have to sleep...naked.'" His smile softened. "However, because I have more respect for you than to lead you on that way—and because I know you'd lay me out soundly if I even tried—I'll rustle something up for you."

Miranda bit her lip before she could reply sharply that he should have shown her a little respect before leading her on to begin with, but she remained silent. Lucas's smile fell then, and she got the feeling he had somehow once again picked up on what she was thinking.

"There's an extra toothbrush in the bathroom medicine cabinet," he said in a hollow voice as he turned away. "It's the same one you used before. I'll put something for you to sleep in on the bed in the spare room."

"Thank you," she replied quietly.

She was thankful he didn't elaborate on the fact that such a donation had been unnecessary before, as they hadn't much worried about clothing. As it was, this was going to be a very long night, she thought morosely as she journeyed slowly up the stairs. And she dreaded to think about what the following morning would bring.

Chapter Eleven

The following day they walked into town for supplies, because despite Miranda's certainty that Lucas had planned her kidnapping and desertion down to the last detail, and despite the surprisingly vegetarian contents of his pantry, he only had food enough for one there—and a significant number of the items were canned products that contained meat. And since they were going to town, Miranda had decided further, they might as well check on the progress of his car while they were there.

As she walked beside him down the dusty, narrow road, Miranda tried to quell the nervous butterflies that were scattered in flight in her abdomen, and focus instead on the fact that she was on the Cape against her will, the victim of yet another deception. But it was difficult to be angry on such a beautiful day. The sun, gleaming like a beacon high in the sky, was still warm against her face, but the air held just a touch of coolness. The coastal wind smelled of a curious mixture of salt and pines, and it rustled quietly

through the tall trees as if spreading secrets. The sound
made Miranda feel dreamy and romantic, but when Lucas
reached over and touched the tips of her fingers with his in
an effort to hold her hand, she tugged it away and wrapped
her arms around herself, as if for protection.

She heard Lucas sigh wearily beside her, but he said
nothing in response to her gesture. In fact they had said little to each other since awakening that morning. Breakfast
had been waiting for her when she went downstairs—canned
fruit cocktail and frozen orange juice. It was Miranda's first
clue that perhaps Lucas hadn't orchestrated the weekend
after all. He knew she much preferred fresh produce over
canned fruits and vegetables, and didn't like frozen juice at
all. On the other hand, she had decided quickly, perhaps his
lack of supplies was part of a strategy to make her strand-
ing seem all the more accidental.

*And perhaps you're becoming entirely too paranoid for
your own good,* she told herself.

They went on in silence until they reached a tiny grocery
store that sat by itself on the side of the road. On the other
side of the road was an ancient-looking gas station with a
faded red-and-white sign that proclaimed in nearly unread-
able letters, Mack's. Lucas's car was out in what Miranda
supposed was meant to be the parking lot, but which looked
to her like little more than a gravel-strewn turnaround. The
hood was lifted up to reveal two legs and a rear end encased
in dingy gray coveralls sticking out from beneath it. The
sight was enhanced by the distant, muffled sounds of metal
clanking against metal and some very colorful swearing.

"Gee, looks like Mack may be having some problems,"
Lucas stated unnecessarily.

Miranda nodded, unconvinced. "Mmm. How convenient."

Lucas glanced over at her with a disappointed shake of his
head. "I didn't plan this," he told her for perhaps the tenth
time since her arrival.

"Fine," Miranda replied blandly. "Whatever you say."

He opened his mouth momentarily as if he was going to offer an argument, but then seemed to think better of it and simply bit his lip. Finally he said, "Look, why don't you go get started on the groceries? I'll see how the car is coming along."

Miranda nodded, then watched him as he ambled carelessly across the street. He was wearing khaki shorts, an old T-shirt emblazoned with the logo of a popular Boston night spot, and a pair of ragged leather tennis shoes. He looked like such a normal, average kind of guy, that Miranda nearly felt like crying tears of frustration. If only that was true. If only he was an everyday kind of man in whom she could fully place her trust. But he wasn't. From the moment she had met him, Lucas Strathmoor had clearly displayed his aggressive ambition and his propensity for ruthlessness in gaining whatever he wanted. She had seen for herself by the lines on his hand that he was indeed a man who was fully capable of overlooking the needs of others in order to satisfy himself first. And she would always know that she couldn't really trust him.

As she watched Lucas join Mack beneath the hood of his car, she turned toward the grocery store with little enthusiasm, tugging down the hem of her white skirt with a nervous, unnecessary gesture. Inside the little grocery, she picked up a basket and filled it with fresh fruit and vegetables but was somewhat disappointed by the selection and quality. To compensate, she collected the fixings for fresh bread and quiche, thinking that since Lucas had cooked for her the night before, she would return the favor for him that evening. As much as she hated using bottled herbs, that was all she had to choose from, and as she dropped the last one of them into her basket, she found it lifted from her hand by Lucas, who held an identical one in his other hand that he had filled with his own nutritional needs.

Miranda wrinkled her nose in disgust at some of the things he had chosen, but out loud only asked, "How's the car coming along?"

"Mack said he can have it ready for me in the morning."

"What exactly was wrong with it?" she asked further, hoping to put him on the spot.

Lucas grinned at her indulgently as he placed their purchases on the counter for an elderly woman in a pink duster to ring up. "Oh, fan belt, radiator, spark plugs, all that car stuff that women find so uninteresting."

Miranda nodded with a sage expression. "Amazing that a little garage like Mack's would have all those things for an obscure, expensive foreign car like yours."

Lucas looked at her suspiciously. "It isn't that obscure. Besides, he's been stocking them for me since I bought the house out here."

Miranda nodded again. "I see."

"You still don't believe that I had nothing to do with Grace's bringing you here, do you?"

"Lucas, can you blame me? It would be just like you to pull a stunt like this."

"Why?" he challenged her bluntly.

Miranda felt herself coloring and glanced down at the floor. "Because... because..."

"Because I still love you and would do anything to keep you in my life?"

"Well, no... not necessarily... not exactly."

He dropped his voice to a near whisper, leaning close to her ear so the cashier wouldn't hear what followed. "Because that's true, you know, Miranda. I do still love you, and I would do anything to keep you in my life. Just tell me what you want from me."

Miranda, too, lowered her voice but was still unable to meet Lucas's eyes when she replied, "It's not a matter of what I want now," she said softly. "It's what I wanted from you before—from the very beginning. I wanted to be able to trust you, Lucas. I did trust you." Finally she looked up to meet his gaze levelly. "But I can't now. You're not the man I thought you were."

Lucas's eyes grew stormy at her statement, and he clenched his jaw tightly in anger at her suggestion that he wasn't to be trusted. He said nothing, though, only threw a handful of bills down on the counter when the cashier quoted his total, then snatched up his change and the heaviest of the bags, leaving the other one for Miranda to carry. He strode from the store without a glance backward, leaving her to follow him whenever she felt like it. Deciding he needed a little time to himself, Miranda smiled a little nervously at the cashier, then took her own time in gathering up the sack of groceries and walking out behind him.

She kept her distance for much of the walk home, thinking they must look ridiculous to anyone who would be watching, a throwback to the ancient mentality that a woman should walk ten paces behind her man. Then she reminded herself that Lucas wasn't her man, nor was she required by law to do anything she didn't want to do. With several quick steps, she caught up with him, matching her stride to his.

"Lucas, wait," she said quietly, tugging on his sleeve to make sure he knew she was there. "I shouldn't have said what I said."

Immediately Lucas came to a halt. He studied her for a long time, then must have decided to forget about her comment, because he nodded slowly and said, "It's okay. Don't worry about it. I guess I had that coming."

Miranda wished with all her heart that things could be different between the two of them, but knew her wish was in vain. However, they managed to come to some kind of unspoken agreement then, because after that, they made the rest of the walk home in relatively companionable silence.

By the time they arrived back at the house and retired to the kitchen to unpack the groceries, much of their antagonism had dissipated, and Lucas did his best to replace it with the light banter in which they used to indulge so frequently.

"Hold it," he said as he delved into the sack of groceries he set on the counter. He picked through the contents gingerly and reluctantly, as if they were radioactive. "I think I have the wrong bag here. Tomatoes...broccoli... spinach...ew, granola. Gross." He reached quickly for Miranda's bag. "Where's my stuff...the bologna, the blue Kool-Aid, the Snickers bars, the white bread, for God's sake?"

Miranda chuckled and shoved her bag at him as if the contents had gone rancid. "Here. Take them. I want no part of your nutritional downfall. If I'd realized what I was carrying, I would have dumped it by the side of the road."

Lucas wiggled his eyebrows suggestively. "It's nice to know how much you care."

Miranda refrained from commenting, fearful that she might say something that would return them to their earlier animosity, and finished unpacking the groceries in silence.

For the remainder of the day, Lucas followed her around trying to get her to talk about the state of things between them, and Miranda did her best to change the subject with every other breath. At one point, she tried to retreat to the beach for a little solitary relaxation, but Lucas found her there and joined her. When she got up to walk along the shore, he decided a little walk was exactly what he needed, too. And when she went back to the house in search of a good book, he was right behind her to recommend one— then pulled a novel from the shelf entitled *Second Chances*.

By dinnertime, Miranda was nearly exhausted from the hours spent evading Lucas's advances, and despite his presence at the kitchen table rambling on incessantly about nothing, she put the meal together in pointed silence. She also ate in silence and cleaned up in silence, certain Lucas would get the message eventually. She should have known better. As soon as the last dish was dried and put away, he went to the cabinet where he stored his wine and retrieved and opened a bottle before she could object. When he placed a glass in her hand, she took it wordlessly, then spun on her heel and exited the kitchen.

"Good idea," Lucas murmured from close behind her. "The living room is much more comfortable."

Miranda halted and turned to face him, taking a sip of her wine for fortification before she spoke. "Yes, and the bedroom upstairs is even more comfortable."

For a moment, Lucas's expression was identical to what it would have been if she had just thrown ice water on him. Then he quickly recovered and smiled with maddening charm. "Yes, it is," he agreed heartily. "I'll just go get the bottle and join you there."

"No, you won't," she told him firmly. Instinctively she raised her hand to place her open palm against his chest to stop him—and immediately regretted her action.

His skin was warm beneath the softly faded fabric of his T-shirt, his muscles taut and firm. She felt his heartbeat quicken to a rapid pace when she touched him, and her own pulse responded in kind. Before she could jerk her hand away, Lucas wrapped his own around it, tightening his grip when she tried to pull free.

"Don't," he whispered softly. "Just let me touch you for a minute. It's been so long..."

Miranda felt a warmth meander through her body until it pooled in a heated circle somewhere between her heart and her loins. It had been a long time, she thought. Too long...

But not long enough to make her forget why she couldn't allow herself to fall under his spell again. Once again she tried to tug her hand from his, and on the third attempt, she succeeded. Lucas let her go, but the expression in his eyes told her she wasn't going to get away as easily as she'd like.

"Go to bed, Miranda," he said softly. "And try to sleep peacefully if you can. But dream, too. Dream of me. And then tell me it's over between us."

She swallowed with some difficulty, willing herself not to succumb to the absolute certainty she detected in his voice. It was over between them, she assured herself. It was. He might still be able to make her feel giddy and aroused, but a relationship needed more than hormonal activity to keep it alive. It needed good, healthy roots that were well grounded in trust. With a silent shake of her head, Miranda assured both herself and Lucas that whatever lay lingering between them, however steadfast, lacked that particular fruit.

Without saying good-night, Miranda turned and headed for the stairs. But unlike Lucas, she hoped never to dream again.

Miranda wasn't sure what caused her to awaken in the middle of the night, but she realized immediately that she was freezing. She reminded herself that it was late August, that normally temperatures soared into the eighties and nineties this time of year, and reached down to pull the bedspread up over her. But it was made of a lightweight, gauze fabric and in no way offered any amount of warmth that would penetrate her chilled limbs. Lucas had left a faded navy T-shirt and an exhausted pair of gym shorts on the bed for her the night before, but Miranda wore only the shirt. The shorts had been large enough to hold two of her, and as it was, the shirt nearly reached her knees.

At the moment, however, she wished it went down to her ankles, because she was shivering from the cold. Glancing over at the bedside clock, she saw by the glowing green numbers that it was just past three. Something must have gone wrong with the air conditioner, she thought, because there was no way it could be this cold, even out on the Cape. If she had any hope of getting warm, she would either have to find more clothing to put on, or figure out where Lucas kept his blankets.

As she rose from bed, Miranda wrapped the gauzy bed-spread around herself twice for warmth, then realized too late that such an action would force her to take tiny steps when she walked. She struggled until she had freed one arm, then tiptoed across the room toward the closet. She discovered two extra pillows, a box full of paperback books and another set of sheets, but surprisingly no blanket. She pushed her sleep-rumpled hair out of her eyes and pivoted around, then took several baby steps across the bedroom, opened the door and shuffled out into the hall.

She found the thermostat with little trouble, but in the darkness couldn't tell where it was set. However, she pushed the needle as far to the right as she could, hoping that in placing the setting at its highest, the air conditioner would shut off. But she never heard the telltale click that indicated she had succeeded.

"Cripes," she muttered under her breath. "With all the work Lucas put into this house, the least he could have done was make sure the air conditioner worked."

Miranda was familiar enough with the house to know that all the rooms upstairs were bedrooms, and that the closet at the end of the hall held only recreational supplies—beach chairs, games, puzzles, and the like. She recalled that there was another closet downstairs in the living room near the front door, and decided that if Lucas didn't store extra linens in the upstairs hall closet, where it would make much more sense, then he must keep them in the main closet, where recreational supplies would be much more appropriately stowed.

"Just like a man," she whispered to herself.

It took Miranda a little longer than usual to manage her descent down the stairs because her tightly swathed body forced her to make quick jumps from step to step. And she was concentrating so hard on not tumbling forward that she didn't realize there was someone in the living room waiting for her until she reached the bottom step. By that time it was too late for her to turn and run back up the stairs, and she never would have succeeded anyway because of the awkwardly wound bedspread. When she fully understood the implication of the sight that met her eyes, however, Miranda wasn't entirely certain that she did want to escape. Not just yet, anyway.

She didn't know what Lucas had planned, but as she gazed at him lying shamelessly naked on top of a very appealing wool blanket before a roaring fire in the fireplace, Miranda decided there was no reason she had to leave right away. It was warm down here, after all, she told herself. Maybe she could just sit by the fire until it chased the chill from her body. As for Lucas, she had already seen him naked on a number of occasions, she reasoned, so there was nothing to threaten her in that, was there?

Still, she thought, the warmth she felt creeping from her toes and fingers through her legs and arms, gathering together quickly and catching fire somewhere between her heart and her stomach, had little do with the fire on the other side of the room. No, Miranda realized quickly that it was Lucas's state of abandon that was probably responsible for the particular heat she was experiencing at the moment. However, she thought further, it was rather a nice heat, a welcoming heat, and a warmth that brought her body back to life after long weeks of dormancy. Surely no one would object if she enjoyed it for just a little while longer.

As Miranda took a few tiny steps forward, she noted for the first time a silver ice bucket dripping with condensation near the fire, a freshly uncorked bottle of champagne reaching from its midst. Beside it was a solitary crystal flute half-filled with the sparkling pale gold wine, a single perfect strawberry resting at the bottom. Lucas held an identical treat in his hand, and as Miranda drew nearer, he lifted his glass in the air.

"I knew you'd come," he said with quiet confidence. "Dreams can be annoying as hell sometimes, can't they?"

Miranda tried not to smile, but found it nearly impossible not to. "Dreams had nothing to do with it," she assured him. "And considering the fact that you've rigged your air conditioner to its Antarctic setting, then started a raging inferno down here, how could I resist?"

Lucas wiggled his eyebrows, then took a brief sip of his wine. "To which raging inferno are you referring?" he asked slyly.

Miranda pointed at the fireplace with her free hand. "That one. Is there another I should know about?"

Lucas placed his open palm over his heart and inhaled a melodramatic sigh. "This one. It's been raging out of control since I met you, and your presence here this weekend has only thrown gasoline on the flames."

"Mm-hmm, I see," Miranda said. Inevitably her gaze journeyed over his naked body, and she tried in vain to still her overly aggressive pulse rate. He was even more glorious than she remembered, his body stained a golden bronze from his work in the sun, every solid muscle of him flexed hard and rigid as if mocking her. Why did he have to be so magnificent in form and so questionable in motive? Miranda wondered to herself. Out loud, however, she only said, "In fact, I see a little too much. You think you could do something about . . . that?"

"About . . . what?" Lucas asked, feigning ignorance.

"Lucas . . ."

He made a face at her, one which clearly indicated his disgust at her unwillingness to throw herself into his arms, but wrapped himself up in the blanket in much the way Miranda had with the bedspread, except that his chest and arms were left bare. She murmured her thanks, then took a seat on the sofa well away from Lucas's position seated on the floor with his back against a chair.

"Champagne?" he offered, lifting the untouched glass from the hearth to hand it to her.

There was no use in trying to evade him any further, Miranda decided. He was determined that they should hash this thing out in whatever way he could manage, and she was just too weary to fight him off any longer. Reluctantly she leaned forward and curled her fingers around the stem, then lifted it to her lips to sip cautiously. For a moment, neither spoke, but simply gazed at the other thoughtfully. Finally Miranda broke the silence.

"You've gone to an awful lot of trouble for nothing," she told Lucas.

"I don't know what you mean," he replied indifferently. "Apparently there's something wrong with my air conditioner, and I got cold, so I built a fire. That made me thirsty, so I opened a bottle of champagne. I assure you there were no ulterior motives involved."

"Right," Miranda agreed with a doubtful chuckle. "A perfectly logical chain of events. It wouldn't occur to you to turn off the air conditioner or open some windows, no. And simple tap water would never satisfy the sophisticated thirsts of Lucas Strathmoor, would it?"

Lucas took another sip of his wine. "As a matter of fact, no. But not because my thirsts are sophisticated," he assured her, setting his glass down with a soft clink exactly where he had picked hers up. Slowly he began to make his way toward her on his hands and knees, and she couldn't prevent the stark image of a prowling wolf that embedded itself in her mind. "Just the opposite, in fact. My thirsts—and my hungers—are of the most basic, most primitive variety, Miranda. Mere champagne does little to quench them. In fact," he added, now crouched on the floor beside her, looking to her as if he were about to pounce, "there's only one thing that's ever even come close to satisfying me."

In one swift, graceful motion, Lucas was on the sofa beside her, his hands planted firmly on either side of her—one on the arm of the sofa and one on the back. His eyes were a dark and stormy gray, and his bare chest rose and fell in ragged breaths. Miranda swallowed with some difficulty.

"Wh-what's that?" she stammered in a shaky voice.

Lucas leaned in until only a hairbreadth separated their bodies. Miranda could feel the heat of him reaching straight down into her soul, warming what little was left cold inside her.

"You," he said simply before taking her mouth with his.

It wasn't the kiss of a hungry man, she realized vaguely with no small amount of surprise as Lucas tugged gently at her lips with his. Instead it was the kiss of a man who was apologizing, asking again for her forgiveness. His motions were gentle, tender and solicitous, as if he were requesting that she be the one to set the pace for them. Miranda didn't know what to do. So instinctively she kissed him back.

It was apparently all the encouragement Lucas needed. As soon as she offered him that small acquiescence, that tiny indication of surrender, he deepened the kiss, leaning forward to press his body more intimately against hers. Miranda wrapped one arm possessively around his neck to pull him closer, but even after struggling with the bedspread, her other arm remained awkwardly imprisoned. When Lucas realized her dilemma, he sought to aid her, and together they managed to tear the bedspread free enough to enable her to embrace him fully.

After that, things went along very nicely. As her thoughts became little more than incoherent realizations that everything Lucas was doing to her was quite exquisite, she drifted away from all the worries and concerns she had harbored earlier that evening. Instead she focused on the warm sensations rippling through her body, and concentrated on what she could do that would make Lucas feel as wonderful as she did. Eventually, however, even those thoughts turned hazy, and Miranda was left only with her feelings and responses.

And respond she did. As Lucas cupped the back of her head with his hand, holding her more firmly so that he could deepen his kiss to enable even more extensive exploration, Miranda opened to him willingly, taking advantage of his position to venture a little further herself. Tangling her fingers in his hair, she tried to pull him closer.

She tugged eagerly at the coarse wool blanket wrapped around Lucas's waist until it was free, then tossed it carelessly to the floor. In response, Lucas dug his fingers beneath the gauzy fabric in which Miranda was still swaddled, yanking feverishly and without concern for the numerous, ragged sounds of tearing, until it, too, had joined the blanket on the floor. Then he eased her back down on the sofa beneath him, lying prone atop her with his body supported by his elbows on either side of her rib cage. Miranda raked her hands down his bare back, fingering every rigid muscle she encountered until her hands splayed gently over his taut buttocks. He was as glorious as ever, she thought feverishly. And he was hers.

At the feel of Miranda's hands brushing possessively over his body, Lucas's already eager arousal turned into an incandescent need. Their hearts clamored heavily against each other, and their ragged respiration mingled in the warm air surrounding them. It occurred to him then that they were joined in nearly every way except the one that would bring them the most pleasure. With deft, confident fingers, he lifted the hem of the T-shirt Miranda wore, spreading open his palm against her flat belly before guiding it up over her heated flesh to cradle her breast. With his other hand, he pushed the softly faded fabric out of the way, then lowered his mouth to taste her.

Miranda gasped and arched her back at his action, pushing herself more fully toward Lucas's hungry lips. He opened them wider then, closing his fingers more tightly around her swollen flesh to take even more of her into his mouth. As he curled his tongue around the rigid bud more insistently, circling and laving and tasting, Miranda groaned and tangled her fingers in his hair to pull his head even closer. At her encouragement, Lucas dropped his other hand to the waistband of her panties, pausing to see if she would protest. When no objections came, he dipped his fingers inside the lacy cotton fabric and caressed the most feminine part of her.

Miranda caught her breath in a strangled sigh, then buried her hands more insistently in Lucas's hair. The fingers that brought her such pleasure mimicked the motions of the mouth that wreaked such havoc on her senses, driving her perilously close to the point of no return. Suddenly her decision to end their relationship seemed like the most grievous wrong she had ever done herself, and all she wanted was to make love with him from now until the end of time.

"Lucas, please . . ." she whispered softly.

"Miranda, don't tell me to stop," he murmured hoarsely against her heated skin. "I don't want to stop until I've made love to you for hours and we're both too exhausted to do anything but lie in each other's arms."

After a moment's pause, she told him quietly, "I wasn't going to ask you to stop."

"You weren't?"

Miranda shook her head slowly, and it took a moment for her implication to register with Lucas. Once it did, however, he began to smile, a smile that was at once delighted, satisfied and, Miranda realized with some trepidation, victorious.

"Did . . . did you bring anything?" she asked him cautiously. She was unable to quell the little stab of uncertainty that pierced her heart at the realization that she had probably capitulated to him as easily—and in exactly the same way—as he had planned.

Lucas's expression became puzzled. "What do you mean?"

"You know . . ." she said with a meaningful shrug. When he still didn't seem to understand what she was talking about, Miranda sighed with resignation and concluded with a shy whisper, "Birth control."

Lucas gazed at her warily for a moment before replying, "No, I didn't come prepared. As I've already told you a dozen times, I wasn't expecting any visitors this weekend."

Miranda tried to ignore the small jolt of pain that shot through her at her realization that his statement suggested there might be visitors other than herself. Certainly that wasn't what he'd meant, she told herself. But her words were less eager, less impassioned than before when she told him, "Nor was I expecting to visit."

Lucas narrowed his eyes at the note of reluctance he now detected in Miranda's voice. "We could still make love," he said softly.

Miranda shook her head. "I could get pregnant."

"Would that be such a terrible thing?" he asked carefully.

For a moment she didn't answer. She'd never given much thought to the idea of having children. Although from time to time she indulged in the normal fantasies of what motherhood might be like, she'd never fully considered all the consequences that getting pregnant would involve—simply because she'd never had a serious enough relationship with a man for the topic to arise for consideration. And now that it did, Miranda decided that getting pregnant probably *wouldn't* be such a terrible thing—as long as the father of her child was someone who loved and respected her. Someone who would be around to help nurture and teach their child. Someone who would never think of lying to her.

And all that kind of left Lucas Strathmoor out of the running, she thought sadly.

"Under the circumstances," she said quietly, tugging the T-shirt back down modestly over as much of herself as it would cover, "yes. It would be a pretty terrible thing."

Lucas observed her wary gesture and listened to her softly uttered declaration, then dropped his chin to his chest in defeat. He still lay supporting himself atop her, but he couldn't force himself to move, couldn't make himself meet her gaze. Only one thought permeated the cloudy confusion that swirled around in his brain—Miranda didn't want to have his child. Whether she didn't love him enough, didn't trust him enough, or didn't respect him enough, mattered little to Lucas. He understood it was probably more accurate to assume that her decision resulted from a combination of all three. Worse than any other realization, however, was that Lucas had to admit he had done nothing that should inspire her to feel otherwise.

"Do you hate me that much?" he asked before he could stop himself, glancing back up quickly to meet her gaze levelly with his.

Miranda caught her breath at the tone of desperation and hopelessness she heard in his voice. "Oh, Lucas, no," she was quick to assure him. "It isn't that at all. I could never—"

She couldn't even say the word aloud. But she couldn't tell him she still loved him, either. It would only prolong their inevitable separation. As much as Miranda might still care for Lucas, she couldn't quite let herself trust him. There was still a big part of her that simply could not forgive him for the way he had used her, and a part of her that wouldn't quite be convinced that he would never do it again. Whatever they might have had together was over before it had even begun, and no amount of talking would change that.

"But you don't trust me, either, do you?" he asked her evenly.

This time it was Miranda who looked away, unable to meet his gaze as she replied softly, "No."

"And you don't love me."

She said nothing in response, but continued to stare unseeingly out into his living room, no more willing to meet his steely eyes than she was to lie to him.

"There's nothing I can say that will change your mind, is there?" he asked her. "No apology, no explanation will suffice, will it?"

Miranda shook her head silently.

"I blew it, didn't I?"

Instead of replying, she simply continued to stare at the flames dying gradually in the fireplace. She didn't look up when Lucas rolled away from her and wrapped himself up in his blanket again. Nor did she move to help him as he collected their champagne glasses and the ice bucket and took them to the kitchen. And when he paused at the foot of the stairs to tell her good-night before going up to bed, she didn't respond at all.

Instead Miranda reached down for her own cover and wrapped it tightly around her again, curling herself into a ball at the corner of the sofa nearest the lessening warmth of the nearly extinguished fire. She was still cold. But this time it had nothing to do with the temperature in the house. This time, the hottest fire at the center of the earth wouldn't even come close to warming her.

Less than ten hours later, Lucas sat in her driveway, watching her leave him. He had never felt more helpless in his life. And helplessness was something Lucas Strathmoor hated feeling. Normally it was virtually alien to him, completely outside his experience. But then again, normally, if he wanted something he took it. Whether by buying it outright or sneaking around to acquire it, eventually he wound up with precisely whatever he went after. Yet Miranda True had completely evaded his every maneuver. She wouldn't be bought, she couldn't be acquired, and every attempt he'd made to take over her affections had come to naught. The raid on Miranda's heart, which he'd thought would be the raid to end all raids, had failed dismally. And now Lucas didn't know what he was going to do.

Their drive from Yarmouth had seemed endless, and had been made in almost total silence. Miranda had evidently wanted to put as much distance between the two of them as possible, because she had leaned against her door with so much determination that Lucas had feared she would tumble out of the car if he took a turn too wide. Now she pushed open her front door and entered her house, closing the door behind her again without even offering him a final glance.

It was over. Every bone in Lucas's body told him that was true. But his designing mind and his unfulfilled heart refused to be put off so easily. There must be something he could do that would make Miranda see reason, he thought. Some promise he could utter, some gesture he could make. If only he could think of something...

As he put his car into reverse and backed out of her driveway, Lucas wished he could go back in another way as well. Back to when he first met Miranda True, when none of his odious deeds lay between them. If only he hadn't doubted her the first time he'd met her, if only he'd had a little faith in her, or been able to see her for the woman she was. If only he hadn't been so caught up in his own problems then that he'd resorted to taking advantage of her the way he had. If only, if only, if only...

If only he hadn't acquired all those companies as a result of his association with her, he thought further. That was what really bothered Miranda, Lucas realized. That he had turned such a profit as a result of their relationship. Panwide, of course, had been the nail in his coffin, the acquisition that had caused Miranda to feel most betrayed. But all of them, all seven companies that he had purchased after her unknowing input, stood between him and his ultimate happiness with the woman he loved. If he hadn't gone after those...

His musings halted abruptly and began to rewind. And then with the force of a speeding freight train, it struck him. There was indeed something he could do to win Miranda's affections back, Lucas realized, but it would take some time. It wasn't something that would be easy, and it was going to cost him plenty. Not only would he be making a tremendous sacrifice, he was facing an enormous hassle to get the whole thing orchestrated. Simon was going to have to help him out. Lucas chuckled mirthlessly. That was the least his friend owed him after the part he'd played in this epic tragedy.

Because what Lucas was planning was without question something that must be done. It was the only way he would make Miranda change her mind about him, his only chance to prove to her how much he loved her and how unequivocally she could place her trust in him in the future. Tremendous sacrifice, hell, Lucas thought. The enormity of what he was about to give up was nothing compared to what he would lose if Miranda didn't come back into his life.

Lifting the phone from its cradle beside him in the car, Lucas punched the same series of numbers that had started him down his road to ruin. This time, however, he hoped the road would land him elsewhere. With any luck at all, this time he might just find paradise waiting for him at the end.

"Lawler," he said when his associate picked up the phone at the other end of the line, "I need your help."

Chapter Twelve

Once the realization set in that there was no hope for a future with Lucas Strathmoor, time began to drag for Miranda. Every morning she awoke at her usual time and went about the same daily rituals she had gone about for years. But she no longer approached the day ahead with the zeal and anticipation that had once punctuated her every action. Gone was her interest in the way her gardens changed from day to day. Gone was her excitement over discovering some new product for the store. Even Marcy gave up hope of snapping Miranda out of her funk, and simply resorted to continuously quoting the age-old adage about time healing all wounds.

Miranda never said the words aloud, but she knew in this case Marcy's assessment of the situation couldn't be more wrong. No matter how much time passed, no matter what the future might bring, there would never be a point in her life when Miranda would be able to put thoughts of Lucas completely behind her. Perhaps the pain would dull somewhat over the years, but she would never feel completely healed, or completely whole, again.

And there would be no more romantic involvements, Miranda decided resolutely. She knew that in making such a decision at age thirty-two she would appear hopelessly jaded, to the point of being melodramatic, but she was two for two in the broken romance department, a one-hundred-percent failure rate. She simply couldn't trust her own judgment where men were concerned.

And what did she have to offer a man, anyway? First she had given her heart to Patrick Lyndon, who had promptly turned his back on her when their relationship had become public, because of the social stigma attached to her position in his parents' household. Then for an encore, she had placed her faith and trust in Lucas Strathmoor, who had disregarded her affections in order to latch on to her moneymaking potential instead.

From such experiences, Miranda could only conclude that the lifelong love and respect she could offer her partner must not be much of a marketable commodity by today's standards. Clearly men wanted something more than she was able to give.

As summer gradually drew to a close and the Massachusetts nights became kissed with the promise of cooler times to come, Miranda went about her seasonal routines with little interest as well. Her yards drifted out of the soft pastel and bright primary colors that erupted in summer, and into the harvest golds and rusty ambers that heralded the arrival of autumn. She selected the best of her vegetables from the garden to stock her own pantry or sell in the shop, and transplanted some of the hardier flowers into potted arrangements of saffron, sienna and scarlet in anticipation of the upcoming fall holidays. Piece by piece, Miranda began to put her life together again. But it wasn't the same as before.

She missed Lucas.

Despite everything he'd done, she missed him with every cell in her body. He had become such a part of her life, such a part of her daily routine. At times she found herself wanting to pick up the telephone and invite him over for a casual dinner, just to try to win back some of the warmth and comfort that his presence in her house had brought with it. But on those occasions, Miranda reminded herself that such warmth and comfort was gone forever—it had been as false and affected as Lucas's loving responses to her had been. Even the cats seemed puzzled over his disappearance, and Miranda often caught Bix staring at her with an expression of extreme censure.

"Oh, you didn't even like him," she reminded the big black tomcat on one such occasion as she prepared a squash casserole for her dinner.

Bix threw back his head and emitted a ragged, plaintive cry. If Miranda didn't know better, she'd almost think he sounded kind of lonely.

"Hungry is probably more accurate," she said out loud.

As if he knew a feeding was imminent, Bix rose and curled casually around Miranda's ankles, his rumbling purr almost deafening in the otherwise silent room. Soon enough he was joined by the other cats, and by the time Miranda got the casserole in the oven, the combined sounds of four cats purring and meowing made her feel as if she had wandered into a construction zone.

"All right, all right," she said with a soft chuckle. "I'll feed you."

She went to the cabinet where she stored their food—an organic vegetable mixture she carried in her shop—and reached in blindly for a can. Oblivious to what she was opening because she was too busy trying to dodge the furiously dancing cats, it wasn't until the can sat open on the counter before her that Miranda realized what it was.

Corned beef hash.

The only reason she had ever allowed such a thing into her house was because Lucas Strathmoor had loved it for breakfast. She had thought she had cleared every reminder of him from her home, but somehow this had slipped by her. Unbidden tears leaped into her eyes, and Miranda mustered every bit of willpower she had to keep them from falling. But it was no use. She had promised herself she wouldn't cry over Lucas, and until now she had kept that vow. But this unexpected reminder of him caught her off guard.

The cats, having smelled something much more to their liking than the product they normally ate, were going crazy around her. Bix stretched to his full, impressive length and reached his paw up to the counter, and in his overzealousness, snagged Miranda's hand slightly with his extended paw. It was only a tiny pain, but it brought more tears than she could hold in. For a moment, she only stared at the can of hash and tried vainly to stop crying. Bix reached up again, and Miranda glared down at him.

"This stuff will kill you," she told him sharply, rubbing her nose viciously when she couldn't prevent a sniffle. "Fat, cholesterol, salt—it has absolutely no nutritional value whatever."

Apparently Bix didn't care. He meowed with rusty insistence again, and a chorus of agreement rang out from the other cats.

Oh, why the hell not? Miranda thought miserably, a feeling of defeat spreading lethargy throughout her body. It could be their way of finally saying farewell to Lucas, too. She scooped out four equal portions into four identical bowls and set them on the floor. Then as the cats dug into their feast, she slid down against the cabinets herself, until she was seated near them. It was early October, the evening just barely warm enough for Miranda to have the windows of her house open. As she crouched in the corner of her kitchen watching the cats consume the final reminder of

Lucas Strathmoor, a cold breeze whipped through the screen to stir her hair and remind her of how soon winter would be here.

It was well past ten o'clock when the phone rang, and Miranda glanced up from her book with some distraction. She rarely received phone calls because hers was an unlisted number, and no one called this late in the evening. She shifted her glass of wine to her other hand as she answered the phone, tucking her sock-enclosed feet beneath the hem of her flannel nightshirt.

"Hello?" she said softly, certain it must be a wrong number.

Her suspicion was confirmed by the silence that met her at the other end of the line, but ever courteous, Miranda tried again.

"Hel-loooo?" she intoned good-naturedly.

"Miranda."

It was a man's voice, but not one she recognized, and for a moment her heart hammered fearfully behind her rib cage. This was all she needed to top off the day, she thought. An obscene phone call.

"Who is this?" she asked pointedly, trying to keep her voice as calm and even as she could manage.

Another brief silence met her question, followed by a deep, masculine sigh. "Miranda, this is . . . it's Patrick. Patrick Lyndon."

Now it was Miranda's turn to be silent. For long moments she simply stared out into her living room, clutching her glass of wine as if it were the only thing keeping her from sliding inescapably into a past life she had no desire to visit. She hadn't spoken to Patrick for more than twelve years, wouldn't have been able to identify his voice any more than she would have recognized Napoleon's. His voice now was deeper than she recalled it being when they were young, a little rougher, and very weary.

"Miranda? Are you still there?"

His question brought her out of her reverie, and Miranda replied quietly, "Yes. I'm still here, Patrick. How ... how are you?"

He drew in another deep breath, and his relief when he spoke again was unmistakable. "I'm fine. Better than ever now, actually." There was another pause before he continued, "I was afraid you wouldn't want to talk to me."

Miranda shrugged, knowing he couldn't see her, but helpless to stop the action. If he knew how instrumental she had been in his family's loss of their company, he would be the one who had no desire to talk to her. "I ... it's been a long time, Patrick. I'm surprised to hear from you, certainly, but ... I wouldn't hang up on you, if that's what you were worried about."

"It was." Another long silence followed, as if he were wondering as much as Miranda why he was calling. "I ... How have you been, Miranda?"

She set her wineglass down on her steamer trunk before replying, hoping the gesture would give her some time to recover from the shock of speaking to Patrick Lyndon after all this time. She certainly wasn't going to bring up her recent trip into heartbreak with a man who had taken her there himself so many years ago, so she simply replied vaguely, "Not bad." Then, no longer able to keep her curiosity in check, she asked bluntly, "Patrick, why are you calling me?"

"I wanted to thank you."

Now Miranda was really confused. "For what?"

"For helping my family get back the company," he told her. "I don't know how you did it, Miranda—or ... or why— but we can't thank you enough for whatever it was. We didn't think we'd ever have Panwide to call our own again. But when Strathmoor said—"

"Whoa, whoa, whoa," Miranda interrupted him. "I don't know what you're talking about, but I assure you, I was anything but helpful to you where your family's business was concerned. In fact, I was—"

"You were the one responsible for Lucas Strathmoor selling it back to us."

Miranda was certain her hearing must have gone. "I was what?"

Patrick went back to being silent for a moment before he spoke again. "Lucas Strathmoor sold Panwide back to us," he explained, sounding to Miranda as if he were choosing his words very carefully. "And he did it, he said, because of an obligation he had to you."

"What?" she repeated.

"Those were his exact words," Patrick told her. "When he called us last month, he said we could have Panwide back for exactly what we received for it. Then he said something like, 'Normally, I wouldn't dream of surrendering a potentially profitable company like this, but I'm doing it because—' and this is a direct quote '—because of an obligation I have to Miranda True.' That's what he said," Patrick concluded. "What was he talking about?"

"I have no idea," she replied. "Didn't he say anything else?"

"No. And I didn't press him. As it was, we had to scramble to get the money together, because we'd already spent most of what we received from the sale to get ourselves out of hock. It was just this afternoon that we were finally able to sit down and settle the terms of the agreement."

"You saw Lucas today?" The question was out of her mouth before she realized she had uttered it, and immediately she was sorry she had. There was no way Patrick would be able to mistake the note of melancholy she detected herself, and she was sure her intent in asking it would be equally clear.

"Yes, I did," Patrick told her, his voice softer now than it had been. When she offered no comment to his statement, he went on. "I know it's none of my business, Mir-

anda, but are you and he...I mean, did you...were
you...you know."

She had set herself up for his question, Miranda thought,
so she might as well offer him an honest answer. "Whatever Lucas and I had together ended more than a month
ago."

"If you'll forgive my asking, did you tell him about the
two of us?"

"Of course not, Patrick. That's personal." Miranda
sighed in resignation. "But he did find out about us
from...another source." She wasn't about to tell him it was
through a background check Lucas had done on her.

"Then if you'll now forgive my meddling, it doesn't
sound to me as if it's over at all."

"What do you mean?"

"Just that Strathmoor glared at me throughout the
meeting. I thought maybe it was because he resented selling
the company back to us. Now I think maybe it was because
he wanted to lay me out for...for the way I treated you while
you were living in Saint Denis." Before Miranda could
comment, he rushed on. "And he asked me to call you to
tell you about this. I don't think that's the act of a man who
wants things concluded with you."

"Maybe not," she said thoughtfully.

She spoke with Patrick for a long time that night, surprised to discover she no longer carried any of the emo-
tional baggage of her youth that had once weighed upon her
so heavily. Patrick told her about his wife and two children, went on at length about how well his parents were enjoying their retirement, and filled her in on much of the
gossip that kept the residents of Saint Denis going. Miranda was too polite to tell him she really didn't care much
anymore what went on in the town where she'd grown up,
and instead marveled at the fact that she had made such a
clean and total break from her past. When she hung up the
phone, it was with an unfamiliar, almost giddy sensation,

something akin to a feeling of renewal. She had no idea what had prompted Lucas's decision to sell Panwide back to the Lyndons, but in the deepest recesses of her heart, a tiny flicker of warmth ignited.

And as the week progressed, that flame gradually grew higher and began to burn brighter. Because throughout the week, Miranda received phone calls similar to the one she'd had from Patrick—seven of them, to be exact. Some were from people she had never met in her life, whose names she would never have recognized. Some were from people she had met perhaps once or twice through her relationship with Lucas. But each of them told her the same thing—Lucas Strathmoor had offered them the opportunity to buy back their companies for exactly what they had received for them, and he'd done it, he said, because of an obligation he had to Miranda True. And they all thanked her for whatever she'd done to allow them their fresh start.

By the time Miranda received the last call on Friday afternoon, she was nearly in tears. When Marcy found her in the stockroom dabbing at her eyes, Miranda told her it was because of a splinter, then excused herself to make a phone call.

Her fingers were trembling as she punched the buttons that would connect her to Lucas's home number. She knew before it even began to ring that he wouldn't answer—he always let his machine get the phone whether he was home or not, then either picked up when the caller identified him or herself or returned the call later. His usual stringent, to-the-point message had been changed, however, and Miranda couldn't help but smile as she listened to the voice she had been denied for weeks.

"Unless you're Miranda True, I'm unavailable," the recording at the other end of the line recited. "And if you *are* Miranda True . . . then you'll know where to find me."

Miranda laughed a little uncertainly as the recording concluded with its usual beep, but didn't bother to leave a message. Instead she settled the phone back into its cradle, stood there gazing at it only long enough to decide she and Lucas really needed to talk face-to-face, then grabbed her purse.

"I'll be gone for the weekend, Marcy," she said to her assistant as she blustered quickly through the store, unwilling to waste another moment. "You won't mind working with Denise and Toni tomorrow, will you?"

Marcy looked as confused and dazed as Miranda felt. "Well, no... but..."

"Thanks," Miranda said hurriedly as she exhaled deeply her relief. "I have to go out of town."

"Where?" Marcy asked. "Is everything all right?"

Miranda's smile was dazzling when she replied, "It will be."

Marcy smiled back. "Does this have anything to do with that delicious Mr. Strathmoor you've been moping over for the past several weeks?"

Miranda nodded. "It has everything to do with him."

"Good," Marcy said with approval. "It's about damned time."

Miranda had her hand on the front door and was about to exit when she recalled something very important. "Marcy, I have to go to Yarmouth right away, and I don't have any way to get there. I just remembered that I don't own a car."

Marcy shook her head hopelessly. "Didn't I warn you that you were going to find that inconvenient someday?"

"Well, mass transit is so efficient," Miranda tried lamely to explain, "and fewer cars on the road would help keep the plants from suffering."

Marcy reached for her purse. "Take my car."

Miranda held up her hand to object. "But then how will you get around this weekend?"

"I'll manage."

Then Miranda had an even better idea. "Could you maybe give me a lift out to the Cape? I'll pay you overtime."

Marcy drew the store keys out of her purse and jangled them meaningfully. With her eyes sparkling happily and with a very mischievous grin, she said, "I'll just lock up after us, shall I?"

"But we have to make a quick stop by my house first," Miranda told her as they left. "I'm not getting stranded without a few creature comforts this time."

She's not coming.

The thought paced and circled sadly through Lucas's brain as he stared out the window watching the moon rise slowly in the night sky from behind the black silhouettes of the pine trees surrounding his house. The wind kicked up once more as it had been all evening, bending the tops of the trees gracefully to the right before releasing them again. It was going to storm, Lucas thought as the moon slipped stealthily behind a fat cloud. All the signs were there.

He was sure that by now Miranda had received every phone call he'd instructed be made, and he had been so certain she would have telephoned him and left a message on his machine. But he'd called home a little while ago to play back his messages, and none had been from Miranda. He had gambled with her affections once and lost them. This time he had gambled with his own, so certain he would win hers back. But he had lost again. And now he had nothing left to bargain with.

Lucas turned away from the window and gazed hopelessly at the elaborate scene he had gone to such lengths to set up. A fire danced and crackled in the fireplace with inviting warmth, and on the wide hearth sat a sterling silver champagne bucket dripping with condensation. Inside was a bottle of the best champagne he'd been able to find, chilled by now to a perfect temperature for tasting in the two long-stemmed crystal flutes he'd placed nearby. And in front of it all was the pastel-hued, Indian-print blanket he'd wrapped himself in on that night so many weeks ago when he had succeeded in chasing Miranda completely from his life forever.

Lucas sighed in defeat and ran a hand dispassionately through his hair. He'd even brought protection this time, in case she still objected to getting pregnant. Pretty damned optimistic of him, he thought now. As usual, his overconfident, arrogant disposition had landed him nowhere.

He crossed to the dining room, where he'd lain the table with newly purchased china, crystal and silver, upon which he'd spread a vegetarian feast of fruits, cheeses, fine breads and condiments. He was about to blow out the candles when he heard a noise outside that brought his attention around. The noise was made by a car, he realized hopefully as a hot flame licked at the walls of his stomach. But as quickly as his spirits lifted toward the sky, they came crashing back down to earth. The noise was, more accurately, made by a car that was leaving. He drew in a breath to extinguish the first of a dozen candles, then halted at the quick rapping of a knock on his front door.

Lucas turned toward the sound, thinking it rather ominous and somehow fitting in light of the gothic surroundings of his darkened house that was about to be rattled by a thunderstorm. But instead of moving to respond, he simply called out quietly, "It's open, Miranda."

Even though his statement must have been too soft for her to hear, Lucas wasn't surprised when the door creaked slowly inward and Miranda stepped cautiously from behind it. She was dressed casually in a pair of lovingly faded blue jeans and a pale blue cotton sweater, with her hair bound loosely just above the ends with a length of blue ribbon. In one hand she clutched a small flowered canvas duffel bag, and in the other a large wicker picnic basket. Lucas smiled. She looked as if she were well prepared this time for a weekend at the beach.

"Hi," she said softly, smiling a little nervously.

"Hi," he replied just as quietly, willing himself to stay put and not sweep her up into his arms as he longed to do. He didn't want to scare her off by being too aggressive. There would be time enough for holding later.

"I was beginning to think you wouldn't come," he continued, remaining resolutely beside the table, still uncertain of what she was expecting, still unsure of how to act.

The wind whipped up and gusted around the house outside, catching the front door in its grip and slamming it shut with a loud bang. Miranda flinched and took several more steps inside.

"Why did you do what you did?" she asked him, unwilling to wade through small talk that would only waste more time. "Why did you sell all those companies back to the original owners? You lost so much money in the process."

Lucas took a step forward, then paused. "Because I knew it was the only way I could prove to you that what I wanted from you had nothing to do with professional and financial profit. I lost so much more than money when I lost your trust. Those companies meant nothing to me, Miranda, compared with how important your love has become. Tell me I still have that, because without it, I have nothing."

"You still have it," she told him immediately, her voice scarcely louder than a whisper. "Oh, Lucas, you never lost it."

Miranda finally discarded whatever reserve remained, and she stooped to set her duffel and basket on the floor before rushing toward Lucas. Throwing her arms around him in a fierce embrace, she murmured against his neck, "Lucas, how could I not come? I've missed you so much."

"I've missed you, too, Miranda," he murmured against her hair. "I've missed you so much."

For long moments they only held on to each other, recalling how good it had always felt to be embraced this way. Eventually Miranda pulled reluctantly away, gazing at Lucas hungrily because she simply couldn't stop staring at him.

He looked magnificent, she thought. As handsome as she thought him to be in his expensive dark suits, Miranda found him irresistible in his snug-fitting, faded jeans and his aged, pewter-colored corduroy shirt. And he smelled divine, she realized, closing her eyes to inhale deeply and fill her lungs with the scent that was distinctly Lucas Strathmoor—a combination of pine, smoke and something else that was wonderfully elusive and masculine.

When she opened her eyes again, it was to find Lucas studying her face with an odd expression. "What is it?" she asked him.

He shook his head slowly back and forth and said absently, "I think I had honestly come to the conclusion that you were out of my life for good, Miranda, forever. I guess I'm having trouble believing you're actually here. There's still a part of me that's afraid you're going to leave again. And I don't want to lose you. So if you're planning on going, do it now. Don't let me feel hopeful only to be disappointed."

Miranda smiled up at him and threaded her fingers lightly through his dark hair, loving the way the wavy locks seemed to want to wind around her fingers in an effort to trap them. "Didn't you notice that I actually packed a bag this time?" she asked him lightly. "I'm not going anywhere unless you decide to send me away."

Lucas pulled her closer, wrapping his arms snugly around her. "That's never going to happen," he stated firmly.

"Lucas—"

"Miranda—"

They spoke as one and ceased as one, then both began to laugh a little uncertainly.

"You first," Lucas told her.

"No, you first," she replied.

"Then let's sit down, because we need to talk."

Miranda nodded her agreement. "Okay."

He stepped away from her only far enough to allow them to cross the room, but kept her hand clasped lovingly in his own. As he moved away from the table, Miranda noted for the first time the elaborate banquet Lucas had arranged, and she began to smile.

"I guess we won't be needing all the food I packed after all," she told him.

"We can have it tomorrow," he told her. "Since you're planning on staying the entire weekend this time."

His voice rose only slightly on the last part of the sentence, turning it into just the tiniest hint of a question. Miranda nodded with much confidence to reassure him, and Lucas seemed to breathe a little more easily.

When she was comfortably seated on the sofa near the fireplace, Lucas reached for the champagne and freed the cork with a resounding pop. After filling the two glasses with pale gold effervescence, he sat beside her and handed one to her, then lifted his own in a silent toast. She did likewise, touching the rim of her glass against his with a nearly inaudible ping, and they both sipped heartily as if quenching a mighty thirst. Finally Lucas broke the silence that had risen between them.

"Don't take this the wrong way, Miranda," he began slowly, almost warily. "But why did you come here tonight? Not that I'm not eternally grateful, mind you, but...I'd like to know your reason."

She took another thoughtful sip of her wine before responding, then said quietly, "Because I remembered something that I had forgotten."

Lucas's expression was puzzled. "What's that?"

After setting her glass down on the stone hearth, Miranda reached for Lucas's glass and did likewise with it. Then she took both of his hands in hers, holding them palm-up in her own. "These," she said as she cradled them gently, rubbing her thumbs over the warm flesh of his palms. "Your hands."

"What about them?" Lucas asked quietly, as if by speaking too loudly he would taint a sacred tradition.

Miranda studied his hands for several moments, and when she lifted her gaze to meet Lucas's once again, her eyes glistened with the presence of unspilled tears. "To me, Lucas, hands are like a window that looks into the soul," she told him. "People carry their hearts in their hands."

She dropped one of his hands back into his lap, and with her free fingers traced over a number of lines in the palm she still studied. "And in spite of all those other qualities you harbor as a smokescreen to hide your true nature, you're a decent man, Lucas Strathmoor. An honest man. But I conveniently chose to forget all that and focus instead on your lesser traits. It made things . . . easier for me."

"Easier in what way?" Lucas asked her, his voice belying none of the hope and happiness that swelled in his heart.

Miranda continued to gaze at his hand as she spoke, stroking her thumb over the sensitive flesh between his thumb and wrist. "Loving someone is difficult," she told him softly. "It's easier to push a person away and tell yourself there's no longer any risk of losing him than it is to embrace him and suffer with the constant fear that someday he'll betray you."

Lucas hesitated for only a moment before asking, "Do you love me, Miranda?"

She looked up at him then, her face rosy and glowing, though whether from the warmth of the fire or the heat of her emotions, Lucas wasn't sure.

"You know I do," she whispered roughly, a single tear spilling from the corner of her eye to wander down over her cheek.

"Then say it," he petitioned quietly.

"I love you, Lucas."

It occurred to Lucas that her answer to his next question might even be more important than the one to which she'd just replied. "Do you..." he began uncertainly. He sighed deeply and tried again. "Do you trust me?"

Another tear trickled from Miranda's blue eyes as she answered him softly, "Oh, Lucas. Yes. Yes, I trust you."

Lucas brushed her tear away with a chaste kiss, then vowed, "I'll never betray you, Miranda. Because I love you, too."

She said nothing then, only continued to gaze into his eyes as if searching for the answers to so many questions left unasked.

Lucas captured her hand in his, squeezing it hard. "Do you believe me?" he asked her urgently.

Miranda nodded slowly, and the gesture caused another tear to fall. "Yes," she replied quietly. "I believe you with all my heart."

Lucas exhaled his relief on a long sigh. "Then before we go any further, there are a couple of other things I should own up to."

Miranda gazed at him levelly, tamping down the fear that trembled around her heart. She didn't want to hear about it if Lucas had lied to her about something else. She wasn't sure if she could stand it. Just as she was about to silence him with a kiss and tell him to keep whatever secrets he had private, he began to speak again.

"Remember that weekend when Grace brought you to the house?" he asked her slowly, weaving his fingers through hers lest she try to escape from him again.

Miranda released a silent sigh of relief herself, trying to hide a smile when she knew what was coming next. "Yes," she told him evenly, her voice belying none of the playfulness she felt quickly replacing her fear.

"That...that wasn't Grace's idea at all," Lucas confessed, his eyes fearful, his expression worried. "It was mine. I planned it all. I lied to you when I kept insisting I'd had nothing to do with it."

Miranda opened her mouth to tell him she had suspected that all along and certainly bore him no grudge now as a result of his actions, but he hurried to continue before she had a chance.

"And when I told you I was having car trouble that Mack was trying to fix?"

"Yes?" Miranda replied calmly.

Lucas licked his lips anxiously. "That was a lie, too. You're right, I can fix my own car, and frankly, Mack wouldn't have a clue how to go about servicing it. As it was, he broke my radiator hose that morning when we were in town. I could have killed him."

Miranda bit her lip in an effort to keep from laughing. "Lucas Strathmoor," she pronounced, trying to look disapproving. "What am I going to do with you?"

"I'm sorry, Miranda, truly I am," he apologized wholeheartedly, still not meeting her eyes. "I panicked. I was desperate to talk to you, and that plan was the best I could come up with. I didn't mean to lie to you, I just...panicked. It was wrong, I know and I'm sorry. I—"

When he heard Miranda chuckling, Lucas immediately halted his profuse apologizing and glanced up to meet her gaze. When he saw the laughter flickering in her eyes, he smiled at her curiously. His confusion only compounded Miranda's mirth, and she began to laugh in earnest.

"You haven't answered my question," she said through her giggles. "What *am* I going to do with you?"

He took the champagne from her hand and placed it beside his own on the hearth, in exactly the same way he had done that night so many weeks ago in his blatant attempt to seduce her. Then with one swift, graceful movement, he circled her shoulders with his arm and pulled her down until she lay on her back with her head resting in his lap. When his eyes met hers again, Lucas saw that there was something else besides the laughter catching fire there, and he, too, began to chuckle—the chuckle of a man about to enjoy the most intimate kind of pleasure.

"What are you going to do with me?" he asked, turning her question back on her again. "I have a few very good ideas."

Miranda reached up to tangle her fingers in the dark hair at Lucas's nape, then pulled his face down toward hers. "So have I," she told him in a throaty whisper. "So have I."

As the wind kicked up around the house again, hurling a fistful of rain at the windows, Lucas kissed Miranda with all the fury of the approaching storm. And as the fire in the fireplace grew brighter and burned hotter, so did their passions become inflamed as they never had before. Throughout the night they pleasured each other, their union this time even more explosive than before, because this time they came to each other with no secrets, no shadows, nothing to hide. And when the sun arose the following morning on the two forms cuddled beneath an Indian-print blanket on the sofa before the fire, it was to shine on a love that would grow and flourish forever.

Epilogue

"Come on, you little bundle of joy. Auntie Grace is going to teach you all about building a financial empire."

Lucas reclined carelessly on the cedar bench beneath the huge sweeping oak tree in the front yard, absently rubbing his thumb over the soft patch of fur behind the ear of the big black cat that slumbered peacefully in his lap. He shook his head as Grace Devon lifted ten-month-old Isobel out of her well-shaded playpen.

"What if she doesn't want to build a financial empire, Grace?" he asked her with a smile. "What if she wants to wear berets and go to France to paint cathedrals?"

"Nonsense," Grace murmured without looking away from the baby she rocked carefully in her arms. Her next words were offered in the same perky, breathless, child-pleasing tone of voice she would use if reading to Isobel from *The Three Bears*. "What woman wouldn't crave riches...and power...and a flock of men scurrying around whenever she told them to jump, hmm?"

Lucas chuckled. "If anyone can teach my daughter how to hold her own when swimming among sharks, it's you, Grace." His gaze was drawn to where Miranda waded hip-deep through the tall grasses that would soon turn into a burst of yellow sunflowers along the side of their house, and inevitably he smiled. "Of course, Isobel will be learning more than a few lessons from her mother in that department, too." Miranda had captured and tamed the biggest shark of all, Lucas thought. And he couldn't be more pleased about it.

As if she'd known he was watching and thinking about her, Miranda looked up then, the wide straw hat she wore shielding her eyes from the bright noonday sun. With her loose-fitting floral jumper only hinting at the new life growing inside her again so soon, she looked like the occupant of a pastoral Renaissance painting. Immediately Lucas was filled with a warm and fuzzy sensation he had finally begun to get used to after eighteen months of marriage, and he sighed with complete satisfaction. His wife. Her husband. Their daughter. And another child would make an appearance soon.

Had anyone told him when he was a wild inner-city youth, smeared with the remnants of a recent oil change in his father's garage, that someday he would find himself seated so peacefully surrounded by nature and loved ones, Lucas would have laughed in that person's face. He suddenly felt the need to hold Miranda close in his arms, but before he could rise from his seat to approach her, she began to make her way out of the garden toward him. As had become their habit, she had somehow detected his thoughts once again. Or perhaps he had detected hers, Lucas thought with another smile. Either way, it had become a common enough occurrence for them.

Miranda picked her way carefully through the rest of the garden, a small spade in one hand and a handful of weeds in the other. Their new yard had been a particularly compelling challenge for her, because except for the sunny patch from which she was now departing, most of their property lay in shade, thanks to the numerous oaks and elms. When she and Lucas had realized Isobel was on the way, they had decided neither of their homes was appropriate for raising a family—Miranda's was too small, and Lucas's had no yard. So they had sold both and pooled their resources to buy this big federal-style home in Cambridge. Miranda loved it. She had more yard to work with than she'd ever imagined she would be able to call her own.

A little plot of land and someone to love, that's all she'd ever really wanted in life. Miranda remembered thinking those exact words the day Lucas Strathmoor had come barreling into her yard, her house, her life. Now she had a huge plot of land and several someones to love. She curled her hand protectively over her belly and smiled. This one would be a boy, she decided. Somehow, she just knew. She watched as Grace carefully transferred baby Isobel into Lucas's arms, and was filled to the point of tears with happiness. How could she have been one of the lucky few to have received everything she wanted out of life? Whatever she had done right, it must have been a doozy.

She joined the scene she had been watching, taking her seat close to Lucas to tickle Isobel's face with a dandelion blossom. The baby chuckled and blew a bubble, and Miranda and Lucas laughed.

"I'm glad you gave up corporate raiding," she told him with a smile.

"Why?" Lucas asked, linking the fingers of his free hand with hers to offer them a gentle squeeze.

"Because I plan to keep you busy from here on out."

"Oh? Doing what?"

Miranda took a deep breath and settled their two hands over the barely discernible rise of her belly. "Oh, this and that." She turned his palm up in her hand and gazed idly at the two of them together. Suddenly she laughed out loud, delighted by what she saw.

"Lucas, look," she cried out in amazement. "Your line of the heart matches my line of the heart. They're almost exactly alike."

"What does that mean?" he asked her dreamily.

She glanced up at him with an uncertain shrug. "I'm not sure," she told him honestly. "But they're both very long, starting well into the mount of Jupiter. That means a long-lasting affection."

Lucas grinned indulgently. "I don't need my hand to tell me that," he said softly. "Regardless of everything else, I'll always love you."

Miranda grinned back. "Yeah, me, too."

Lucas gazed down into the deep blue eyes of Miranda True and smiled back. When she had told him she wanted to keep her name after they married, he had immediately agreed. It was, quite simply, *her* name, he'd thought then, and it shouldn't—couldn't—be changed. He, too, was glad his most recent raid had been his last, and glad that it had been his most successful. He had indeed won Miranda's heart utterly and completely. Only instead of making him greedy for more, as his corporate conquests had always done before, winning her love had only made him anxious to give—his own heart to Miranda True.

Now the only thing he wanted from life was exactly what he had found—respect, love, trust. They were the only things that were important, Lucas thought resolutely as he kissed her lightly on the lips. And he had found them all with Miranda.

* * * * *

S SPRING
FANCY

**Three bachelors, footloose
and fancy-free... until now!**

Spring into romance with three
fabulous fancies by three of
Silhouette's hottest authors:

ANNETTE BROADRICK
LASS SMALL
KASEY MICHAELS

When spring fancy strikes, no man is immune!

Look for this exciting new short-story collection
in March at your favorite retail outlet.

Only from

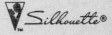

where passion lives.

Take 4 bestselling love stories FREE
Plus get a FREE surprise gift!

Silhouette®
SPECIAL EDITION™

COMING NEXT MONTH

#805 TRUE BLUE HEARTS—Curtiss Ann Matlock
Rough-and-tumble cowboy Rory Breen and mother of two
Zoe Yarberry knew that getting together was unwise. But
though their heads were telling them no, their hearts . . .

#806 HARDWORKING MAN—Gina Ferris
Family Found
The first time private investigator Cassie Browning met
Jared Walker, he was in jail. Cassie soon discovered that
clearing Jared's name and reuniting him with his family
were easier tasks than fighting her feelings for him!

#807 YOUR CHILD, MY CHILD—Jennifer Mikels
When confirmed bachelor Pete Hogan opened his door to
Anne LeClare and her child, he thought he was saving them
from a snowstorm. But the forecast quickly changed to sunny
skies when they offered him the chance for love.

#808 LIVE, LAUGH, LOVE—Ada Steward
Jesse Carder had traveled far to rekindle the flames of an old
love—until she met sexy Dillon Ruiz. Dillon brought Jesse's
thoughts back to the present, but was their future possible?

#809 MAN OF THE FAMILY—Andrea Edwards
Tough cop Mike Minelli had seen Angie Hartman on the screen as
a former horror movie queen! Now he sensed vulnerable Angie
was hiding more than bad acting in her past!

#810 FALLING FOR RACHEL—Nora Roberts
That Special Woman!
Career-minded Rachel Stanislaski had little time for matters of the
heart. But when handsome Zackary Muldoon entered her life,
Rachel's pulse went into overtime!